She's
LIKE THE
Wind

ELIZABETH J MARIE

To order additional copies of this book, contact:
Bookwhip
1-855-339-3589
https://www.bookwhip.com

Contents

For my best friend Tallie

Your *heartbreaking* passing taught me that life is short. You taught me
to have courage, be strong and most importantly; to believe in myself.
If it weren't for your friendship and strong sense of self; I wouldn't have
been able to find the voice inside me, to follow through with my dreams
and live the life I want to live.

Words will never be able to define how much I miss you but somehow, I
find the strength to put one foot in front of the other knowing that you're
always beside me in spirit, giving me the strength to go forward and to
never give up on life.

"You see," she said, "your first love isn't
the first person you give your heart to—
it's the first person who breaks it."

—Lang Leav

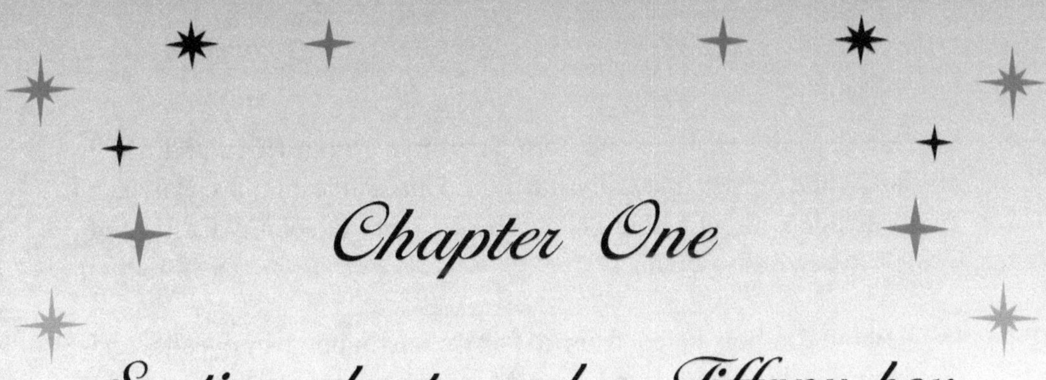

Chapter One

Seating charts and a Tiffany box

Sitting at her dining table in her brownstone in Tribeca, Harriet sips on her coffee as she looks down at the seating chart for her upcoming wedding reception. Her impending nuptials to Damon Bennett, a 32-year-old banker from Manhattan, occur in less than three months and as each day comes to pass, she is slowly finding that all the floundering wedding jitters she's tried to bury deep down inside are getting the best of her.

Looking down to her hand, her white gold princess cut tiffany engagement ring comes into view. Rubbing her right index finger over its stones, she loses her train of thought. Momentarily caught by the sparkle from the sun catching light off the ring and casting crystal-like reflections onto her ceiling, she moves away from the chart towards the seat of her front bay window.

Watching people pass by down on the street, making guesses as to where they are off to and what they might do for work. As she takes another drawn out sip of her coffee, her eyes glance down once again at the ring, and her mind is brought back to Damon, particularly on how they met.

They hated each other at first. Meeting when Harriet planned his older sister's wedding but she learnt a long time ago that first impressions are never as they seem. It's the most obvious cliché in any epic love story. Most of the greatest love stories that Harriet had ever read about or watched on screen began in hate and despise. Elizabeth Bennett and

Mr Darcy. Margaret Hale and Tom Thornton. Robin Hood and Maid Marian. Anne Shirley and Gilbert Blythe. But of all examples, Harriet's favourite tale without a doubt had to be the story of Johnny Castle and Francis "Baby" Houseman.

Like Baby; Damon haled from a family surrounded by wealth and tradition. He is a sixth generation Manhattan Bennett and from the moment Harriet met his mother, she strongly felt that Mrs Bennett would never approve of their relationship due to Harriet's lack of title and family background. Whereas Harriet in this scenario is like Johnny, having grown up in an average family with a modest home in Hartford, Connecticut. Her father isn't a fortune 500 stockbroker but instead, a licensed plumber with his own business while her mother is a stay at mother, who now; helps run her father's business and organises the weekly book club within their neighbourhood.

Funnily enough, after a few heated exchanges and a date, Harriet and Damon began seeing each other. After three years together, living together for practically two, they became engaged and are now soon to be married up until there had been no talk of marriage and babies. Harriet had come to assume that they were simply enjoying each other and were busy with their careers. That was until Damon proposed and an elated Harriet accepted.

Resting her head against the cool glass pane, a private thought sends a smile to her lips as she remembers the sight of her family's faces when Damon and she drove to Hartford to share the news. Her father's face displayed tells of elation and joy whereas her mothers showed disinterest.

Changing her train of thought, she looks down to the steps leading up to the apartment, and she smiles, once more. Taken back to the night that Damon proposed, she remembers the moment when she realised that her life was never going to be the same.

✸　✸　✸

Nine months earlier . . .

Harriet is sitting on her window seat, listening to the stereo play the Dirty Dancing soundtrack, with a glass of wine. She has had a long day of bridezillas and unsatisfied parents that she is trying to unwind by letting Patrick Swayze soothe her soul and by looking out at the stars in the night sky. A past-time she enjoyed as a child but rarely gets time to do as an adult.

Looking down on the street, she watches Damon pulling up in front of her apartment in his BMW, and upon the departure of his car, she watches as he smiles up at her and waves. Placing his briefcase and keys down in the hallway, he moves further inside the

apartment to find Harriet still seated at the window seat. Meeting her, he leans down and kisses her forehead before taking a sip of her wine and a seat opposite her on the sill.

As he watches the beautiful creature that sits opposite him, a smile is brought to his face as he slowly clues in on the music that plays in the background. When they first met, they shared indifferences regarding the movie but as time passed, the music just became another fixture in the apartment especially if she's had a trying day at the office.

Grinning at her, he smiles. "Another eventful day at the office, honey?" Smiling gently back at him, she replies. "Oh always", as she moves from the sill to the floor and rests her back upright against the wall.

Stopping to look at her, concerned at her answer, he sees the exhaustion in her tired eyes. Feeling the need to spread some sunshine across her face, he figures its finally the right time to ask her. Slipping his hand inside his jacket, he softly pats around the pockets in search of the little blue box and is overwhelmed with relief, when he finally finds it in the breast pocket.

Smirking to himself, he can still remember the phone conversation he had with Harper when he asked her to come with him to Tiffany's and help him pick out a ring for Harriet. Unfortunately, their entire time in Tiffany's he was bombarded with questions on how and where he was going to ask. Unsure but mostly scared to death, he just laughed along with his sister at her enjoyment at his pain. He can also remember how relieved he was when he arrived back to the apartment that morning to find Harriet out, giving him plenty of time to find a hiding place for the ring.

He tried, but he failed. He thought of places he could hide it but knowing that there was a possibility that Harriet could find it and start asking questions, terrified him, so he took it to work with him the next day and placed in his drawer until he found the right opportunity. Grinning, as he finally finds the words to introduce the subject of marriage, his attention is focused on her reaction.

"Just think of all the experience you're gaining. I mean, you'll be a pro by the time we get married."

With confidence, he stands to watch her as she fathoms a response; first in her head then in words. He loved that about her, that she never made a decision without at least taking a moment to mull it over that was unless it was about him of course. She at times, had the sharpest of tongues, a trait in which he came to face to face with when they first met or say whenever his mother was around.

Harriet, who has now changed her focus from outside to Damon's face catches the last words of his comments and looks at him with confusion.

"Wait - What now? When we get married?"

Damon, who is now in the kitchen, grabbing a beer and taking something out his pocket begins to walk back to her at the window.

"Well yeah, I mean don't you?"

A shell-shocked Harriet freezes in her place. Her mind racing with thoughts on how to even to begin to respond to his declaration.

"Damon, when did. I mean, we haven't even. I didn't even know; I mean I never thought -"

Smiling cheerfully as he takes a seat on the carpet next to her, beer in one hand and the blue Tiffany box with its white satin bow neatly tied, resting inside the other.

"Harriet, listen. I know we've never talked about it and I'm sorry if I've shocked you with this. It's just that well, we've been together now for three years and when I think about my life and my future, there is one only thing that is constant. That is you.

I love you, Harriet."

With tears streaming down her cheeks, she takes a slow but deep breath before wiping away the waterfall that is now her cheek.

"I love you too Damon. I just never thought in a million years that you wanted to get married?"

Slowly nodding, he opens his palm to show the small blue Tiffany box. Surprised that the box is still in one piece and not crumpled

up into a million pieces like the knots in his stomach, he reaches over to take her right hand and open the box on her palm. Watching intently for her reaction but deeply terrified of hearing a negative response, he takes her left hand inside his as he fights back his doubts to produce a smile.

"Harriet Arabella Lancer, would you do me the very great honour of marrying me and becoming my wife?"

Rendered speechless, Harriet's ability to speak is lost, and she can't help but nod her head profusely in acceptance. Leaning towards him, she kisses him softly. Pulling her arms up around him, Damon breaks the kiss to look down at her hand to see the ring. Only in the blurred moment of her acceptance, she forgot all about it, and he smirks at the sight of the small powder blue signature Tiffany box, with its delicate white satin ribbon, sitting on the floor beside her.

"Do you even want to see the ring?"

With a glowing smile that spreads sunshine across her cheeks and gives off sparks from her eyes, her moment of euphoria weakens as she begins to realise that she has no idea where the box had actually ended up. Bending down to her knees, she searches around for the box, and Damon can't help but laugh at her oddball behaviour.

"God, we're engaged no more for ten minutes, and you've lost the ring?"

Whacking his shoulder, she grins back at him. "Well, you distracted me!!!", she says as she smiles back up at him. Finding the box at her feet, she picks it up and slowly begins the untie its blue satin blue bow, savouring every moment she can. Once the box lid is free, and she is rendered speechless to find a gorgeous white gold princess cut engagement ring sparkling up at her.

"So you like it then???"

Looking up at him, she nods as she lets the tears stream down her cheek once again. Yanking Damon down to meet her, she watches on as she takes the ring from the box to slide it on her finger. Resting his back against the wall of the front bay window, he opens his legs and positions inside them, her back to rest against his chest. Contented, Harriet rests her head in the crook of his neck and for a moment, allows herself to become lost at the sight of his strong neck. Following the column of

A contented Harriet, lets herself settle against his chest for a moment before allowing her eyes to follow the column of his neck, up past his profoundly defined jaw. They take their rest on his piercing powder blue eyes as he looks back down at her, pulling her tighter into his arms.

Looking away from him, her focus drops to the ring, and it doesn't take long for her mind to become consumed with thoughts of the tasks involved now that they're engaged. Looking away from the ring and out at the night sky, she begins to rubs her forehead until it dawns on her that she'd have to call her mother to tell her the news.

The smile that was once posted upon her lips has now died at the thought of having to tell her mother.

"Oh god . . . I better ring my parents, let them know."

Reaching for his beer beside him, he takes it by its neck and takes a long pull. Smiling as he swallows, he shares that he has already been to see her father.

"Your dad already knows!"

Turning in her spot, she looks up at him. "He does???"

"Yeah well, I kind of had to ask for his permission and all. I mean, I didn't want to not ask him and risk upsetting the "the family".

Knocking her head back, she is consumed by laughter. Damon watches as her laughter fills her body and she shakes her head back at him. His use of the quotation marks whenever he refers to her family still continues to amaze her, a trait of his that she has become very familiar with especially during their heated arguments when he refuses to state names, particularly if he's talking about her or someone she knows.

Wiping her face, her cheeks are now the brightest shade of pink at his assumption that her family is somehow involved or is connected with the mafia. Knowing that it's in no way true, at least she thinks.

"Oh my god. You and your funny Italian beliefs!?"

"What? Come on, you of all people; I mean don't you think some of your relatives are scary? Uncle Sal for instance?"

"Uncle Sal owns this apartment", she responds, her voice still raptured by giggles. "But, I do appreciate you asking my father. I know he would've cherished you asking him."

He smiles, and before nipping at her neck, he takes a finger and curls a length of her dark chocolate brown locks around it.

"Well, what can I say. I am an old-fashioned guy!"

Shaking her head at him, she can't help but say, "Speaking of old . . . I guess we'll have to tell your mother?"

"Yeah, I guess so. I mean my father and Harper already know, so I guess 'we' should tell her."

Snapping a hellish look back at him, she turns and wiggles her finger defiantly back and forth at him.

"Oh no. This - ", pulling her fingers into the same curled quotation trait he is always making at her, "one is all yours!!!"

Rolling his eyes, he reaches for his beer to take another pull. "Harriet, she'll respect us more if we do it together."

Standing, she stomps off into her kitchen only to reappear with a glass and wine bottle. Slamming the glass down on the table and filling the entire glass to its rim, she begins firing back at Damon.

"Every time that woman is near me, it's like she feels she has to insult me."

He stands and meets her, knowing that their relationship has never run smoothly, this mostly due to this mother. Harriet has literally done everything she has possibly could to get into his mother's good graces but just won't warm to her.

Before she can take a drink, Damon takes the glass from out of Harriet's grasp and turns her to face him.

"Don't worry; I'll protect you!"

Harriet, who is silently fuming, shakes her head at him as a contradictive smile creeps up over her lips.

"You always say that, Damon. Yet -"

"No, Harriet!!!", frustrated he declares, "I'll protect you!!!"

Reaching down, he takes her hand and rests it on his chest. "This isn't just some game. Don't you get it!!! Your heart lives inside this heart. I want to spend the rest of my life with you!"

Brushing a lock of hair away from her face, he looks down into her eyes. Cupping her soft chin, his eyes move over her face.

"I love you, Harriet. I have from the moment I set eyes on you, and you told me off for insulting Dirty Dancing!!!"

She smiles back at him. "You deserved it!!!", as a tear falls down her cheek.

"Well if I knew then what I know now, the effect that Dirty Dancing and that Patrick Swayze bloke has on women, I would've watched it sooner."

Looking up, her eyes trailing the strong column of his neck to his lips and resting on his eyes, Harriet just shakes her head and then places her head back down on his chest.

Pulled back to reality by the ringing sound of her phone, Harriet shakes some sense into herself and allows her machine to take the call as she sips her coffee. Looking back out towards the front bay window, she watches as her busy neighbours scurry along the street's sidewalks before gazing up past the street and building skyline, to the clear blue sky speckled with white pillowy clouds.

The site of them reminded her of how much she used to love watching clouds make shapes when she was younger. The hours she spent on the trampoline in her backyard, just watching the clouds float by and change as she made guesses as to what shapes they formed. Looking back inside her apartment her focus returns to the seating chart.

Taking a deep, elongated breath, she rubs her hand over her forehead. The act of having to seat the guests into a manageable order is causing more problems than she had originally anticipated. Trying to seat two families from two very different backgrounds and the calibre of guests each family were requesting an invitation for, wasn't going to be as easy as she thought it would be.

Walking back to the chart, her finger trails down the guest list her father gave her. Rubbing her forehead again, her finger stops dead against the names of her childhood neighbours, Mr & Mrs Michaels. Closing her planner, she moves into her kitchen and empties her coffee cup. Placing it in the sink, she turns and heads upstairs to get ready for a long day at work.

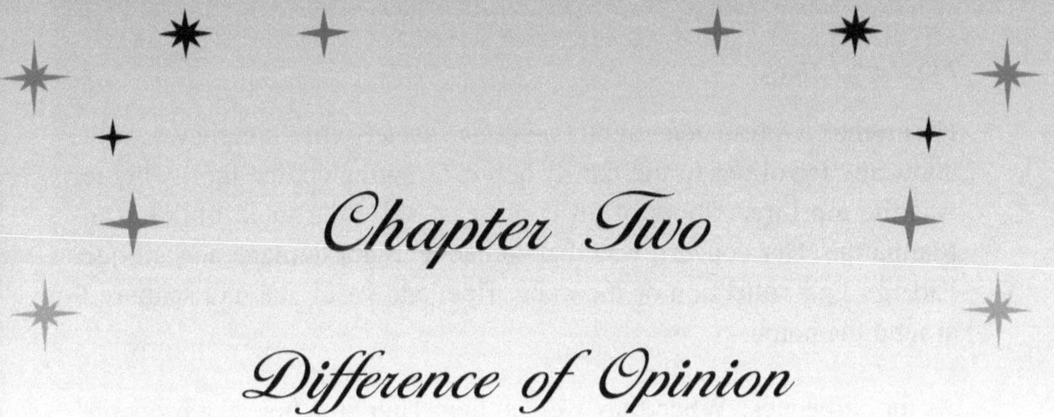

Chapter Two

Difference of Opinion

Shortly after the proposal, in which Damon and Harriet had to attend an extremely awkward Bennett family dinner to announce their engagement, the happy couple travelled to Hartford to share their happy news.

Taking the 176 exit to Hartford in transit to Bristol Street where Harriet's family home is located, Damon couldn't help but notice how different the streets are in the town she grew up in compared to his in Manhattan. Glancing over at his fiancé, he notices that her attention is preoccupied with the outside view, fixed on the streets of her childhood hometown.

Returning his attention to the road, he imagines her as a little girl. Riding her bike down the streets, going trick or treating with friends. Her family and neighbours having barbecue's in their backyards and maybe even attending a holiday parade here and there. Before he knows it, he is succumbed by a wave of jealousy. As it swells and crazily pounds on his chest, he silently wishes he had grown up in a community like this, in a house with a backyard.

Skimming the rearview mirror, he notices a young boy on his bike, and he thinks back to the time, in fact to the only time he ever rode a bike. It was during senior year, and he had borrowed a mate's motorbike only to smash it later into a tree. Luckily enough for him, he walked away injury free and his parents paid for a new motorbike plus sent a cheque to the school to cover the cost of any damages but mostly to keep the accident quiet and off his permanent record.

His mother, a fourth generation Forbes and society wife, simply wouldn't allow any frivolities in the family home. Growing up, the family home was the top three floors of an upper east side apartment building in Manhattan. Her concern was that someone might damage her antique Faberge Egg collection or the many fine jade vases she had scattered around the home.

As for barbecues? When they were at their Hampton house, a property with shorefront views, deck, tennis court and swimming pool; his father would allow the wait staff to grill steaks for them, but they still sat inside at the dinner table, never allowed to eat their food out on the deck. Beverly Forbes-Bennett never cooked or even knew how to cook. Damon and his sister Harper always had their food prepared for them. The only thing close to being hospitable that his father knew how to do, was to fix himself a scotch on the rocks or to empty the crystal distiller before retiring to his separate bedroom every night. That of course was on the nights he was actually home.

It was only when he began dating Harriet that Damon learnt how to use a frypan. When they first started dating, she was happy to meet him out, but as their careers grew busier, Harriet would elect to stay in and cook. Over time she slowly showed him to cook various types of meals from Macaroni and Cheese to a simple stir-fry until recently, Thanksgiving Dinner in which Damon's sister Harper and her husband attended.

Sprung from his reverie, he sees Harriet is watching him. Her mouth is twitching as it fights backs her giggles, she smiles. Enamoured at the way her smile paints a glowing ray of sunshine across her cheek and sparkle in her eyes, he can't help but smile happily back at her.

"I bet it's different than what you expected."

Nodding, he willingly admits. "I think it's lovely. It must have been great growing up here!"

"Yeah, it was okay. I mean, it wasn't a fairy-tale, but I survived."

Unaware of his envious behaviour, Damon shields Harriet from his festering irritations that swell deep inside him from her comments. Constantly overrun with ill thoughts and reminders from his family of how different they truly are from each other. He has always been made aware of their differences. But the dream of living a simpler future with a loving and exceptional woman that had been eluding him finally became a possible reality the moment he saw her in her uncle's tailor shop for the first time.

He knew it was no longer a dream when he saw her in her purple lace cocktail dress at Harper's wedding dinner rehearsal that he realised he had begun to fall. Then when she didn't attend the wedding because she had to go home for her brother's wedding, he found himself strangely missing her and in a desperate move to see her again, he willingly nominated himself to deliver payment in person at the offices of Enchanted Events in hopes to see her again.

Looking out at the homes, a glimpse of what might be passing through his mind. A scattering of images play with his mind. Standing in their driveway, a smiling Harriet beams at him as she watches as he holds the handlebars of their daughter's bike as she takes her first ride. Flash to Harriet and him jumping up and down in elation on the sidelines of their son's soccer match as they watch him score a goal. Another flash and he sees them up late Christmas Eve, wrapping their children's Christmas presents together. To the last flash, a glimpse of them sitting hand in hand on a porch swing on the veranda of their home outside of the city. Her head resting on his, his body relaxed into hers.

His attention is pulled back into the car by the touch of Harriet's hand on his arm.

"See this house coming up, the one with the olive tree garden and green shutters. That's my parent's house."

"I know Harriet."

Shaking her head, she places her hands over her face, embarrassed. "Sorry. I forget that you were only just here a few weeks ago", she smiles apologetically.

Slowing down, he pulls into the driveway, stopping the car in front of the two-door garage. As Harriet steps out and looks around the street, she muses over how the place looks as if it hasn't aged a day. Gazing up, she catches the sun rays peeking through the leaves of the Manchester redwoods as they cast shadows over the footpaths that line the street. Moving towards the boot, she eyes the street light at the end of the driveway. The sight of it reminding her of her favourite time of the year in Hartford was always Christmas this being that because each lamp in the town was decorated with big red bows and fairy lights. Almost as it were one of Thomas Kinkade idyllic Christmas paintings.

She looks over at him, catching him assessing the place, assuming he's seen her mother's olive tree garden. His financial assessment concludes that the property owned by Harriet's parents involves a two-storey, four-bedroom colonial, with possibly two bathrooms and a converted two door garage.

"I know right. It seems out of place. An olive tree garden in the front yard in a home in Hartford but she had to have one."

Laughing, he pops the boot with a button on his remote before walking around to help unload the car. The boot is almost empty when they are joined by her father's presence.

"Harriet, my sweet. Good to see you", he gently says before extending his hand towards Damon, "Damon, always a pleasure".

Picking up a suitcase, her father begins walking back inside as Harriet looks around to notice the obvious absence of her mother.

"Dad, where's Mom?"

Looking back over his shoulder as he makes up his way up the front steps. "Oh, she's inside, getting your room ready."

Shaking her head, Harriet isn't surprised one iota. "Of course she is."

A watchful Damon eyes her discomfort. Looking to her, he inquires. "That's sweet . . . isn't it?"

Harriet's reply is just to scrunch her face up and rolls her eyes. Stopping she turns into him before letting him in on some of her mother's traits that he will eventually come to know.

"Yeah, sure it is. Something you need to know about my mother: she'll do anything to get out of having to do any heavy lifting".

As they walk into the house, her father takes their bags off them and walks on ahead to place them in her room which is at the back of the ground level of the house. Growing up, she had shared a room with Paige until she turned thirteen. Much to her mother's disgust and protests that she didn't need her own room and the fact that she'd just be fine sharing with Paige; her father who thought it was time she had her own room, so he and her uncle converted the downstairs office into a bedroom and built an office onto the back of the garage.

Stepping further inside the lounge room of her childhood home, a small smile of familiarity creeps over her lips, as she notices that nothing has changed. The light blue walls are still plastered with photos from their childhoods with many of her and Will's high school photos now replaced with photos from their graduation and of Will's wedding.

Taking a deep breath, Harriet takes Damon's hand, that is held out to her and laces her fingers inside his. As they take a seat on the lounge.

"So . . . What do you think?", she asks.

Grinning back at her, he smiles politely. "Its . . ."

Interrupting him, she answers for him. "I know, pretty average well at least to your place!"

Touching her nose with a finger, he remarks. "I was going to say, homely."

"It doesn't exactly compare does it?"

His warm eyes, smiling back happily, meet hers. "I love it, Harriet. I don't think you realise how lucky you are!!!"

Their private moment is interrupted by her father presence as he joins them and places a tray down on the coffee table in front of them. Arranged on the tray is a selection of sandwiches, scones, slices of tea cake and brownies causing Damon's eyes to almost fall out of their sockets as he takes witness to all the delectable goodies in front of him.

Shaking her head at him, she looks to her father curiously. "Dad, is Will and Sophie coming?"

Her father looks back sorrowfully and nods. She nods in understanding. She knew her mother wouldn't have put on a spread like this for her and when her mother does finally join them, she sits in the single armchair opposite her daughter, without a greeting or a simple hello.

Gloria Lancer pours herself a cup of tea, she takes the cup and saucer and sits back in the chair. After taking a long sip of her tea, she places the cup on its saucer and looks at her daughter.

"So Harriet, what is the meaning of all this?"

"Well. Damon and I just thought you'd like to know that we're engaged."

Her face devoid of congratulation, Gloria immediately looks at her husband and spits out. "Did you know about this?'

"Yes, my dear I did."

"And you weren't going to tell me until now!?"

Intervening, an annoyed Harriet speaks up on behalf of her father. "Please don't talk to him like that. He knows because Damon asked him for my hand."

Meeting her daughter's eyes, Gloria's ice-cold eyes cut an eerie disapproving look. "Excuse me, missy, I'm talking to your father."

But to Gloria's dismay and disgust, Harriet has had enough. Finding her voice, she speaks. "Oh come *OFF* it!!!! You're just taking it out on him *because you* weren't told first, *because* something is finally not about you and *because* it's something to do with me!!!"

Narrowing her eyes at her daughter, Gloria coldly snaps back. *"Don't you dare* talk to me like that in this house!!!"

Frank interrupts, attempting to put out the fire between the two forces of nature. With a soft voice and sweet but concerned eyes, he eyes his wife. "Gloria sweetheart, for god sake. Your daughter's engaged. Aren't you the least bit happy for her?"

Shaking her head at them all, Gloria just sits in her chair. Disappointed, Harriet looks to her father sadly before resting back at Damon

Standing, Harriet prepares to leave. "Right. So Damon and I are going . . ."

"Oh, here you go again, making a scene. Always making a scene!!!"

Looking at her mother, her eyes glassy and full of anger and disappointment, she teeters out. "What scene? We came here to tell you some amazing news, and you're picking for a fight! God!!! I mean, I knew this wasn't going to be easy, and I know you hate me. You know, I never wanted to come back here, but Damon wanted to meet you. For reasons I don't know why!!!"

Looking at her sympathetically; Damon takes Harriet's wrist gesturing for her to sit down. Taking a deep hurt breath, she sits.

Rubbing her forehead, her voice breaks. "Look, be happy or be mad, care or don't care or whatever but we wanted to tell you in person. Come or don't come, there's going to be a wedding whether you like it or not."

Purposely ignoring his stewing wife, Frank looks to Damon. "Damon, dig in. Would you like a coffee or tea?"

Nodding happily back as Franks hands him a plate. "That'd be great Mr Lancer."

"Oh and please call me Frank."

"Okay, Mr Lancer. I mean, err, Frank."

Taking a piece of tea cake and a brownie, Damon sits back into the sofa, next to Harriet. Their shoulders brushing each other, he can feel the warmth emitting from within her. As Frank hands him his coffee, Damon turns his attention to the countenance between father and daughter. Feeling a grin form over his lips, Damon smirks as he watches Frank quietly hand his daughter a cup of tea and she smiles sweetly back at him as Gloria immediately disappears from the lounge at the sound of the ringing doorbell.

Sipping their drinks and sharing quiet glances between each other, they become aware of the guests and the reason behind the lovely spread of food laid out before them when they hear Gloria exclaim. *"My darling!!! It's good to see you!!! Sophie, always a pleasure."*

Harriet looks at Damon and shakes her head in disapproval. Standing, he places his now empty plate on the coffee table and holds his hand for her. Standing she meets him, and as they wait for Will and Sophie to enter, he takes his arm around her and scoops her into his chest. Glancing upwards, her eyes follow the length of his neck to his mouth and rest in his eyes. Feeling embarrassed, she sighs and buries her face in his chest.

"I'm sorry for before. My mother is selective with her affection."

Leaning down, his softly kisses her forehead. His fingers take on a mind of their own as they search for her hair before losing themselves inside her dark brown and caramel toned locks. Knowing her pain, he realises he'd be nothing more than a fool if he didn't immediately forgive her earlier behaviour.

"It's okay. You've met my mother right?"

Smiling, she looks up at him, and they share a private giggle until they are interrupted by Will and Sophie presence. Seeing his sister, Will immediately approaches her and pulls her into a hug before Sophie happily kisses her cheek.

Taking a seat, Harriet inquires. "It's good to see you both, have you been?"

Nodding at her, Will smiles. "Likewise stranger. We've been good. Really good. The house is coming along nicely!!!"

"And Sophie, how are you?"

She responds happily with, "I'm good, thank you for asking."

"So . . . what's going on, Harriet???", Will anxiously interrupts and meeting Damon's eyes, Harriet and Damon share a smile. Nodding at each other they look back at Will and Sophie. "Damon and I are engaged!!!"

Uprooted from their seats, Harriet and Damon immediate begin to feel as if they are playthings being jostled here and there again, being submerged in hugs and kisses.

"Are you serious?! Wow!!! That's, that's amazing!!!", Will excitedly snaps at them both.

"Let's see the ring then!!!"

Lifting her left hand, she shows a positively beaming Sophie, "Congratulations!!!"

"Thank you. We're . . .", turning her attention to Damon, "We're very excited!!!"

Smiling briefly, Harriet feels a nauseating sensation beginning to build in her stomach. In desperate need of fresh air and aim to escape without causing alarm, she looks for an immediate exit. There are two. Using the pretence of visiting the ladies, she stands and quickly escapes out the back door.

Standing, fixed on the other side of the door, she feels stuck. Looking up from her feet she takes a scanning view of the backyard and her breathing labours as she is comforted by familiarity. Noticing that nothing much has changed to the backyard apart from her parents having extended the patio and built a large wooden pergola covered in a lilac-coloured wisteria, in the middle of the yard. Peeling herself off the door, she steps down off the patio in search of one thing. Hidden at the very back of the yard, still standing upright and left untouched as if it were stuck in time, is a trampoline. Her trampoline.

Reaching it, she places her hands on its side railings. The cold steel, cooling her shaking nerves as she climbs into the middle of the aged black mesh. Lying flat across its width, she buries her face in her hands. Overwhelmed with thoughts and plans of the engagement, her mind is overrun by thoughts of her return to Hartford. She theorised her mother's reaction and truly wanted to believe that her mother would be happy for her. What a fool she'd been.

Her need for a quiet reverie is interrupted by a sound being carried from over the fence. A voice that she couldn't forget, even if she tried.

"You goddam lousy good for nothing waste of space!!! You've chewed up my work boots again!!! That's it; I'm giving you away!!!"

Leaning up from the trampoline, she looks over the fence to watch as Nate searches his backyard for his shoes. His odd behaviour comes of no surprise to Harriet, still after all these years, so his talking to a dog wouldn't be any stranger than usual.

Nate, on the other hand, in the hope of making a quick exit back inside, is stopped from returning inside by the sight of someone lying on the trampoline in his neighbour's yard. Feeling a deep burn cut across his chest, he fights with his better judgement to find out who it is or to just go back inside. Instead, he finds his heart compelling his mind, and an undeniable force edges him closer to the fence for a closer look. Standing on his tippy toes, the tells emanating from her stomach pain is proved true when he gets a real glimpse of her.

The one and only Harriet Lancer. The girl who stole his heart when he was eleven and still after all these years, he has never really been to escape everything that is her. She will always be the girl that no other will ever compare to. They hadn't spoken in years — ten in fact. If you don't count the moments in which they've been forced to speak briefly with each other over the years, make that argued; most recently being at Will's wedding but the memory of why they aren't on friendly terms, continues to elude them. Stepping away from the fence, the cold reminder of their history gives him the momentum to move back inside.

His attempts to disappear unnoticed are thwarted when Harriet sees his shadow near the fence and causes her to stand up on the trampoline.

"Nate???"

Turning around slowly, he faces her. "Oh, Harriet. *Hello?!* I . . . Uh. Sorry but I'm running late for work . . . so ah,"

Watching his escape, she sighs a sigh of relief. Relieved, she mumbles. "Oh well okay."

Stopping at his door, the reason as to why she is home bothers him. She *never* comes home unless she *has* to.

"How long are you back for?"

"Ah . . . just for the weekend. I have to be back in New York on Monday. I have a lot of work to do!!!"

"Really?"

"Yes actually, well for the next year at least."

As she stands on her trampoline, she scrutinises his every action so intently. Desperately; she wants to draw out the moment, in the hope that his curiosity will peak and get the better of him so that she can tell him her news.

"Well, that's great Harriet. I'm happy to hear that you're doing so well. I . . . well, I better get going."

As he makes to walk inside to leave for a walk, he is stopped by Harriet's sweet but soft voice once more. He missed her voice especially when she was calling his name. For the longest time, he felt that when she called his voice, it was like being called home. It made him feel safe, and it made him feel loved. For the longest time, she was his heart's home.

"Nate. Don't you at least want to know why I'll be so busy?"

He already had guessed. He knew probably before she did. On the occasion when Will came back to Hartford to visit, or the Lancer's invited him over for dinner, they would always openly talk about Harriet and how well she is doing. Well, Frank and Will did at least. But in the last couple of years, their conversations shifted and came to include Damon. Sitting around the barbecue next door or watching Friday night football alongside Will, they all talked about how all they thought that it wouldn't too long before they talked marriage.

Feeling helpless and irrelevant, the more they talked about them, the more Nate felt like his heart was going to shrivel up and die. It had been happening more frequently than often lately, a deep burn around his heart and when he saw Damon's BMW in the Lancer's driveway a couple of weekends ago or better yet forget Mr Lancer's cheery disposition later that night when Will invited him over the fence for dinner, he knew the possibility of ever having her tied to him had finally slipped from his reach.

Disinclined to show his pain from her happy news in front of her, he plasters on a fake jaunty smile before facing her to ask the question to what his heart will never be ready to hear. "Why will you be so busy, Harriet?"

"I'm getting married."

And just as he had predicted, in her clearest yet concise voice, it struck him like a knife right into the middle of his heart.

"Is it Damon Bennet that you're marrying?"

"Yes. His name is Damon Bennett. Why?"

"He's the brother of the girl whose wedding you were planning when you came home for Will's wedding, right?"

"Yes!!! That's right!"

"When you stopped speaking to me???"

Hastily jumping down from the trampoline, an irritated Harriet shakes her head at him. Having hit a nerve, she moves towards the fence to meet him. "I stopped speaking to you for a reason. Besides, you stopped speaking to me a lot longer before Will's wedding remember!!!"

Stepping back, she begins to make a move back inside the house. She is stopped midway by his now ragged voice.

"Do you love him?"

Infuriated, she snaps as she turns to meet him. But her anger immediately diminishes at the sight of a lost Nate looking to the ground, unwilling to meet her eyes with his hand raking through his dark chocolate brown hair.

"Yes, Nate. I do. I love him. Very much!!!"

Turning she departs and returns inside while he remains watching the space as it dissipates from something to nothing. And like Harriet, he too returns inside his home to finish getting ready for work. Stopping in his kitchen, he makes himself a cup of coffee.

Standing at the window, his coffee pursed between his fingers and his lower lip, his attention is taken by the sight of the trampoline in the Lancer's backyard. The now empty trampoline. Closing his eyes, his mind cruelly plays with him and causes him to think back on when his infatuation with Harriet began and if it had ever ended.

The one thing that he has always been sure of is this. What started as a seemingly innocent, sweet and youthful love turned out to be his greatest undoing. An undoing that will undoubtedly haunt him for the rest of his life.

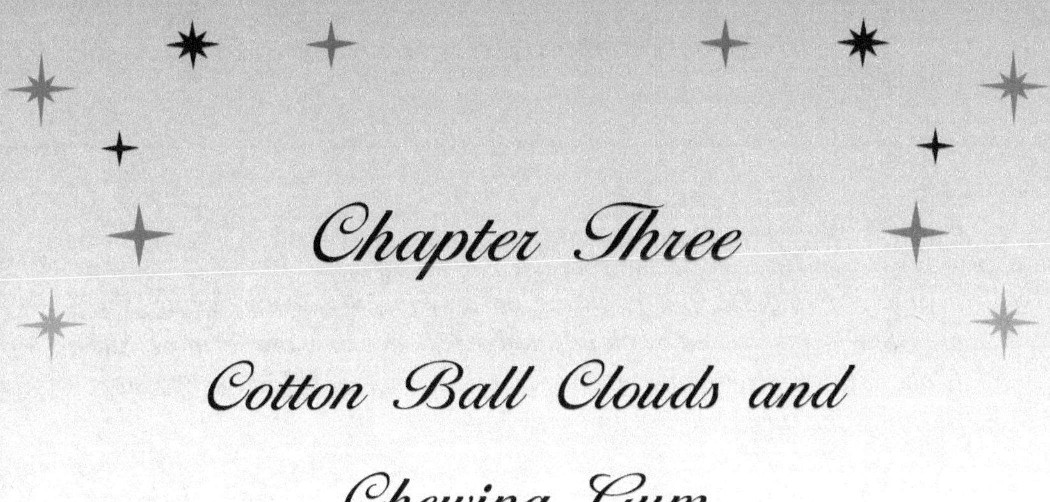

Chapter Three

Cotton Ball Clouds and Chewing Gum

Walking back inside, Harriet is stuck. Fixed against the door, her mind cruelly recalls what just transpired between her and Nate.

The truth is, she had never been sure of what Nate truly felt for her. If he did feel or say something, it always came across as some joke or like he was chasing a good time. As a teenager he became quite the charmer and one more than occasion, he fragrantly demonstrated his talents in front of everyone. But around Harriet, in private moments he led her to believe that he felt something more than just friendship.

Nonetheless, as time would have it, their wants and dreams drove them in different directions. The moment she received her high school diploma, she moved to Dartmouth to begin college and later again to New York for her career. While Nate stayed in Hartford to run the family business. Mistakes were made, and after many heated words were exchanged in private over the years, her trips home became fewer, and before long, he was just some boy she knew that lived next door.

Peeling herself off the door, she enters her room and takes a seat at her window. Gazing up towards the cornflour blue plastered sky and white meringue puffed like clouds, she feels a wave of warmth unfold over her. Lowering her forehead against the cool glass pane, she recalls the time when Nate first sprung her watching the clouds.

❈ ❈ ❈

Nineteen years earlier . . .

A nine-year-old Harriet is sitting on a swing at school during first play. She is memorised by clouds and the shapes they are forming. She is about to start swinging when someone comes up behind her to start pushing. She turns around and sees Nate.

"Oh Nate, you scared me", clutching at her throat in shock, she stops swinging. And as he sits next to her on the empty swing, he peers around at her, "What on earth were you looking at?"

She looks up into the sky, "The clouds."

"The clouds? Why on earth for?"

Ignoring his vulgarity, she replies instantly. "Because they're fascinating. They look like puffs of smoke or cotton balls but at times make the oddest of shapes."

"Harriet, you think way too much!"

Looking around her to see where all the other boys his age are, she remains curious as to why he is there.

"Nate, why aren't out playing soccer or running with Will and the boys?"

He avoids looking at her face and muffling out a reply; he admits to her why he's missed yet another play-time.

"Err. I had detention."

"What for this time???"

Turning away from her, deliberately avoiding her eyes, he quietly responds. "I kind of put chewing gum in Halley Sawyer's hair."

Smiling, trying hard to suppress her need to giggle and be serious, Harriet smirks. "Why do you do such stupid things?"

Flashing his cheeky smile at her, he replies immediately. "Don't know? I just do. Besides, I thought you didn't like Halley anyway?"

"I don't either Nate, but I certainly wouldn't put chewing gum in her hair!"

She looks around and notices Halley wasn't at school today. Come to think of it, she hadn't been to school all week.

"I haven't seen Halley in a while; she hasn't been in class all week!"

Watching her hair, its light curls bouncing in time with the wind, he loses his train of thought. He couldn't imagine how he'd feel if she had to have her long russet-like locks cut off. Feeling guilty, he knows he has wronged, but he also knew the kind of person Halley was and of the pain that Halley was deliberately causing Harriet.

"Yeah, apparently they couldn't get the chewing gum out of her hair, so she had to get a haircut."

"Oh . . . That's awful. So seriously why'd you do it?"

His sweaty hands, clutching embarrassingly at the chains of the swing, he realises he's about to admit to why he did it.

"I don't know. I might've heard from someone that she was giving you a hard time about the whole Dirty Dancing thing."

Her eyes are exploding at his confession, she immediately becomes embarrassed and flushed. Shielding her discomfort, she attempts to laugh it off, "Um Right. You know, I'm sure it's just a phase."

"Yeah . . . sure. Just a phase!"

"Besides, I think everyone goes through a phase. Kinda like when you and Will would pretend you were Rocky and Rambo or was it Jean Claude Van Damn? Anyways, you two would run around the backyard with guns and boxing gloves", then with a shrug of her shoulders and a sweet tone in her voice, she tilted her head and glanced his way, "But hey maybe I'm wrong."

And as the school bell rings as if on cue, to alert all students that play time has ended and to return to the land of the alphabet, chalkboards and erasers, a smug Harriet jumps off the swing and starts to head back to her class.

"Bye Nate!"

Watching as she walks away from, he is left completely dumbfounded. His hands a puddle of sweat against the swing's chain and on standing, he drops them to his pants to wipe them free of sweat. As he moves one foot in front of the other, he begins the journey back to his class.

Still quizzical lost by event just now, he can't help but try to fathom the effect that Harriet has on him. How did she do it? How was she able to make fun of herself yet make him feel as small as possible at the same time?

Stopping to take a drink at the coolers, the cold water rushes across his lips and helps to cool his overloaded mind, currently scattered with memories of Harriet smile. There was something always magical about the way she smiled that undid him.

Maybe it was the way that when she smiled, it seemed to light up her face like a rainbow lights up the sky after a shower sending waves of bright shades of pink to her cheeks and causing her chocolate brown eyes to sparkle as they danced in the sunlight.

It was there and then that a realisation had crept upon him. He had fallen in love with her. At eleven, he had fallen for his best friend's sister and next door neighbour and that his life was about to become more complicated than he could ever have anticipated.

❋ ❋ ❋

Removing herself from her room, Harriet re-joins her family. Entering the kitchen, she grabs a water bottle from the kitchen fridge while a quizzical Damon, who has been wondering where she has been, catches sight of her and sees that she is a million miles away. Fixed at the kitchen window, she stares over at Nate's house.

Will, whose attention has gone from his mother's to the bizarre behaviour of his sister, stands and meets her in the kitchen.

"Harriet? Woo-hoo . . . Earth to Harriet!!!"

Pulled from her thoughts, she glances up to look at him, "What? I mean, hey Will."

"So . . . where you'd go?"

Taking a sip of her water, she slowly shrugs and looks down at her feet, purposefully avoiding his eyes.

"Oh . . . just outside. Sat on the tramp. Can't believe it's still there!"

As he chuckles, he moves to cross his arms over his chest. "Yeah, I think she's keeping it in case she gets any grandchildren."

Smiling, she looks up from her feet. "I think you'd make a great dad, Will."

As her attention slowly returns to the view of Nate's house, she feels Will's presence beside her at the sink.

"So . . . did you see Nate while you were out there?"

Scratching her eyebrow, she awkwardly responds. "Um yeah. I did. It was weird actually. To see him after all these years."

"Yeah, I know. But he's good though. He owns the shop in town, and he's seeing someone."

Her breathe, slowly hitching at the news that he's seeing someone, replies. "Well . . . that's . . . that's good."

Turning away from the window, she looks over to Damon only to become immersed with laughter. He is glaring back at her and rolling his eyes as her mother rattles on about family news and that she has left him there, all this time, to fend for himself.

"I like him, Harriet!"

Turning to look at her brother, she nods her head in agreement. "Yeah, I do too!!!"

"He's a keeper."

Nodding, her attention still fixed in the direction of Damon. "Yeah, I know!"

As he begins to make the walk back to Sophie, she stops him. "Will??? . . . Thanks."

"It's okay. . . besides, you'll have to face to rest of Mom's lot at the party tonight."

"What party???"

Avoiding her question, he puts his arm around her neck and playfully pulls her back over to everyone, deliberately changing the subject. "Come on; let's go have some cake before Damon eats it's all!!!"

Looking up the ceiling, she breathes out a deep sarcastic sigh.

"Woo-hoo . . . I can't wait."

Chapter Four

The Engagement Party

Fixed against the grey plush leather of his BMW, Harriet and Damon are headed towards the Sheraton Hartford South Hotel.

After Damon asked her father for her hand, Frank Lancer immediately went about putting together plans for an engagement party for them. Frank had Damon organise the New York side of things while he handled the details there in Hartford.

Pulling into a park, he turns off the ignition and looks out at the venue before glancing back to his fiancé. Mildly concerned, he stays transfixed in his seat as he watches her take a deep breath at the sight of the hotel before her eyes come back to meet his and she laces her fingers within his.

Looking down at their entwining fingers, she opens his hand so she can trace the lifeline of his open palm, softly from left to right.

Glancing back up, her now worried eyes ask. "Are you ready for this?"

Grinning back at her, hoping that she is just nervous, he smiles reassuringly. "Yes."

Exasperated by the unknown eluding them inside, she looks back out the window. That is until she feels Damon yank her attention back on him as he takes her hand and forces her to look at him. Watching as a smirk twitches over his lips and spread across his cheeks, he smiles as he takes a strand of her hair and curls it around his finger.

"Harriet, I have never been more certain!!!"

Leaning back in her seat, she closes her eyes and softly nods. Opening them, they exit the car and head towards the hotel entrance. Once inside, the couple sights her parents standing just inside a room alongside Will and Sophie, Paige, Uncle Sal and Aunt Wanda and walking into the room herself, Harriet is shocked at the sight before her.

Circling slowly, her eyes are overwhelmed by the sight of a large crystal chandelier hanging from the ceiling. Draped from the chandelier are lilac lavender chiffon that stretches out to all four corners of the room. And if the chandelier didn't already create enough sparkle for the room, the fairy lights placed under the chiffon drapes help to cast moonlit shadows off the floor and ceiling as if you were walking on a moon dust-covered cloud with bewitching stars sprinkled across your night sky.

Glancing down, her eyes look towards the tables. Taking a hand, she reaches out to feel the table's white cotton tablecloth and smooths her palm over the material. Perched in the centre of each table are simple but tall glass vases, filled with lavender roses and surrounded by smaller glass vases holding tea light candles that flicker away behind the place cards for each guest.

Continuing, she finally stops at the table which has been set just for Damon and her. Overwhelmed by the sheer beauty of the room and warmth from the men's act, tears well in her eyes and begin to spill down her cheek. Particularly touched and astounded by the fact that Damon remembered that her favourite colour was purple and her favourite flowers are roses. Placing her clutch down on the table, she fixes the tears away from her eyes and looks down to smooth her dress out. A dusty pink chiffon boat neck cocktail dress paired with her pale pink slingback heels. She was going to wear the purple lacy dress that she wore to Harper's wedding dinner rehearsal but instead chose to wear pink.

Turning, she notices guests beginning to appear inside the room. Her cousins and mother's relatives have arrived early to reserve the best tables for themselves causing her father's relatives to no doubt to elect to sit quietly near the back of the room and wait patiently to see the newly engaged couple. She always felt bad for her father's family and seeing that she preferred them to her mother's, she decided that if she were ever to get married, hers was going to be a different affair. Mostly because she would be paying for it herself. She always wanted it that way. It gave her the power and financial freedom to say, do and invite whomever she wanted. From the moment she left for college, Harriet was determined to never ask her parents for anything that she couldn't get for herself, and she didn't.

From the moment she started working at Enchanted Events and began building a clientele, she had begun putting money away for a rainy day, and her wedding was now the perfect excuse to use it. She worked hard, worked her way up through the ranks and became highly sort after and in demand for events. Elizabeth respected her and loved her work so much so that Harriet knew that Elizabeth was practically a heartbeat away from promoting her to partner any day now.

Plus, the perks that come from working in an event management company is that you get to finally use your clientele services on yourself and that most would give their services at discounted prices. She also knew, without even having to ask them, that her godparents would supply the formalwear and do the party's hair and beauty. Also, seeing that Harriet and Damon lived in Tribeca, well that meant that they could just go home after their wedding and leave for their honeymoon the next day. Damon anticipated that his family would crawl back to Manhattan leaving the only accommodation she'd have to organise would be her own family's as they would have to travel from Hartford and stay in New York.

Taking focus of the guests that have seated themselves at the back of the room, she sees her Aunty Mara, her father's sister. Smiling happily, she goes to greet them. Opening her arms, she pulls her Aunt into a warm hug.

"Aunty Mara, thank you so much for coming!"

Cheerfully, she hugs her niece tightly. "Oh, honey. We wouldn't miss this for the world. Your young man seems very nice!"

Glancing over at Damon, Harriet's eyes meet his. "Yeah, he's a peach."

Pulling back from the hug, she stays rooted next to her Aunt as her Uncle meets them on his way back from the bar with Harriet's father and drinks in tow.

"Congratulations, my dear," he says as he kisses her on the cheek and hands a drink to Mara. Looking around the room, he chuckles. "Thank you so much for inviting us. I was surprised when your father called and told us he was pretty this on. I thought that was your job."

Shaking her head in genuine surprise, she smiles back at her uncle. "I didn't even know. Will told me just this morning. I'm so happy you're both here. I haven't seen you both in so long. I'm planning to come back to Hartford in a couple of weeks, we will have to catch up and have dinner."

Turning to look over at Damon, she can't help but laugh at Damon as he is being swallowed up by her aunts and cousins. Knowing that she should go and save him, she lets it go for another ten minutes to talk with Mara and John before leaving to rescue him.

Reaching around to hug them both, she beams. "I'd better go rescue the damsel in distress. I promise to come back in a little bit so we can talk more okay."

Nodding away, they shush her off, and she begins her way back to Damon, and her trip back would've been a fast one considering the distance between them if it weren't for the sight of a couple walking past the room's doors. Caught out, she almost loses her footing at the sight of Nate with his arm around a blonde. A blonde who looks oddly familiar to her. But before she has the chance to put a name to the face, a worried Damon is at her side, checking to see if she is okay.

"Hey? Are you okay?" he asks, concerned.

Dazed, she shakes it off. "Yeah, no. Just lost my balance. These heels are as thin as a chopstick. Seriously, I'm fine."

Touching her chin, the pad of his thumb swipes over her cheek causing him to smile. "Okay. You're good then."

Blushing, she glances away, but her eyes can't help but make their way back to his. As he slowly leans down to kiss her forehead, he whispers, "You should probably take it easy on the champagne tonight."

Grinning, she argues back. "Oh really? I do, do I now?"

"Of course not. This is your party. Drink as much as you like!", she replies instantly, elated.

Closing the distance between them, Harriet reaches up and softly nips at his lips. Taking his hand from her cheek, he moves it to her hair and places his other hand around her waist, trapping her against him. Her kiss on his lips, light and soft to begin with evolves into a passionate and rather heavenly embrace between them. Pulling apart, they feel the eyes of their guests on them and decide to make a move to their seats, when they hear a tapping off the microphone so that the festivities can officially begin.

Tapping on the microphone to make sure it's working properly, Harriet's father starts. "Good Evening everyone, I just would like to say a few words on behalf of my beautiful daughter Harriet', smiling over at her as she happily glances back, 'I just, we, Gloria and I would just like to say how happy we are for Harriet's engagement to Damon Bennett. Damon, I have never seen my daughter happier than she has been these last couple of years so I just wanted to formally welcome you to the family and we all wish you our deepest congratulations! We hope that you will live a long and loving life together. So let's all raise our glasses to the newly engaged couple, to Harriet and Damon. Salute!!"

"Salute!!!"

Nodding at Frank, everyone watches as Damon makes his way to the microphone and to briefly hug Mr Lancer. Placing the microphone to his lips, he begins.

"Good evening everyone. It's been lovely meeting you all, and I especially can't wait to get to know you all better when this beautiful woman", glancing over at Harriet he gleams happily, "and I marry."

Happy beyond compare, Harriet finds herself become momentarily overwhelmed by the attention from everyone's eyes in the room. Feeling a wave of claustrophobia begins to spread over her, she posts a fake smile across her lips before looking down at the table to close her eyes. As the location of the hotel's exits flashes across her mind, her attention is brought back to the celebration by the soft voice of the gorgeous Greek-like Adonis speaking into the microphone before her.

"Now, I don't know if you all know how Harriet and I met, so I just wanted to share a little story. . .'

Grinning mischievously, he glances at her before continuing. 'I met this beautiful woman when she was planning my sister's wedding. We didn't like each other at first, mostly because I snubbed Dirty Dancing . . . What?! Apparently women go crazy over this movie!!!"

Hearing the room break out into laughter, an immediately flushed Harriet looks down to the table and shakes her head before meeting his eyes sarcastically as he laughs into the microphone.

"Sorry, I couldn't help it. I fell fast and before I knew it, what I felt was beyond my control. She completely amazes me. I love this woman. She is my everything and to honour this moment in our very long and happy life together, I thought we should dance to our song. .'

Harriet looks at him, confused. *But we don't have a song?!* And as if by magic, a giggle builds in her belly and fills her body when she hears the opening chords to "I've had the time of my life" play over the room.

Lost in giggles and a frosting of tears, she shakes her head. *No, he didn't.*

Standing before her, he reaches out to take her hand and leads to her the floor. Lacing his fingers in hers and positioning her back in front of him, he places her arm around his neck and gently runs his fingers down her arm, resting them in hers. Harriet knew this move. *She dreamed about this move.* Ideally, in her dreams, it was Patrick Swayze that was standing behind her but her sparkling bright eyes and upturned lips splashed over her face couldn't any bigger than now in this moment all because Damon had learnt the dance and surprised her with it.

As they move into the first steps and leg lift of the Mambo, the room now exploding in laughter and joy, Harriet can hear Paige's wolf whistle overpowering the music and when the song's instrumental interlude approaches, Damon, swings Harriet out turns to face the room before ushering everyone to come join them on the floor and isn't long before all of her family have joined in on the dance.

Taking her hand, he curls her back into him and out again. Spinning her around, they join hands, and he takes a firm hold of her by her waist. Not expecting the anticipated lift, a surprised Harriet is astounded when he varies the move by picking her up in a newlywed lift and spinning around on the spot.

Then finally as the song begins to lull out before the chorus is sung for the last time, Damon places her back on her feet to take her left hand and drapes it over his shoulder and place her right around his waist to sway slowly together for the remainder of the song. That is until her favourite part comes up, you know the part in the movie where Patrick and Jennifer are swaying back and forth in each other's arms, and he is singing to Jennifer as she gazes back up at him, well, Harriet can't help but melt as she gazes up at Damon as he mouths the lyrics back down at her and sways them back and forth.

Running her hand through his hair, her fingers wavering in his golden locks, she is unable to contain her joy. Grinning ear to ear, her body bursts with glee at the sight of him, trying to be Johnny Castle. Pulling her closer, she feels his lips softly nip her nose before whispering, *"I love you, Harriet."*

Tickled, she finds solace by placing her forehead in his neck. "Damon, you know that you're the reason why I keep smiling, don't you?"

Pulling back from his arms, she meets his eyes as they softly look back at her. "I love you!"

Nodding, he leans forward and kisses her forehead softly. "I love you!"

"Damon?"

"Yes?"

"Thank you, for all of this. I don't know . . . words can't -"

Drawing her back into the warmth of his arms, he grins. "I know, honey."

Their private reverie is interrupted at the of sight Sophie and Will, who are wheeling out a two-tier, lavender quilted with pearl decor engagement cake. Watching as Will lights the sparklers sticking out from the top tier, Damon and Harriet join hands as they cut into the bottom tier and softly kiss over the gilded flashes shooting out from the cake.

Reaching for the microphone that Damon had resting on their table, Harriet decides it's finally her time to say a few words.

"Thank you, everyone. Damon and I would like to say thank you so very much from the bottom of our hearts -"

Beaming, she turns toward her parents, Will and Sophie and Paige. "Dad, thank you for organising all this. Mom, Will, Sophie and Paige; thank you for celebrating this with us and welcoming Damon into the family. It's always great to see the Lancer's out. I won't deny the fact that I do get busy in New York, but I do enjoy coming home and seeing you all. Lastly, I would also like to acknowledge my godparents Sal and Wanda, I love you both so much and thanks to you as well for being ever so supportive and I'm so lucky to have you all in my life!"

And as she turns around to place microphone down on the table, she catches Nate watching from the door. Ignoring the sight of him, Harriet encompasses herself back into Damon's arms as he brushes her cheek and they discuss having a piece of their cake.

Then once the cake had been devoured and all the champagne had been drunk, guests began to sparse from the party by going home.

After helping to clean the room and speaking with the staff at the Hotel, Harriet is coerced into staying out a little longer by having a drink at the bar. Before departing the room, an ever grateful Harriet hugs her father.

"Dad, thank you for tonight."

He smiles at her, "Anything for my love."

Looking at her mother, her enthusiasm pains a little, but still, she knows that she must thank her mother too.

"Mom, thank you. Damon and I really appreciate tonight."

Gloria smiles politely at her daughter then gathers all her things. "It was a lovely party, Harriet. .', nodding she looks over at her husband, 'Frank, come on. We'd better get going and leave the young ones to party."

Exiting the room, they depart as Frank passes Harriet to the hotel's front entrance, he winks at his daughter.

"Go on, honey. Go on and have fun!"

She watches them walk off when she feels Damon's warmth on her back. Leaning back into his chest, her body tingles at the touch of his lips against her neck and her legs quiver as he moves over her ear.

"Did you have a good night?"

Looking upward, "I had a great night. Thank you, Mr Bennett!!!"

"What did I say about you calling me Mr Bennett?"

"Hmmm . . . remind me again what you said about being called Mr Bennett?"

Giggling, she shows wondrous magic when she catches him smiling back. Burying his face in her neck, he places soft kisses on her shoulder and back before pulling up to meet her smiles again.

Taking her hand in his, he pulls her towards the bar. "Come on, let's go get a real drink!!!"

Chapter Five

Post Celebration Insults

"Harriet??? Was it weird being back in that room?"

Looking back at her brother, she shakes her head. "No . . . why???"

"Don't you remember, you had your 18th in that room."

"Oh . . . yeah", slapping her forehead in amazement as they enter the bar, she childishly groans. "Gosh . . . It's been ten years already. God, I'm old!!!"

Standing while the women search the room to find a booth big enough to sit in, the men wait for drink orders. When the women have finally taken their seats, Sophie and Paige's jaws slowly drop as they watch Damon take everyone's drink orders.

"He's very well mannered. Will, see how he waited until everyone was seated then took our orders.", Sophie teases.

Laughing at their behaviour, Harriet is almost reduced to tears as she watches the two of them are completely mystified by Damon's etiquette and then over at her brother's clear disinterest. Her somewhat joy at the moment is brought to an immediate halt and quickly changes to an uncomfortable revolt at the sight of Nate and Halley Sawyer entering the bar. Noticing the change in his sister, Will follows the breadcrumbs of her focus to see Nate standing at the bar with Halley in hand.

Standing, without even thinking, Will invites them over to join their party.

"Hey, Nate. Didn't think I'd see you here tonight. Please, come join us!!!"

Watching Nate and Halley move towards their table, Sophie meets Harriet's eyes and takes a deep breath as she begins prepares herself for the delightful company of Halley Sawyer, an unenthusiastic Harriet slumps back into soft cushioning of the booth, and Paige looks to the ceiling.

Disgusted, Paige leans and whispers to Harriet. "Oh god, Halley is coming to sit with us?"

Overhearing Paige, Will glares at Paige before they sit down. "Hello Halley, how are you?"

Looking up from her nails, a displeased Halley glances at Will. "Halley, you remember my wife Sophie and my sisters, Harriet and Paige."

Stunned at much Harriet has changed, she spits out. "Harriet? Harriet is that you? Wow . . . haven't you changed???"

Feeling awkward at her response, Harriet frowns a grimaced look back. "Um thanks, Halley', uncertain of what to say or do she finds herself bumbling out uncomfortably, 'looks like you haven't changed a bit."

On hearing Harriet's comment, Halley sits up straight. With her nose twitching and her eyes glassing over with fury, Halley summons her inner bitch and searches the table for immediate payback. Coolly, she smugly asks. "So what are you doing in town?"

"Oh, we're all here tonight for the engagement party!", Sophie replies.

"*Oh really.* Who's getting married now???"

"I am!!!", Harriet snaps instantaneously, and as her response leaves her lips, the others can't stop themselves from looking back to Halley as she squirms in her seat uncomfortably.

As the topic of conversation changes to the party and the women go about ignoring Halley, Damon appears with a tray of drinks and hands out everyone's drink. Taking a seat next to Harriet, he takes his arm and places it around his fiancé before looking up at everyone. Acknowledging the new additions to their group, he immediately stands and reaches his hand over to introduce himself to them.

"Excuse me where are my manners. Damon Bennett, Harriet's fiancé. A pleasure to meet you both."

Astonished, a gobsmacked Halley is rendered speechless. As she slowly closes her mouth, Halley sits upright and straightens her posture. Revolting in their seats as they watch her, the women watch a somewhat cringe-worthy performance from Halley as she takes the length of her blonde hair within her fingers and flips it onto her neck before standing to return his introduction and shake his hand.

"Nice meeting you Damon, I'm Halley", batting her eyelashes as she watches enviously as he takes his seat next to Harriet.

"So, how do you know Harriet, Halley?", Damon asks curiously.

"Oh, we went to school together!"

Intrigued, Damon responds with "Really?" before looking at his fiancé. Harriet nods silently at the news, her confirmation interrupted by the sound of Halley cackling uncontrollably and snorting rudely.

"Yes!!! She was crazy for Patrick Swayze back then. Always writing Mrs Johnny Castle all over her books and then re-enacting the

dance all by her lonesome at lunchtime!!!"

Tightening his arm around her, Damon feels Harriet tensing and in an attempt the lighten the mood, he smiles proudly at Halley.

"Ah, thank you, Halley, for that information. But I'm actually already quite well aware that she is indeed a Dirty Dancing fan."

Sensing defeat, Halley snaps back. "That must be why the whole hotel had to listen to that ridiculous song. Don't tell me, she made you dance to that Damon!!!"

Brushing his knuckles against her cheek, a starry-eyed Damon looks at his Harriet. "Actually, Halley', he begins before glancing over at her, 'knowing of how fond Harriet was of the dance and the music, I took some dance lessons and planned the surprise especially for Harriet."

"What? When?", replies a surprised Harriet.

"*Oh* . . . I just went to a couple of classes during the week"

"*Really???*"

Feeling the eyes on them from everyone around the booth, Damon nods happily while Harriet smiles blissfully at the group.

"Well, I thought it was awesome!", replies Paige.

"It was great. I thought it was romantic that he surprised Harriet with it!" responds Sophie as she meets her husband's eyes with a smile.

Shaking his head, Will smirks at his wife. "Yeah, I think Harriet enjoyed it." Looking over at Damon, Will is curious as to whether it be a recurring event at the wedding, "So since you're such a pro-Damon, are you going to do a repeat dance at the wedding?"

Looking to his fiancé, Damon smiles, "I'm game if you are!!! Will, do you think your mother would join in?"

Shaking his head, Will answers immediately, "Um. I'm just going to go ahead and say no. But Dad probably would!!!"

Shaking their heads, the entire party except Halley can't help but laugh at Will's comments. Halley feeling uncomfortably left out doesn't understand the joke, and as she goes to ask Nate what the joke is about, she catches Nate watching Harriet. Feeling Halley's eyes on him, he looks away and to her but somehow he knows there will be hell to pay when they get home later that night.

When the table lulls into a quiet spell as they all sip their drinks, the small silence is broken by the sound of Nate's voice.

"So, did you have a good night?"

Not sure at who the question was directed at, Damon and Harriet both look at him and then at each other, before answering.

"Yeah, I think we did!!!", replies Damon.

On hearing the response, Nate looks down into his beer bottle before emptying its contents. As he places the now empty bottle on the table, he leans in towards Halley to whisper. "Wanna get out of here?"

A disgusted Halley who has been watching him this whole entire time stands up immediately and without a goodbye, storms over towards the bar's exit. Concerned that she hasn't broken a nail or her brain, Paige asks him, "Is she okay, Nate?"

Locking eyes with Harriet, he replies frustrated. "She'll be fine. It's probably just her time of the month or something!"

Standing to leave, he looks to the table, "Um. So anyway, I guess that's my queue. We'll leave you to your celebrations. Night everyone."

Standing up to speak with his friend, "Come on mate, stay? Halley will be fine."

Shaking his head, Nate declines. "Nah, I'd better go. We'll talk later okay mate. It was good seeing you are finally happy, Harriet!"

Upon hearing him saying her voice, her eyes travel from her lap up to meet Nate's with a brief smile and polite nod.

When Nate and Halley have finally left the bar, Paige lets slip. "God!! What a bitch!!!"

"Paige . . . shhhhh. Not so loud!"

"What! It's the truth!!!"

Sophie laughing with Paige remains curious too. "Where does she get off?"

"Sophie? Please, that's my best friend!", a disappointed Will snaps.

"Honey, I know that he is your best friend and he is welcome to join us anytime as long as he chains her up before he leaves the house!!!"

As the table erupts in laughter, Harriet can feel tears falling down her cheeks as she looks over at her sister in law.

"Oh my god, Sophie. I didn't think you had a mean streak in you!!!"

Shaking her head and pointing her index finger at Harriet, Sophie replies instantaneously. "Oh no. I'm not mean, I just have 'Bitch radar' and she my friend is a bitch!"

Wiping the tears away from her eyes with her drink napkin, Harriet and Damon share a smile as Paige looks over to Will.

"Why is Nate even with her anyway? I thought he would have no trouble getting himself a nice girl?"

Will shrugs, "I don't know. He mentioned to me recently that he's ready to settle down and that she can be quite nice once you get to know her or something like that. I wasn't really listening, I'm just confused as you are, Paige."

Sophie, rolling her eyes, "Well, let's hope he wakes up to himself soon because I don't think I can stand having her around!!!"

Paige, nodding in agreeance. "Still, I don't get it. Growing up, I just always assumed he was into brunettes, not blondes!"

Feeling her chest grow tight, Harriet begins to shift uncomfortably in her seat. Playing her reaction down to hearing both Will and Paige's comments on Nate's relationship, she wipes her eyes and stretches in her seat.

Watching her, Damon leans forward and asks, "Feeling tired honey?" as he gently rubs her back. Smiling over her shoulder at him, she nods, and they stand to leave.

"We should probably get going. Mom won't like it if we wake her up. That, and we have to drive back to New York tomorrow."

Taking her hand, he leads out of the booth and stops in front of Sophie and Will. Reaching in for hugs, they thank them both for being there.

"Sophie, Will. Thank you so much for all this."

Smiling happily, Sophie nods, "No sweat honey. Um, listen I know you're an expert and all but if you need anything, please let me know okay."

"Sure. That'd be great. We should be back in a few weeks so would it be okay if we all catch up then? I know Paige will be back at college, but I know Sal and Wanda will want measurements as soon as."

Sophie looks at them quizzically, "Wait . . . what?"

"Well, um if it's okay with you. I've been thinking about having three bridesmaids. My friend from work, Karen, Paige and I was going to ask you, Sophie. Damon is having two friends of his, and he was going to ask Will to be a groomsman so -"

But before Harriet can finish, Sophie yanks her into a hug. As Damon and Will shake their heads at the behaviour of the girls, Paige can't help but gag and mimic throwing up in the background.

"Yuck!!! Get a room!!! Email me sis if you need something, okay otherwise I'm sure Mom will tell me!"

Will unexpectedly snaps, "Yeah, I bet she will!!!"

Shaking her head at her family as they move out of the bar, Harriet reaches for Damon's hand, and they leave the hotel.

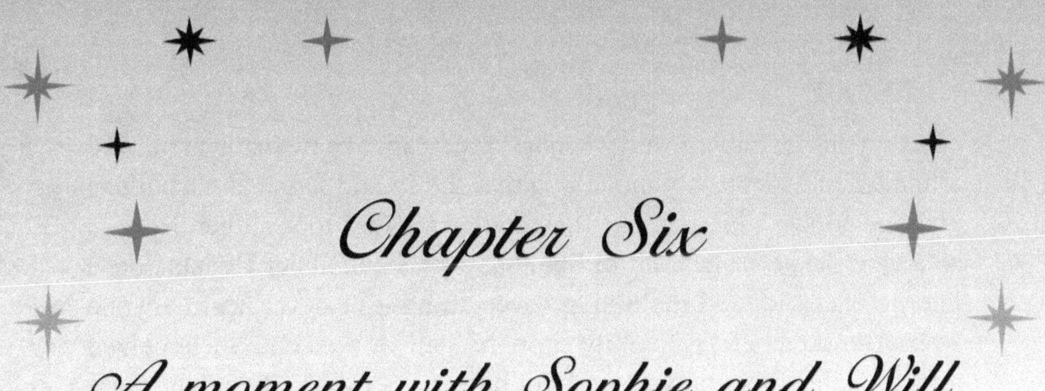

Chapter Six

A moment with Sophie and Will

On their way home to Star's Hollow, Sophie is seated behind the steering wheel shaking her head at her husband, who is at this point in time in the evening, experiencing an aftermath of having one too many drinks at the Engagement Party.

After they were married, Will and Sophie bought a house in Stars Hollow which they've been slowly taking time to renovate. The location of the home in Stars Hollow meant that they could live and raise a family in a nice little town with everything they could possibly need while giving them enough space away from their parents especially his mother.

Sophie, who is watching the road and purposely keeping her husband awake, speaks over at him.

"I can't believe Harriet has asked me to be her bridesmaid!"

Watching his wife, an inebriated Will smiles. "Why? Why wouldn't she?"

Shrugging her shoulders and pursing her lips, she watches the road. "I don't know. I just never thought she would."

Sitting up in the seat, Will starts. "I know that it seems that Harriet is one tough cookie to crack, but she's that way because she's never had it easy and my mother definitely never made it any easier. I still remember the day when Harriet came home from school after the principal announced her class ranking and they got into a huge argument about it. She had her heart set on Dartmouth, and when her acceptance came in the mail, Dad told me that Mom pretty much said that she should forget about college and just go get a job because they couldn't afford to send her. He was so angry, I'd never heard him like that ever. I called her a couple days later to check in, and she told me everything. I've never heard anyone so heartbroken before. Luckily enough, it all worked out. She received a full scholarship and won a school bursary. So yeah, she might seem a little rough, but Harriet's had it harder than any of us. She's worked hard to get where she is, and we both know firsthand, she is good at what she does."

Nodding understandably, she remarks. "It sure was interesting seeing Nate there tonight? And not just on any night either, the night of Harriet's engagement party. And you know what, I think I even saw him lurking at the door too during the night, I mean, at least I thought I did?!"

Breathing out a deep sigh, Will nods in agreeance. "Yeah I know it's all so strange. I mean I know he's kind of protective of her, but sometimes it's all just so weird between them. I mean, you remember how he was acting at our wedding right?"

Sophie glances a look over at her husband, confused. "Honey, you don't think they . . . um . . . well, you know?"

Confused by her meaning, he snipes. "No!!! I don't know . . . *what?!*"

"You know what I'm talking about!"

"No, I don't. Spit it out, *Mrs Lancer*!"

"Hey, don't take that tone with me, *Mr Lancer*!!!"

"Well, I'm sorry, but maybe I just like thinking that you are trying to suggest that my best friend was interested in my little sister?"

As her voice slowly rises, she glares back and counts off her theories on her fingers back at him. "Okay. 1 – She's not your little sister. She hasn't been little for like over ten years now. 2 – I'm not saying interested. I'm thinking it was more than that because no man looks at a woman like he did all night. Whether he was in the room or not."

"He wasn't looking at her!!!"

"Bullshit Will."

"What?!!"

"You heard me. I'm calling bull – s . h . i . t!!! He never took his eyes off her the whole entire time at the bar and before he left, he

asked Harriet but Damon answered and hello . . . Halley. Need I say more?"

Rubbing his forehead, completely failing to see her logic, he snaps. "What? He's with Halley because he likes her!"

"He's with Halley to get a rise out of Harriet!!!"

"So what *are you trying to say exactly*, Sophie???"

"I am just pointing out. I honestly think that maybe something happened. It'd at least explain for all the awkwardness between them."

Annoyed at his wife's comments, Will looks out his window and into the darkness of night. He can see the street lamps of Star's Hollow main street within his sight. Taking a moment to think about Sophie's comments, he can't help but be reminded of the time when he came home for Spring break during his third year at Ole Miss. He had spoken to Harriet about coming home early with him, but she still had classes to attend. But if any memory specifically came to mind right there during that car road home, it was the memory of the way that Nate behaved when Will stopped by to see him and the topic of Harriet had come up.

※ ※ ※

51

Ten years earlier . . .

Nate is completing a final check on a car with an apprentice when he sees Will pulling in. Walking over, he greets his mate.

"Will! Hey, when did you get in?"

"This morning. Decided to come home for Spring Break. Catch up with my mates."

Curious at his comment, Nate is confused. "They let you do that?", to which Will just shrugs off.

"Probably not. But I literally had nothing to do. No assignments or exams and we're not training, so I came home."

Nodding, Nate shrugs, "Well okay then." Signing off on the paperwork in his hands, he hands the clipboard he's holding off to a young man that approaches him. Turning he looks back to Will, who is now leaning against his bonnet taking in the sights.

"Wow, Nate. You've really got this place running well!"

"Yeah. Took a bit."

"No mate, this is awesome!", Will replies.

Nate smiles at his friend. "Yeah, we finally got sponsorship money in and dad's handling the chain setup so. . ."

"So are you just doing repairs?"

Nate replies, "Actually we've widened our services. We now offer smash repairs and all car services. I have a guy that restores classics, he works three days a week, and I have a guy starting next week who builds cars from scratch. We've got a couple of clients that are corporate racing sponsors, and they're looking to invest in us to build stunt and demo

*cars. Which means we can take on more people and apprentices",
as he's being handed another clipboard to sign and give back to yet
another employee.*

*Ecstatic for his friend, Will nods happily. He was afraid that Nate would
feel left behind, what with being stuck in Hartford and not being able to
go to college like he so desperately wanted to. He also knew that with
Nate's SAT scores and his swimming record that most colleges from
around the country were offering him full scholarships. But now that
Nate had begun working for his father's company and that the business
was running so well, college had become something that Nate no longer
wanted.*

*Walking towards his office, Nate ushers Will to follows him and once
inside, gestures for him to sit.*

*Curious to know if he still swims, Will asks. "So do you spend any time
in the pool these days?"*

*Looking over his shoulder as he's pouring two coffees from the
kitchenette, Nate shakes his head.*

*"I try to swim occasionally, but I don't really get the time anymore.
We're pretty busy here, and I've made a commitment."*

*Will, taking the cup of the coffee that Nate hands it to him, he nods into
the cup.*

"So how's Harriet?"

*Will looks at him, questionably. "Well, you know her, busy as usual.
Why, do you want to know if she has any single college friends?"*

*Shaking his head, he replies. "Just thought I'd ask. You know official
big brother duties and all."*

Taking another sip of his coffee, Will adds, "Well, she went to a frat party a few weeks ago. Tells me she's met, someone."

With a not-so-subtle response, Nate's head shoots straight up from papers on his desk and looks at Will, a little wounded.

"Really?"

Chuckling ever so more no, Will's entire body is shaking with laughter.

"Yeah but this is Harriet remember. I mean she thought she was going to marry Patrick Swayze when she was like ten."

Trying enormously to hide his discomfort, he looks down into his coffee to avoid the eyes of his best friend.

"Nine not ten, but I guess . . . I guess you're right."

Sitting up in his chair now, Will remembers the purpose of his visit. "Anyway, so I wanted to ask. I mean it's not like its only reason why I came by or anything, but she's coming home in a few weeks for her eighteenth. Dad, Sal, and Wanda are planning a party for her at The Sheraton. Oh god Nate, mate you've gotta come. I won't survive if you don't come."

"Ah, mate. I don't know."

Scratching his head, Nate is 99.9% certain that he shouldn't go. Whereas the other 1% is screaming at him to go and see Harriet blow out the candles on her birthday cake. He'd love nothing more than to just do that, but he knows all too well, that just watching wouldn't be enough and it'd drive him crazy. He'd ultimately want to be near her. See her smile. Hear her laugh. Make her laugh.

"All of Harriet's slutty college friends will be there."

Politely encouraging his friend, he grins. Placating the comment of her slutty friends immediately to the back of his mind, he unwillingly accepts.

"Sure. Why not."

Slapping his desk, Will sends a shake across Nate's desk causing his coffee mug and computer to tremble and standing from his chair, Will smiles down at him.

"Awesome. Cool well, I'm off. Got things to do. Girls to see."

Nate shakes his head and smirks. Watching Will's back walking out of his office, he hears him yell out, "Later mate!", as Nate returns to his work.

※　※　※

"Honey . . . Honey . . . What's wrong? Are you going to be sick? If you're going to be sick???"

Will opens his eyes and sits up straight in his seat. Sophie is looking over at him, concerned he is about to spew all over the interior of the front seat.

"No. I'm fine. I just remembered something."

"About what???"

"Nate."

Glances over her husband, curiously, "And?"

"Well, I don't know. I'm beginning to think that something did happen but", wiping his mouth and adjusting his jaw to glance over at his wife, "Sophie we can't just go talking about this freely, okay? I mean, she's getting married and this is the happiest I've seen her since she got into

Dartmouth and moved to New York. Plus, if something did happen between Nate and her, I doubt she told anyone about it let alone Damon. So for now, we have to keep this theory to ourselves okay."

Taking his wife's hand in his, they share a single nod before her attention returns to the road. Taking a left, she indicates as she slowly pulls up in front of their two-car garage and turns off the car's ignition.

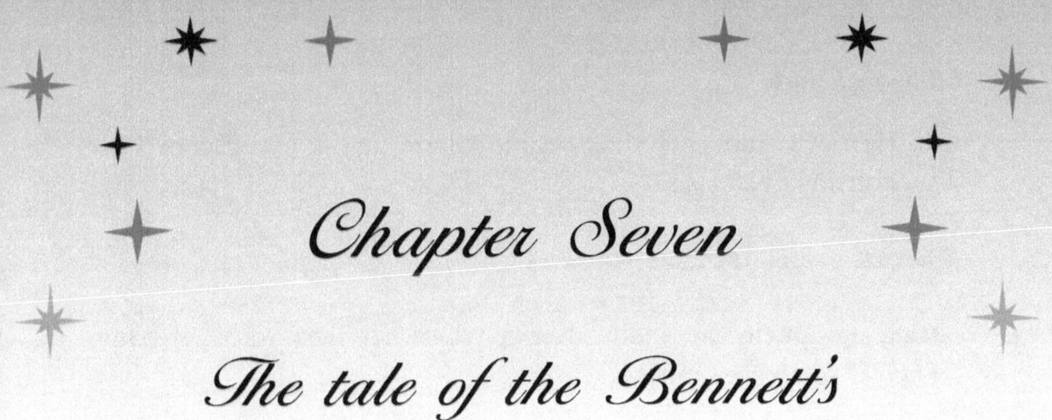

The tale of the Bennett's

Having left Hartford after her father cooked them all breakfast, Damon and Harriet are seated in Damon's BMW on their way back to New York. Pulling out onto the I-95, Harriet looks over at her fiancé as he stares out at the open road. His mind, swimming in deep thought is plucked from its depth by the touch of Harriet's soft hand on his.

Looking over at her, he sees her face glowing with happiness. "Damon, you know if I collected a star every time I've smiled this weekend, I would have enough the light up the night sky for the rest of our lives. I love you so much. Thank you for this weekend."

Shifting his focus from her back to the road, with one hand on the steering wheel he reaches over with his other, to take her right hand and lightly brush his lips against her knuckles before lacing her fingers amongst his.

"You know, I've been thinking -'

"Hmmm . . . What's that?", she responds.

"That your mother isn't that much different from mine!"

Smirking, her eyes go large with emotion. "You think??? God, can you imagine what'll be like when they meet?", she says as she arrives at a dead stop. Her mind immediately becoming lost in the vision of her mother and Mrs Bennett arguing in the middle of The Plaza's ballroom with Harriet's Aunts standing behind Gloria giving Mrs Bennett the disconcerting evil eye.

"Harriet, hey. Harriet, are you okay?"

Sitting upright in the chair, Harriet wipes her face with her hand. "*What???* Yeah no, I'm fine."

"Are you sure? Because you kind of just spaced out just then!!!"

"It was nothing, I'm fine. Promise!"

Knowing the topic of their mothers has brought an unpleasant lull between himself and Harriet, seeing that she is now avoiding his eyes and watching the scenery out her window, Damon feels the need to put her worries at bay by sharing more of himself.

"You know, I never realised –'

Looking back at him, she asks. "What did you realise, honey?"

"That families could be like that. I mean, I know you don't have the best relationship with your Mom, but at least you know your family loves you!"

Taking a deep breath, she shrugs before agreeing. "Yeah, I guess."

Puzzled by his comment, knowing that the conversation could only go either two ways; an optimistic North or an awful South, she can't help herself but ask more about his childhood.

"Damon, I'm *scared* to ask you this but was your childhood a *happy one*?"

Scratching his eyebrow, he takes a deep breath before he openly responds to the question. In earnest, he gently smiles over at her as he courageously admits that maybe his childhood hasn't been as precious as hers.

"I don't know. Honestly, I can't really remember or if my memories are mine to have."

Pausing, he stops and thinks of how he can describe to it her best. Continuing, he begins. "My family aren't huggers. *Emotion is not to be shown, they are inappropriate and to stay bottled up,* at least I think that's what my Grandmother told me when I was like five. A string of nannies pretty much raised Harper and I until we were old enough to attend boarding schools. My parents are socialites, well at least my mother is, and she was always out, doing something so having Harper and me at home was simply inconvenient for their social calendars. We came home from school during the holidays, but we were often whisked away by my father to Europe or the Hamptons while my mother would stay in Manhattan. She once told Harper that everything she ever needed, was right there in Manhattan. My parents were pretty much sleeping in separate bedrooms by then."

Lost in his words and the hidden innuendos of his comments, a speechless Harriet finds her voice has vanished only to be overcome with anger and rage at listening to how people from money live, most especially treat their children.

"When I graduated from boarding school, I returned to New York. I think I spent, maybe three months kicking around before I departed for Harvard to study Commerce."

Smiling, she interrupts. "Isn't it interesting. I was at DU, and you were at Harvard. I'm surprised we didn't run into each other during my freshman year!"

"That would've been interesting indeed", he replies smugly back at her. Knowing that he is having a joke at her expense, she slaps his shoulder. Taking his hand off the wheel, to rub his arm he snaps at her. "Um . . . ouch!!! That really hurt!!! What was that for?"

She smirks back at him, "You know what for!!!"

"It still hurt!!! Geez, what did Will teach you how to box too!!!"

Laughing, she giggles back. "He may have taught me a thing or two!", before she curiously asks him, "So, did you graduate from Harvard and go to work at your father's firm straight away?"

"No, not straight away. I may have procrastinated!", he proudly shares.

"Rebellion???"

He smiles over at her as she asks and she is immediately warmed by the sight of his gorgeous smile. This is the Damon she fell in love with. The warm-hearted, kind and caring man whom she had fallen so quickly and deeply in love with, it sometimes scared her. Never completely sure as to what love truly felt like seeing that she had only ever loved one person before meeting Damon, her heart had remained quite broken. But as she looks upon the translucent powder blue eyes of her fiancé, her mind becomes immediately misplaced when it attempts to pinpoint the moment, somewhat fix the hour in which she had fallen so deeply for him but hadn't realised it until it was too late.

"Just the occasional drinking, hooking up with unsuitable girls, parties and showing up to work late."

Shaking her head, she isn't surprised one bit. "I'm sure your mother would have been so proud. What did your father think?"

Before responding, Damon chuckles at the thought of what his father would think. "He doesn't think much at all. My mother's the boss, and he's along for the ride. I'm not even sure if they love each other". Sensing her discomfort, Damon puts her mind at ease. "It's okay, Harriet. Honestly, my parents' marriage is one of convenience or at least that's what I once heard him utter. Her money, his family's business. Didn't stop him from his wandering eye and living at our Hamptons house most of the time."

Amazed at him, she can't stop herself from uttering a sad but concerned, "Oh", as she fixes her eyes back to the view outside her window. Reaffirming her hand in his, he wills her to look at him. "That's why I think I love you and your family so much. It's okay to show emotions and love, and I can't believe how lucky I am to have met you. I love you so much, Harriet. You know that, right?"

Smiling back at him, she nods quietly. Picking up his hand that holds hers, she lightly brushes her lips over his knuckles before dropping them to her thigh. As her eyes travel up from their hands to clearing city skyline, a sweet, comforting smile forms across each other's lips as they look out at the front windscreen to see the buildings of New York City skyline forming in the distance.

Chapter Eight

Measuring Up

Damon met Harriet unofficially four years ago while she was planning his sister Harper's wedding.

As a groomsman in the wedding party, he was standing on a box being measured by a man he assumed was Sal, the business owner, when he saw a charismatic and beautiful dark-haired brunette woman walking through the shop. Transfixed as she moves through the shop, he freezes in his spot when she stops right in front of him and delves straight into conversation with the tailor whose taking his measurements.

"Hey Sal, how's business?"

Looking down from the box, he watches as the tailor stands up from the floor to look over at her and respond.

"Busy, yourself???"

Smirking, the woman looks down at her schedule. "Oh, you know me. It wouldn't be normal if I wasn't busy. Is this the last suit fitting for the Bennett wedding party?". Looking down into her folder, she lets out a deep breath. "Good, we're on track then."

Watching as Sal places his measuring tape around his neck, Damon sees Sal take a clip folder and write his measurements.

"Do you just want me to fax the bill over?"

Looking up from her folder, she mutters. "Yeah, that'd be great. Elizabeth will fix it up for you. She sent me down here to make sure he showed up."

Watching as she takes the note from Sal and places it in her planning folder, the woman prepares herself to leave.

"Ok Sal, well I'm sure I'll see you again."

Smiling, he replies. "Okay honey. Oh, how's that father of yours?"

Rolling her eyes, she playfully grins back. "Oh . . . he's busy organising a fishing trip!"

Nodding, he then continues to ask, "And you're mother?"

Shaking her head, her body radiates in giggles. It is when she gazes up from the ground to smile up at the man that Damon feels as if his heart has been seized. Lost in the smile that has completely enraptured him, he's immediately mystified by the glow emanating around her. Fixed on the box, he continues to stare that is, well until he is caught staring at her by Sal.

"Thinks she organising Will's wedding of course. You should see her Sal! You'd think she was a Queen, the way she goes about ordering people about!!!"

Shrugging his shoulders, the man sighs Damon before looking back at Harriet. "Oh well, you know Will. You know he would never be able to put a wedding together. Sophie seems okay though, I've only met her briefly, but she seems alright."

"Yeah . . . she's nice. Didn't get much say about the wedding but I've been helping her with that. The wedding is at the Sheraton, so I have their number on speed dial."

"So you are actually planning the wedding!!!", Sal chuckles.

"Officially no. Dad and I agreed to let mom think she's running the show to keep the peace."

"Oh don't worry about her, love. It will be different when you get married.", he replies.

"Um . . . yeah . . . sure!? Like that's ever going to happen. Anyways, I'd better get back to work."

Watching as she kisses Sal on the cheek and prepares to leave, Damon feels the need to stop her from leaving and before he fully realises it himself, his sudden desperation to hear her soft sweet voice speak once more causes him to call out.

"Um . . . excuse me miss but do you need to speak to me . . . at all?"

Looking at him up and down without any hesitation, a small smirk slowly forms across her face as she manages to mumble out a response before exiting the store.

"Ah . . . no!"

Damon, taking an exasperated breath, rakes his fingers through dark sandy blonde hair and turns to the tailor who is now standing before him taking notes.

"Well, she's . . . interesting!", he huffs.

Sal, whose eyes have travelled from behind his glasses perched on the slip of his nose to his clipboard and back up at Damon, eyes him up and down suspiciously. With knotted eyebrows, he gruffs out. "*Hey?!* Watch *your* mouth. That's my *niece*!!!"

Astonished, Damon mumbles. "She's . . . She's. That's your niece?"

"Yes!!!"

"Is she *always* like that?", Damon replies.

Sal, who is now standing behind him, is sampling materials against Damon's legs. Looks around at him, shrugs an okay with his shoulders then nods briefly. "Ah no. *Not always.* She's just overworked. She is working like crazy to please some mother of the bride and her boss, and when she's not working, she's helping out with her brother's wedding. Oh *and* to top it off, her mother is trying to set her up with this awful guy."

"Really? Wow?!"

Shaking his head, Sal looks at Damon with concern. "Hang on, why am I talking about the family to you?"

Scratching his eyebrow, trying to make light of the situation, all that Damon can manage to mumble out is, "I don't know. What's the guy like?"

Sal snaps instantaneously. "Nightmare. Complete mommy's boy!!!"

"This guy still lives with his mother???"

"Yeah. But between you and me, I can't say anything because her aunt, my beautiful wife will kill me if I don't help Gloria find a match for my angel."

Rubbing his forehead with frustration, Damon exhales a long sigh. Relieved that it's not his problem, knowing that his own mother sounds a lot like this Gloria.

"Well, Mr Bennett; I have your measurements, and your suit will be made and ready for the wedding."

As Damon leans down to collects his things, Sal looks him up and down. "Say, you're quite a nice looking young man."

Shaking his head, he affirms the man. "Oh no. No-No. Sorry. I'm off the market."

"Are you married???"

"No, no-no ah, no sir."

"Are you, you know, the gay?"

As his mouths drop in shock, Damon becomes immediately insulted. "*What?!* Of course not!"

Ignoring him, Sal walks off into his office only to return with a card. Smiling at him, he claps. "Then you're still on the market!!!"

A perturbed Damon, replies. "Sir, no offence but I'm really off the market. Plus, I have a mother just like you're sister in law."

Sal stops what he's doing, nods his head and shrugs his shoulder.

"Okay, well hey I tried. I will send all the information to Harriet's office."

But as soon as Sal speaks her name, it hangs in the air, and he becomes enamoured with thoughts of her.

Her name is Harriet. I've heard Harper talking about this woman. She never shuts up about her. She's the one who's giving my mother a run for her money. What was it that Harper was saying last night at dinner about how talented this girl is and how she seems to just know everything she wants but our Mother is putting her through hell. Yeah, that sounds about right. Harper is happy and getting her way, and our mother has to be a stickler about it.

Putting his jacket back on, he looks around the store and notices a desk to the side of the store which he assumes is the man's workstation. Above the desk are three large square chipboards plastered with photos and amazedly, he finds that most of them are of Harriet, the woman he had just briefly met. Peering around him to make sure that Sal guy doesn't spring him, he takes a quick glance around the photos. His heart, filling with warmth at the sight of her as a baby in pink dresses with lacy frills then as a child riding around on a purple bike in what looks a driveway in Connecticut and pulling goofy faces. As a teenager at her prom and high school graduation to being snapped behind a cake lit up with sparklers at her 18th birthday before resting on the picture of her in cap and gown at her College graduation.

Feeling uncomfortable at the level of love and affection that this woman and her family have for another, a wave of jealousy sends a chill over him, and he quickly collects his items and exits out the door. Jumping into his BMW, he feels his eyebrows begin to twitch nervously. Looking into his rearview mirror, he ponders to himself as he stares back at his own reflection.

Well, that was interesting. Harper's wedding is going to be more interesting than I thought it was.

Harper & Glenn

Ceremony and Reception at
The Waldorf Astoria Hotel

Guests – 100 to 150

Three Course Dinner
Swing Band

Canapes and Pre-Reception Drinks

Wedding Car –
Vintage, Grey or Black

H & G

Mr & Mrs Robert Bennett
request the honor of your presence
at the marriage of their daughter

Harper Alice Louisa Bennett
to
Glenn Samuel Christensen

Saturday, the eighteenth of June
at two o'clock
Park Avenue Lobby
Waldorf Astoria Hotel
301 Park Avenue
New York
Reception will follow in Starlight Room

Couture

Bridal Party
4 x Bridesmaids
4 x Groomsmen
2 x Flower Girls
1x Paige Boy

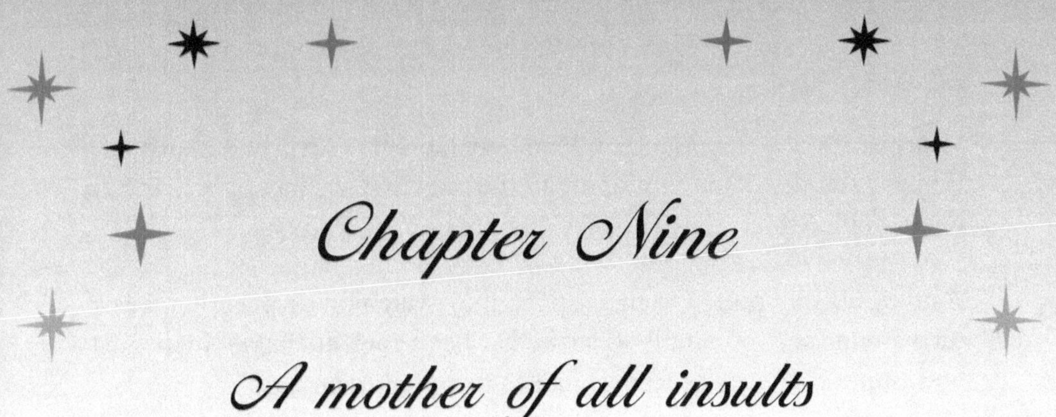

Chapter Nine

A mother of all insults

Entering the Starlight function room at the Waldorf Astoria; Damon arrives with his family and Glenn, to find Harriet poised in front of her planner going over preparations for Harper's wedding rehearsal. It's been a week since he last saw her at her uncle's tailor shop and just like she was then, she is busy completing her work.

Fixed near the room's entrance, he is caught watching her as she adjusts table place settings and is lining up each place card perfectly by Harper before she moves to greet Harriet.

"Hello, Harriet."

Looking up from her smoothing of table linen, Harriet smiles up at Harper. "Hi Harper, how you are feeling?"

Timidly, she confesses. "Slightly nervous but really excited", before turning to her guests as they approach.

Watches as Harriet smiles politely and waits to meet them, Damon begins to automatically feel like he had when he was being fitted for his suit, his mind immediately becoming increasingly overwhelmed with more thoughts of Harriet.

Gosh . . . she looks even prettier today than she did last week.
Come on man!!! Get it together!!!
It's just a young pretty brunette . . . who just happens to be looking extremely beautiful today and who . . . is now smiling at me.

"Harriet, this is my fiancé Glenn, my parents Beverly and Robert Bennett and this", and motioning to the man that she met briefly in her uncle's tailor shop, Harper states, "Is my brother Damon."

As they all stay rooted in their spots, they watch on as Beverly takes a turn around the room only to shake her head back at Harriet in disgust with stone cold eyes as Robert makes to compliment her.

"Well, I say, Miss Lancer, you've done a wonderful job. This room looks wonderful."

"Oh Robert, don't be silly", Beverly interrupts as she swiftly returns to her husband's side, interlocking her arm through his.

"Miss Lancer has had help. Besides she still has heaps of work to get this room up and running for the rehearsal tonight. Not to forget the high tea breakfast tomorrow morning before the wedding tomorrow night. You should do well to remember that I will be checking your work with Elizabeth. Elizabeth and I are old friends. This affair must be perfect. It's the highlight of the season."

Taking a moment to pause, Beverly narrows her eyes coldly at Harriet before ending with, "You can handle it, can't you?"

Straightening in her spot, Harriet firmly nods timidly. With as much grace and class as she can fathom, she takes a deep breath and replies. "Yes. Thank you for reminding me, Mrs Bennett. I should be getting back to work. Excuse me."

A displeased Beverly, immediately feeling that Harriet's comments were rude and unprofessional, straightens her figure before pulling at her husband's elbow. As they move towards the room's exit, Robert can't help but turn and smile apologetically back at Harriet as she picks up her planner.

Waiting until their mother has left, Damon hears his sister speak up. Embarrassed by the way her mother has just behaved and treated her.

"Oh Harriet, I'm so sorry -"

"Harper, its ok. It's the most important day of your life. Of course, your mother wants it to be absolutely perfect."

Nodding, an empathetic Harper awkwardly smiles before turning to her fiancé while Damon notices an upset Harriet looking through her planning, no doubt seeking an excuse to escape the room with. Feeling the tears, a mixture of both anger and grief, well in the back of her eyes, they hear her mumble out.

"Would you please excuse me for a moment. I just have to pop out to speak to management about audio settings for music."

But instead of taking a right towards the manager's desk at the entrance of the hotel, she elects to take a left to the stairs leading the hotel's rooftop. As they watch her disappear out of the hall, Harper turns to Glenn and Damon.

"Poor thing. She's been nothing but wonderful. But mother just keeps well -"

Damon interrupts, "Being mother?"

"Well . . . yes. Anyway, Glenn and I have last minute bride/groom things to do. Do you have to go back to the office, Damon?"

"No. I have work off until after the wedding."

"I was thinking. Maybe you could stay and help Harriet?", she gently insists as he exhales a sigh and nods back at her. "Anything for the bride."

Happily reaching in for a hug, she smiles at her baby brother and whispers. "Thank you".

Placing a contented kiss upon his cheek, she grins. "Besides, you might want to get a few tips from Harriet about planning weddings. Who knows . . . you might be next!!!"

"Doubtful", he quips back as she and Glenn leave too. Standing around, he waits patiently for Harriet's return by taking a walk around the room, to look at Harriet's work.

> *Wow. The room looks pretty good. What on earth could*
> *Harper have meant about me being next? As if!!!*
> *Besides, I don't even think Lucy wants to get married.*
> *Lucy is still in her prime dancing years, and I*
> *doubt she is even thinking about marriage.*
> *Even kids for that matter.*

Walking past a table adorned with a selection of bride and groom flavours, he picks up an elegant candy box and plays with the ribbon that ties the box together.

> *Besides, if I married Lucy, I think my mother would have a coronary.*
> *Ha?! maybe I should suggest marriage.*

Turning around to take in the whole room, he finally realises what a remarkable job Harriet has done and that the hall looks beautiful. Elegantly decorated just a like a palace for a royal wedding. Chiffon and fairy lights draped from all corners of the room to be met in the middle by a beautiful chandelier. The tables decorated with fresh flowers, pearls, and candles. One table is set with a variety of place settings and silverware, sitting on another is a box full of elegantly written place cards which he assumes are to be placed on all the tables.

Noticing a board showcasing the table seating chart, he walks towards it. To his amusement, he finds out that he is being seated between Lucy and his mother. Displeased at the thought of having to be seated next to his mother, he instantly feels like a shuttlecock being hit back and forth over a net. Glancing down to check his watch, he ponders as to

Harriet's whereabouts, but his wondering is cut short when he hears the door open and close.

Observing as she marches directly to the table where all her planning is laid out, he watches as she hurriedly flips through her planner before reaching for her bag only to exit once again. It isn't until she passed him that he realises that the reason for her earlier absence was due to her somewhat shaken demeanour. It all being brought to light by his now visible sight of her swollen eyes and smudged mascara. Evidence that his mother had no doubt caused her pain.

Reappearing fifteen minutes later, Damon sees Harriet return with the function manager. Looking her up and down, he takes note of the fact that her once blotchy face and red-rimmed eyes have now been fixed, and that she is now flitting about the room as if nothing bothered her.

Taking his phone out his pocket, he looks down at his messages. Lucy would be at ballet rehearsal all day, leaving him with an open afternoon. Gazing back up at Miss Lancer, he notices that the function manager has now left and that it's just the two of them alone in the room.

"You know, you can always take a picture!!!"

"Sorry", he manages to mumble out after been caught staring.

Looking down at his phone, he attempts to preoccupy his mind with other thoughts, but he can't help but want to watch her and glancing up from the phone's screen, he stares once more.

"Seriously what? Do you have a problem?", she snaps, feeling his eyes burning into the back of her neck.

"What?! No. I mean, of course not. Sorry."

"Alright then. Do you mind, I have work to do!!!"

"It's just -"

Taking a deep breath, she drops the pen and turns to face him. Leaning against the table, she crosses her arms.

"I just want to apologise. My mother is -"

"Satan???"

Smirking, he grins. "I was going to say harsh, but Satan will do."

Smirking back, she softly emits a giggle before locking eyes with his. "Actually, while you're here. Can I get you to talk to your sister about the music list."

Taking a page out of her planning, she walks towards him and hands it to him. As he releases the paper from her grasp, his fingers graze hers and her soft hands. Pulling her hand back, she returns to her planner as he examines the list, stopping to giggle when he sees "I've Had the Time of My Life" on the list.

The giggle while not annoying, unfortunately, is enough to take her attention away from her work and feeling the giggle niggling away at her, she finds herself asking him. "What's so funny?"

"Nothing. It's just that I never knew that Harper was a fan of Dirty Dancing. She used to make fun of girls that did growing up!!!"

Irritated with herself that she asked and annoyed by his answer, she exasperates. "Really?". Rolling her eyes, she calmly walks over to him and politely snaps the list out of his hands. "Actually, I can take care of this. At least, I know it'll get done."

Collecting her things, she packs up her planning to leave, and she is about to exit the room, she faces him.

"Damon is it?"

Immediately noticing that her once sweet demeanour has disappeared only to be replaced with a strict temperate tone. A tone that he knows all too well. A tone similar to his mother's that she uses when she is displeased with something or someone.

"A **_LOT_** of girls loved that movie! Myself included. So insulting the movie is insulting me. Nice meeting you but I've got this!!!"

❋　❋　❋

Seated in her office, Harriet picks up her phone.

Hannah, is Liz in her office?

Hey Harriet, I'll just find out for you, one moment . . .

Thanks.

Harriet??? . . .

Yeah?

Liz is free.

Thanks, Hannah

Standing, she exits her office to knock on her boss's door.

"Come in -"

Looking up from her computer screen, Liz sees Harriet and motions for her to sit.

"Harriet, just the person I wanted to see."

"You did?", Harriet nervously replies.

"Yes, I've been receiving calls from Beverly Forbes-Bennett all afternoon."

Deflating, Harriet replies. "Oh???"

"Oh no, Harriet. Sorry, this isn't a bad thing. I grew up around that lot, nothing to worry about. I have every confidence in your work. Besides, Harper assures me that she is overjoyed with your preparations."

Nodding, she smiles timidly. "Thanks, Liz."

"So, catch me up. You're off to Hartford tomorrow for your brother's wedding. So you've got the Bennett dinner rehearsal tonight, so that leaves me with -"

"The high-tea tomorrow morning. Marco has all the details, and you'll have my planning on your desk first thing in the morning. The wedding tomorrow afternoon and reception in the Starlight room. But that will all be taken care of because the rehearsal and reception are in the same room, so Marco said his staff will take care of that. You will have to give the room a once over before each event."

"Great. This is fantastic work, Harriet.", she acknowledges.

"Thank you", Harriet happily accepts.

"Harriet, I want to know that the partners and I take a genuine notice in the work that you do. The downside to having a company like this is that there will always be unsatisfied clients as there as satisfied ones. But your client satisfaction ratios currently stand at 50 to zilch. Your work is exceptional and don't let anyone like Beverly Forbes-Bennett, tell you anything different. She was always a prickly and proud kind of woman, the last thing I'd ever want is for you to ever doubt your amazing ability and get ensnared in her web of societal antics. Harriet, I want you to go home this weekend and be proud of your work and reputation. And when you come back Tuesday, hopefully, the partners and I can sit down with you to talk about your next step."

"Thank you, Liz. I'd really appreciate your kind words. And I'd really appreciate the sit down with you and the board."

"My pleasure honey", glancing to her watch Liz checks the time. "Oh, is that the time. I better let you go. You've got a dinner rehearsal to get ready for."

Looking at the time on her watch, Harriet nods. "Oh god. 4:30. I better get moving. The dinner starts at 7:30."

Standing, she exits the office but not before turning to meet Liz's eyes.

"Thank you, Liz."

"Not a problem, Harriet. Anytime!!!"

❈   ❈   ❈

Later that afternoon, Harriet stands in front of her bathroom mirror getting dressed for the dress rehearsal. Electing to wear a purple lace cocktail dress to Harper's dinner rehearsal the dress incorporates two of her loves. Lace and Purple. The dress has a fitted bodice with a lace neckline, a full skirt with tulle lining coloured in a variety of shades of purple, that can only be seen if she were being twirled or dancing.

After finishing her makeup and styling her hair into a thirties' styled wavy side updo, Harriet dusts off her neck, earlobes, and arm with diamonds that her godparents Uncle Sal and Aunt Wanda bought for her on her graduation from college. She does this knowing that she couldn't possibly be without some kind of armour to fend off the haughty up-turned nosed guests at tonight's event, as she slips on her lilac satin pointed slingbacks as she moves into her bedroom to check the time.

Grabbing her clutch from the bed, she heads downs her staircase towards the door to leave. Turning off the lights and locking the apartment, she hears her phone ring. Ignoring it, she lets the machine pick it up.

> *"Harriet, this is your mother. Don't forget, your*
> *brother Will's wedding is on this weekend.*
> *We assume that you are still coming . . ."*

Her forehead wrinkling, she rolls her eyes at her mother's reminder.

> *"Harriet, please remember this is his and Sophie's*
> *weekend, so we expect you to behave yourself.*
> *That means being on your best behaviour at all times, being*
> *nice to your family and keeping your thoughts to yourself.*
> *I know you're busy with that wedding this weekend so I will*
> *ring you later on your mobile to discuss a couple of things."*

Frustrated, she rolls her eyes once more and pulls the door shut behind her.

Chapter Ten

Harper's Dinner Rehearsal

Pulling into the car park at the Waldorf, Harriet arrives for Harper's dinner rehearsal. She has planned the event down to the letter and taken others input under advisement. Smiling happily as she enters the room, she takes pleasure at the sight of the tables. Marco, the function manager being the every bit visionary he is, has beautifully decorated each table with fresh flowers and candles.

Stopping at her small planning table, situated at the back of the room near the bar, she places her things down before checking over each table for perfection and cleanliness. After briefly greeting both bar and serving staff, she checks with Marco regarding the schedule before asking a couple of staff members to light the candles in the room. Once everything is lit and ready to go, she walks to the centre of the room and stands under the chandelier.

Spinning slowly around the room, she double checks everything as she gazes up at the stunning chandelier and back down again, to momentarily get lost in the grandeur, watching as it casts shadows over each table and adding a touch of elegance and magic to the room. The picture perfect society wedding. Her fifty-first society wedding that she has planned herself to date.

✳ ✳ ✳

Standing at the bar with the bar manager, Harriet is discussing the beverage list when Harper and Glenn arrive with their family.

Harper, the soon to be bride, is positively glowing at the site of the room.

Interrupting, she pulls Harriet in an unexpected hug. "Oh my god Harriet, it's so beautiful. Thank you so much!!!"

Pulling out of the hug, Harriet nods happily back at her. "You're very welcome Harper. So how's the blushing bride tonight?"

Taking a deep breath, Harper looks around at all the flurry occurring within the room as she nervously pulls on her necklace. "No more nervous than I was this morning!!! But honestly Harriet, I couldn't have done all this without you!!!!."

Smiling, she shakes her head at Harper. "Thank you, but this is all you. You had a dream, and I helped. It's all good."

"No, it really wasn't. Unfortunately, none of this is about me. It's about my mother. It's about her influence in society, what people will think of her if it isn't perfect."

"Oh. Harper -"

"And it would have remained that way too if it weren't for you. What you've done. How you've personalised it. I . . . this is all truly amazing. Thank you, Harriet, thank you so much. I will never forget this."

"Thank you, Harper." Harriet smiles. "And as much as I would love to stand here talking with you, I believe you have a dinner rehearsal to enjoy, and I have a party to control. So go on, have fun. I've got it handled!!!"

Following Harper on she makes her way back to her table and rests at Glenn's side as Harriet's attention becomes caught by the sight of Damon as he walks into the room with his date. Gazing at her from head to toe, Harriet notices that Damon's date looks like a supermodel with long blonde hair and wearing a dress that is draped in all the right places.

Turning her back on them, Harriet looks away to the bar as Damon and Lucy find their seats.

Looking at his father, Damon notices his father grinning enthusiastically with a scotch in his hand while his mother sits surprisingly quiet next to him with her nose upturned and a cold disapproving manner. It is when Harriet comes into view, watching as she speaks with the Function Manager at the bar that he notices her. Watching her as she stands there talking away with the man, he becomes transfixed at the site of her in that purple dress.

Is that? No, it can't be . . . My, it's Miss Lancer. Is that her date?
No, it couldn't be. Surely she wouldn't
bring a date to an event like this!
Would she??? Quick, in need of a distraction.
I know, drinks. Get a drink order.

Taking down a quick drink order from the table, he moves in route to the bar to where Harriet is now standing with a different man. His inquisitive worries are put to ease when he notices that the man is wearing a red vest over a white dress shirt. Signifying that the man is the bar manager and that she is probably just taking beverages.

He is confident that he won't fall into a puddled mess and embarrass himself in front of her that is until he hears her laugh. Caught in its snare, he feels the laugh capture him and glancing back at her, he completely loses his composure. The pure happiness emitted throughout her laugh was like witnessing a one of a kind work of art. It was magical. So magical that it causes him to forget his order.

"Excuse me, sir. Sir?"

Shaking his head, he looks back at the barman. "Um, sorry. Ah, can I get two Heineken's, a scotch on the rocks and a white wine?"

"Sure, won't be a moment. Let me just put that together for you."

Nodding, he stands against the bar and waits. Glimpsing a look back at her, he notices that she is now standing at the end of the bar, sipping a Pepsi Max.

"Hello, Miss Lancer."

Looking up from her drink, her eyes travel to the face attached to the voice and with a brief smile. She acknowledges his presence before taking the opportunity to take a good look (*well a closer look*) at him.

"Hello, Mr Bennett"

Her eyes, coyly travelling over his fitted grey suit, flit from the elegance of his lapels to the blue dress shirt seated firmly against his chest and come to rest on the dark blue tie around his protruding neck. As she gazes back up his face to meet his piercing blue eyes, she finds that his hair is a lot darker than she originally guessed it was and his smile, is a lot warmer and inviting than she originally thought it to be.

Peeking up from the bar, he catches sight of her looking him, and with a grin, he thinks to turn and ask her something, but his plan is brought to a halt by the sound her ringing phone. A conversation in which he and the entire bar staff couldn't stop themselves from overhearing, even if they wanted to.

Harriet: Hello, this is Harriet . . . Oh god!!! Mom . . . I'm working at the moment, Mom!!!

Gloria: Well, hello to you too. I called and left a message on your home machine. I told you I'd be calling. So anyway, I'm calling about David. He's really excited to meet you. We've invited him to the wedding.

Harriet: No!!! Absolutely not! You cannot invite a date for me, and no, he can't come to the wedding!!!

Gloria: And why not???

Harriet: Why not? What do you mean why not? Because its Will's wedding and I will be busy!!!

Gloria: But you told your father that you agreed to this.

Harriet: When I said that you could set me up I didn't mean for Will's . . .

Gloria: Well sorry, Harriet. But it's too late now.

Harriet: No!!! Absolutely not!!! Look, I've got to get back.

Pulling the phone away from her ear, she pretends she's needed for an emergency. "Sorry, what's that? Okay, I'll be there in a second." Picking the phone up again, she speaks into it.

Harriet: Look, Mom. I've gotta go. I'm needed for an emergency.

Gloria: You don't have an emergency. I know you just want to get me off the phone. Well, the wedding starts at 2 pm.

Harriet: As I told you before, I'll be home sometime tomorrow morning. Everyone, including you, knew how busy I was going to be this week. And as you so happily remind every five seconds, its Will's wedding. They know that I was driving back first thing in the morning. I've gotta go. Bye.

Hanging up, she disconnects, and as she rubs her forehead, for the second time of the night, she feels the people staring at her. Only it's not just staring. She feels as if they're laughing at her current parental discomfort. Righting herself, she braves the attention and walks off towards her table, leaving the bar staff to resume their work and Damon to return to his table with his drinks.

✳   ✳   ✳

After dinner's been served, desserts were consumed and toasts were made; guests began to sparse and leave. The rehearsal had run smoothly just as Harriet had hoped it would and to her surprise, Beverly didn't complain once just as Harper said she wouldn't.

Looking around the room to address the state of the room, she notices that the guests that are left are Harper and Glenn's younger relatives, which at this point have filled themselves silly with bottles of bubbly and are ready to hit the dancefloor. As she looks over to the happy couple, she is warmed by Harper's glowing smile. The smile encompassing her with an emanating flow of golden specks and sparks, as she flits around the room speaking with her older guests and family before finally placing her hand in Glenn's as he leads her to the dance floor to join the rest of their young guests.

Walking the outskirts of the room, Harriet watches the younger crowd dance around before stopping at the bar and take a seat at the bar. Smiling as a waiter hands her a soft drink, she places it down on a coaster and fiddles with the straw. Pushing her hand north, she runs fingers through her hair. Feeling the exhaustion from the past few weeks and the stress of the weekend to come, start to truly overwhelm her. Wanting desperately to be at home, curled up on her couch with white wine instead of the piddly stuff she had been sipping on throughout the night, her thoughts are interrupted by Harper, who has literally run off the dancefloor and ran smack into Harriet.

"Oh, Harriet. I don't know what to say. This has been . . . the most amazing night!!!"

Covering her hand over her mouth, "I'm so glad you are having a great time", Harriet giggles back.

"Oh . . . I wish you were coming to the wedding!!!"

Smiling, she nods softly. "Oh, Harper. I really wish I was too but you know I have to go home for my brother's wedding. Now I've spoken with Elizabeth. She knows everything. Your day will be perfect!!!"

As they both look to the middle of the floor that is now home to the number of young people furiously hell-bent on sleeping when the sun rises in the morning, Harriet sips her drink and ponders over what her brother's wedding will be like. Will it be anything like this? Will her family and Sophie's family be celebrating like this in the middle of the room, together and at this time of the night? How will she react seeing Nate? It's been such a long time since they last spoke with each other, what would she say?

Pulled from her thoughts again, Harriet hears Harper speaking at her with a sweet but perfectly somewhat aristocratically firm manner.

"I know. Look, I just wanted to say . . . that well . . . words cannot express how much I've appreciated everything you've done. I'd really love it if we could catch up and have dinner sometime after I get home from my honeymoon. Would that be alright?"

"I would love that!", Harriet animatedly replies back.

Wiping a tear of happiness from her eye, "I'm sorry. I don't mean to get all *emotional*. I guess I've just always wanted a sister. I grew up around Glenn's sisters, but I don't know, I just don't seem to connect with them like we seem to. And well, you know what these people are like. I mean *really*. I just never, I was really never into all these labels. I hate this society stuff."

Their conversation is short-lived by Glenn when he interrupts to take Harper by the hand back to the dancefloor, and as Harriet watches her run off, she hears a somewhat familiar but particularly loved song of hers begin to croon over the room's speakers. Damon too, who has been sitting at the table with his girlfriend, couldn't help but notice when his sister hugged Harriet then proceed to wipe a tear away from her eye. In fact, if he were sit down and really think about it, he'd also notice how much happier Harper had been throughout the wedding preparation, acting as if herself and Harriet were long-life friends.

Is it when he hears, "I've Had the Time of My Life", begins to play over the room he can't help but shake his head in surprise. Trailing past the young females currently, go crazy and seeing the older women being lulled in a quiet discontent in their seats as the song continues to play. Trailing past them, his eyes lock back on Harriet as he becomes momentarily transfixed on the sight of her softly swaying to the music on her stool. His eyes drifting down the length of her body, stopping at the site of her skirt as it swishes and sways with rhythm, passing down to her biceps then back up again to rest at the site of her long chocolate locks bounce away with life at the soulfully epic lyrics.

Sensing movement on his left, he bashfully gets caught out of this trance by his mother's cold eyes. Having followed his line of focus only to look back at him with intense displeasure. Looking to his right, he immediately becomes privy to the awkward somewhat uncomfortable temperament occurring between his mother and Lucy. Beverley having always shown her dissatisfaction in his choice of girlfriend despite Lucy being an established ballet dancer with the New York ABC institute and whom Damon has been dating for two years, a relationship that has lasted longer than any of his others.

His mother seemed to be desperately hoping that his involvement in his sister's wedding would encourage him to see the reason of their relationship and start making some tough decisions. Surely, if Damon was serious about her, then it's time for him to step up and make the commitment of marriage. If he wasn't, well wouldn't it better to break it off now before things get more complicated? His role in the family company was only going to grow larger, and he knows that Lucy was currently being offered opportunities to dance with other companies around the world.

When the song is over, Damon looks back towards the bar and notice that Harriet has reverted back to her stiff, no-frills or fun manner. Grinning, he smirks to himself. Feeling his chest warm as if he had just witnessed something special, a private moment between the two of them, he smiles briefly before the smile dies and he realises the distance between Harriet and himself.

Turning to Lucy, he finds that she also found herself lulled away by the song. Shaking his head, he realises that he needs to learn more about this Dirty Dancing movie.

"Hey Lucy, can I ask you a question?"

Sitting upright in her seat, she opens her eyes and smiles. "Yes of course."

"Have you ever seen Dirty Dancing? And like 'totally fall in love' with this Patrick Swayze guy and that song that was just playing?"

Blushing embarrassingly, she remarks. "Seriously, are you dense? I'm a dancer. Of course, I've seen it."

Thwarted, he picks up his beer. Taking it by the neck of the bottle in his finger and takes a long pull. He begins to feel like a fool. Particularly stupid by the comments he made to Harriet earlier that day.

"What girl didn't fall in love with Patrick Swayze? Seriously, what kind of stupid question is that?", Lucy continues.

Unwillingly to publicly announce his foolishness, he looks down into the now empty bottle that was his drink. "I ugh. I don't know. I guess I was just asking."

Tickled, Lucy beams back. "I think we should totally watch it when we get back to your place tonight!!!"

"Really?"

Feeling her hand graze his thigh, she runs her fingers lightly along it before raises her eyes to look up back at him. Nodding her head playfully, she leans in to whisper, "Oh *hell* yes . . . and then *maybe* I could *show you* how to *dirty dance*."

Shifting in his seat, he becomes unexpectedly undone. Lost in her show and playful countenance. Swallowing, he breathes out a heavy but excited breath.

"Yes, I think . . . I think I like that plan. I think I like it very much."

❋　　❋　　❋

"Beer please."

Sitting at the bar, Harriet is writing her last notes for the night. Looking up from her page, she unexpectedly meets a pair of cornflower blue eyes staring back at her, as Damon waits for his drink.

"Having fun, Miss Lancer???"

Looking back down to the page, she puts pen to paper as she replies to his questioning. "Isn't that something I should ask you?"

Shrugging, he sighs. "I suppose. But still, did you have fun tonight?"

"I think we both know the answer to that question, don't we Mr Bennett!"

Looking down at his feet, he can't help but smile at the effect he is having on her. "You don't like me much do you?"

"It doesn't matter if I like you or not, Mr Bennett. I'm not here to make friends or enjoy the event. My job is to make sure the bride and groom's wedding is everything they dreamed of", she retorts.

Tilting his head on the side, his eyebrows arching curiously. "Oh . . . well okay then" and when he is served his beer, he makes to close the distance that separates them. Glancing down at her dark brown almost cinnamon speckled eyes, he closes the distance between them at the bar and confides.

"Listen, just in case I don't get another chance, I just want to apologise about the whole Dirty Dancing remark I made. It upset you, and I apologise for that."

Taking a deep annoyed breath, she smugly snorts out. "It's ok. Everyone goes through their phases. *Even spoilt brats!!!*"

Irritated, he drains his schooner. Reaching down to his pants, he fidgets for his keys and on finding them, he turns to her.

"Well, I'd better be going. I guess I'll see you tomorrow night then!"

Closing her planner, she begins to gather her things. "Ah no, sorry. I won't be there."

"Wait? What?!"

Jumping off the stool, she collects her coat and bag. "I've got to go home for my brother's wedding. My boss will be personally handling your sister's wedding."

"Oh okay. Well, have fun. It uh, was nice meeting you, Miss Lancer", he replies.

Smiling gently, she nods at him before disappearing out the back door. Standing rooted at the bar, his watchful eyes on her, follow her every move as she disappears from the room.

Mr & Mrs Alexander Evans
together with
Mr & Mrs Frank Spencer

Request the pleasure of your
company at the marriage of
their children

Sophia Elizabeth Evans
to
William John Spencer

Saturday 15th June
Christ Church Cathedral
Hartford Connecticut
Reception to follow at
The Sheraton South Hotel

Traditional
Church Wedding

Garden Reception at
The Sheraton South Hotel
Guests - 100 to 150

Buffet Dinner
DJ

Bridal Party
3 x Bridesmaids
3 x Groomsmen
1 x Flower Girl
1x Page Boy

Chapter Eleven

Welcomed home with open arms

Pulling up outside her family's home in Hartford, Harriet comes to a complete stop outside the garage door. Looking out her window with her hands still placating the steering wheel, she debates whether to stay or turn the ignition and drive back to New York before anyone notices.

Summer has literally just begun and a smile is brought upon her lips as she looks in her rear-view mirror at a couple of young children, skipping back and forth over a sprinkler in their front yard. Looking back to her parent's garage, her mind is consumed by the memory of when she was ten, and she fell off her bike in the driveway and scrapped her knee. Remembering how her father had come to her rescue, after seeing her fall from the kitchen window while her mother watched on from the front porch and did nothing but lecture her about how she better not see any blood get on her newly steamed carpet.

Opening her car door, she looks around and is amazed to see how much her childhood home was still the same. Her mother's treasured olive tree was looking trimmed and healthy, as for the grass well it was as greener than others in the street. Smirking silently, her heart betrays her mind and allows her eyes to trail slowly from the garage to the house on her right. It too, looked as if it hadn't changed too much. Running her fingers through her hair to push it back out of her eyes, she wonders to herself if the Michaels, if any of them still lived there.

Shaking her head, she lets go of her thoughts and reverts back to her usual demeanour by walking around to her boot and unpack her luggage.

Placing her dress bag over her arm, she shuts the boot and heads towards the house, her suitcase's wheel bumping against the pavement tiles as her father appears at the door on hearing her car arrive.

Ushering her in, he immediately helps her with her things to her room. Glancing around at the mess for Will's wedding as she goes. Placing her luggage gently on the floor near her door, she takes a look around what was once her teenaged bedroom. Her queen size bed still centred in the middle of the room, with its purple spotted doona an array of coloured pillows in different shapes and sizes were strewn across the head of the bed. Her desk in the corner, next to the window that she used as a means of an escape during high school to sneak out to go to parties with her friends or as a means to escape her mother's verbal abuse.

Stepping in her cupboard, she isn't surprised when she notices that some of her old clothing have been placed in boxes on the carpet floor to make room for bridesmaid dresses and groomsmen's suits. Taking a deep breath, she bites her tongue and looks over to her Duchess. Swallowing a deep sigh, she wishes she were back in New York. Sitting in her lounge with a glass of wine and snuggled up with a good book.

Walking to the window, she takes a seat on its bay seat as her mother passes by. "Ah, so I see you've finally arrived, Harriet."

Nodding, Harriet sits silently as her mother continues. "We had to put all of the wedding things somewhere. Besides, you no longer live here, and if I remember correctly, this is still my house."

Silently, she nods once more at her mother. "We have guests arriving soon, so fix yourself up and be ready to join us. We have a lot to do and we don't have time for your New York attitude."

At her departure, Harriet stands and closes the door. Shaking her head, she gruffly makes the short walk to her bed and falls down on it. Looking up at the ceiling, her giant poster of Baby and Johnny practising the lift in the river looks back down at her. Closing her eyes, she takes a deep hurtful breathe as she tries to remember what her friend Karen says about her own poor relationship with her mother. How did it go now? Something along the lines of 'our mother's words only get the better of us if we continue to give them the power to hurt us'.

Opening her eyes, she sits up and glances over to the view outside her window. Why did she have to the room that had the perfect view of the Michael's home. Peeling herself off the bed, she meets the window with her forehead, pressing it against the glass pane. Its warm touch from the sunlight rays startles her at first but then again, her mind has already been consumed with irrelevant thoughts, and she'd only been home for half an hour. Looking to the fence, she wonders when she will see him this weekend. A preposterous thought to ponder she knows, seeing that he is Will's best man and all. His presence always had an effect on her and seeing that they hadn't spoken or seen each other in such a long time, she was secretly hoping that time will have helped to heal their wounds. But then again, with her luck in love. Well, better off not to hope at all.

"Harriet!!! Harriet!!! Stop being rude. Guests are arriving, and we have work to do. Come on!", her mother yells.

Stepping away from her window, she moves into the lounge to meet her mother's so-called guests who turn out to be her mother's family and her arrival in the room, doesn't seem to faze anyone one iota as they seemingly continue to chatter and gossip between themselves.

Taking a deep breath, she scans the room awkwardly before stopping at Will.

"Harriet, you're here. Awesome!!!"

Curious, she smirks. "What do you mean??? I was always coming. Besides, I'm in the wedding party? Aren't I???"

Guiding her away from their mother's earshot, Will drags Harriet to the kitchen where their cousins and uncles have all congregated away from the older women. "Listen, I knew you were coming Harriet. I was just being a smart ass!!!."

Harriet nods in surprise, "Some things never change. How's Sophie?"

"Mom is just having her usual whinge. She pretty much told everyone you were too busy to come. But Sophie and I knew you were driving down today."

Annoyed, she huffs. "Well, I have been busy. There's a society wedding on tonight that I've been planning, but as soon as I knew the date of your wedding, I spoke with Elizabeth and got the time off."

"Wow. Look at that. My little sister's making a name for herself!"

"Gee . . . thanks, at least I think? Besides, how could I forget anyways when Mom calls every fifty seconds to remind me that it's your wedding. You know she left like ten messages for me yesterday, and last night, she called me during the dinner rehearsal."

Throwing his head back, he explodes with laughter. Harriet punches him in the shoulder. "It's not funny Will. It was very unprofessional. Let alone embarrassing. All the bar staff and Harper's brother heard the conversation."

Still laughing at her, "Who's Harper?"

"The societal bride who's wedding I've been planning."

"And what were you doing on the phone near her brother?", he presses.

"I don't know. He was standing near me at the bar when I took the call!"

As he begins to laugh again, she notices his chest booming with cackles when he stops and looks down to smile at her. Unfortunately, their private moment is cut short by the sudden silence that has filled the house. Looking over at their mother then around at everyone besides them, Will and Harriet are taken aback by the looks from their mother and aunts. Smirking at each other, they smile awkwardly before turning back to each other.

Taking his arm around her shoulders, he moves her into the kitchen where her cousins, father, and Sophie are all seated at the dining table. "Whatever!!! I'm just glad to see. Sophie will be pleased to see you!!!"

Taking a seat next to her father at the table, she looks around the room to see who else has arrived. Her eyes panning across the room until they come to a dead stop at the sight of Nate. All her previous thoughts of seeing the boy next door at the event were suddenly answered as she sees him Nate standing in the kitchen, leaning against the cupboards, glaring back at her.

When she sees all the guests suddenly stand to depart for the backyard, Harriet makes a beeline for the kitchen. Her mind pulsing with discomfort sends her in search of aspirin or something stronger before stopping at the kitchen to sink to fill a glass of water.

"I thought you weren't coming."

Glancing at the reflection in the window, she sees him. Standing with his arms crossed firmly over his chest, he glares back at her.

Swallowing back a couple of aspirin, she empties the glass before turning to face him. "How are you, Nate?"

Running through his hand through his dark brown almost black mop, he huffs. "I just. I just didn't think you were coming. If I knew you were coming, I wouldn't –'

Interrupting him, "I was always coming Nate!!!", she snaps back.

His unnerving behaviour at the sight of seeing her fills the room with darkness causing Harriet to increasingly feel as if her heart were piercing her chest with shards of glass. Almost like a piñata that someone has just gone to town on, that someone being Nate. Looking down at her mother's cold kitchen tile, she takes a deep gutted breath and rallies.

"I'm here now, and I'm not leaving. I'm sorry Nate. But this is my family, and I can't not be here. You of all people, know what mother is like!!!"

"Oh, that's rich. Nobody ever has any problems until you show up. This wedding could've just floated on by. We could've all sat back and relaxed -'

"I beg your pardon???", she snaps.

"You heard me!!!"

Moving forward, she breaks from her spot against the kitchen sink and meets his dark chocolate brown eyes that are now surveying her every move. With a broken voice, she coldly hisses. "Thank you, Nate. Thank you so much for reminding me of the painful reason as to why we no longer speak and why I hate coming back to this place."

Straightening, she makes to walk away from him when she feels her upper arm being yanked back to him.

"Let go of me, Nate!"

"What's stopping you! If you hate this place so much why are you back here?", he spits out at her.

"It's _my_ brother's wedding!!!"

Dropping her arm slowly, he backs up. "I mean, right. Of course, what was I thinking? I've never asked anything of you. I just thought that for once, you'd –'

"This is hard for me too you know!!! I hate coming home and being under my mother's thumb. Most especially seeing my brother and knowing what we did. What happened. This can't happen", motioning her hand between the both of them, "I can't do that to him. Not this weekend, not ever." Putting her hands up, she just waves their conversation and her attendance off. "You know what. Why don't you just pretend like I'm not even here? You're good at that!!! I'm sure this weekend will be all over soon enough, and I'll be back in New York before we know it!"

Walking off she joins her family outside whilst he remains to compose himself before joining the party too. Stumped at the way that their friendship has ended up, Nate finds himself thwarted. Walking outside he takes a seat on the brick steps, only looking up to watch Harriet as she floats around speaking with one family member then another. Glancing away, his eyes scan the yard before stopping on the trampoline. Hidden in the very back depths of the yard situated behind a large redwood, he smirks in astonishment at the fact that her parents have still have kept it after all these years.

Glancing back to the party, trailing through the vast number of Lancer family members all mingling and laughing at each other in front of him, he immediately feels unwelcome. Feeling like he did as a child, uninvited and fixed behind that fence looming over at their family and desperately wishing he could be one of the family. Troubled by where his thoughts have led him, he feels his chest begin to tighten as his eyes gaze back to rest on Harriet. Like a moth drawn to a flame, he can't help but be caught by her spell. Only the Harriet he knew or he thought he knew, is completely different to the Harriet before him now. He more particularly never expected to feel this way or to still be in love with her after all these years.

And yet, what happened had happened. They were so far away from each other now that the leftover remnants of the once friendship had evaporated into thin air. Probably never to be seen again. Beaten, he searches his mind for something else to divert his thoughts. Only his heart deceives him, and he takes him back to memories of her in high school. Ones that he remembers as it if they had happened yesterday.

✳ ✳ ✳

Fifteen years earlier . . .

A fifteen-year-old Nate is standing in line during summer break with his friends to see George of the Jungle at the local Hartford cinemas. Almost a sophomore and sporting a bravado around all of his mates, he portrays all that is cool. Like his mates, he spent a copious amount of time in front of the bathroom mirror this morning, spiking his hair with gel and perfecting his look with his black and white Nike Air pumps, Jordan t-shirt and denim shorts.

Standing towards the front of the line, he sees Harriet. Having just turned thirteen a week ago, a fact that he can attest to, witnessing as she blew out the candles on her cake at a barbecue her father organised for her in their backyard. Watching from his parent's back porch as she smiled, thanked each of her guests for coming and kissed her father's cheek for putting together the event.

Smiling at her now, he watches on as she stands in line with her friends, wearing a white shirt and denim overalls and her deep russet hair in loose plaits. His staring is thwarted by Harriet when she turns and catches him. Smiling back, she waves curtly but Nate remembering who he is and the role he's playing freezes and turns his back on her.

During the movie, instead of pay attention to the screen, his mind betrays him with thoughts of Harriet. Observing as she and her friends giggle and smile, his stomach knotting at her ignorance and as soon as the credits have rolled, his grief builds as she disappears out the cinemas with her friends.

Fast forward to a couple of years later . . .

Harriet is a junior at high school. Sitting in the library, she is studying for an English exam as Nate walks in to return an overdue library book. Upon hearing his voice, talking with the librarian at the front desk,

Harriet buries her face in a book, pretending as if she hadn't seen him come in.

"Harriet?"

Feeling caught, she looks up from her book. "Just so I get this right, you are talking to me right???"

"What?! Do you see anyone else?"

Looking around, they both notice that the library is near empty. Defeated, she slumps in her chair. Rolling her wrist, she checks her watch for the time before beginning to pack up her books. Standing, she makes her way out of the library before smiling at Marg, the librarian.

Feeling his feet at the back of her heels she heads towards her locker.

"Harriet, will you slow down!"

"Careful now, people might see. You might lose your street cred!", she snaps.

"What are you talking about?", he retorts instantaneously.

Stopping, she turns and faces him. "What do you want Nate?"

"What?! I can't talk to you now, is that it?", he snaps back proudly.

Inquisitively, her eyebrows furrow angrily back at him. "Nate, do you even know the last time you spoke to me?"

"No –'

"Just as I suspected", she remarks before sprinting off to her locker.

Stocking up her bag with textbooks, she closes its door and spins its dial. As she moves towards the exit, she is met once more by Nate.

"Harriet!"

"For god sakes. Really?! What do you want now? I've gotta get home!!!"

Examining her form as she stands before him, he notices her warm russet brown hair that was once worn in pigtails is now a shade of deep chocolate brown that falls against her profile in soft waves ending below her chest. Gone are the overalls she wore religiously as a thirteen-year-old and reminded him of Pippi Longstocking for she now wore fitted sweaters, boot cut jeans and brown flats.

Rolling her eyes, she huffs having had enough of his attention for one afternoon. "Whatever!!! I'm going."

"Wait!!! Harriet –'

"What!", she snips, "Honestly, what do you want!!!"

Smirking, he foolishly gathers a question in his head and asks. "How many times have you really watched Dirty Dancing, Harriet?"

At a loss, she rebuffs. "Honestly? After almost three years of radio silence and ignoring me, that's what you want to know???"

Smirking, he nods. "Yes!"

His high school experience having turned out to be more than he could ever have imagined, caused for his appearances over at the Lancer's to dwindle over time. With his commitments to swimming, partying and working in his father's auto shop; he spent less time at their home and even less time hanging out with Harriet.

"Yeah well, I guess you'll never know. The answer to a question like that is reserved only for my friends. Last time I looked, I don't even know you!", she smugly answers back.

"Harriet, this isn't like you, you're never cruel. You almost sound like –'

Shaking her head at him, extremely annoyed now at his continued presence, she readies herself to blow.

"Don't you dare say I sound like my mother!!! You know, you were my friend too. You weren't just Will's best friend. But you disappeared, and you expect me to just act like nothing changed?"

"I'm sorry Harriet. I just -'

Turning away from him, she wipes a tear off her cheek. "Yeah well, it's too late. You'll be leaving for college soon, and I'll be able to stop pretending like I once knew you."

As he watches her walk away, he looks down to the ground feeling as if the earth below was going to open up and swallow him whole. Feeling awful, it becomes clear to him exactly how much he too, has missed their friendship. Yes, she's his best friend's sister and practically a sister to him too, but she was also incredibly smart and funny. She used to make him laugh and smile in ways that no-one ever could, and he's missed that, none of the girls his age could ever do that or make him feel the way he did whenever she was around.

Only now, it was too late. He'd be leaving for college soon, and she'd be heading for Dartmouth in a couple of years herself. In the wake of his absence, she had indeed grown up and found her own voice. Not only that, she had evolved into a young woman, more beautiful and charismatic than all others because she had grown up beside him.

She was the only one that he could ever talk to about how he felt to be an only child with absent parents. She understood, and she listened. She always listened. And she also shared the same dream he did. To leave Hartford and never come back.

Chapter Twelve

Will's Wedding

"Ladies and Gentlemen, it's my esteem pleasure to announce the newly married, Mr & Mrs Will Lancer!!!"

Walking into the tent, a tent that she had pleaded with the Function Manager of The Sheraton South Hotel to allow its construction on the hotel's grounds, Harriet follows her brother and his bride into the reception. Looking forward to having a moment just to sit down and relax, a moment's peace to investigate its inside, she notices the tent had indeed been constructed as per Sophie's wishes. Every little detail from the white and blue satin with fairy lights draped across the width of the tent ceiling to circular tables lined with white tablecloths and gold dinnerware beautified the event.

When Sophie had first come to her almost a year ago, begging Harriet to help plan the wedding, Sophie revealed that she had her heart set on a garden ceremony and reception instead of Gloria taking over as she had previously done so with the engagement party. But seeing as Gloria Lancer didn't agree, Harriet helped Sophie to compromise with her obstinate future mother-in-law to have their ceremony in a church and the reception on the grounds of The Sheraton South Hotel.

And that's exactly what happened. Sophie would communicate with Harriet regularly, asking questions or seeking her advice on formal wear and whether to go with a band or DJ. Unfortunately for Harriet that wasn't what her mother was telling her family and friends, informing them that Harriet was simply too busy to come home for the wedding and obviously, still continued to harbour envious thoughts towards her brother.

Taking a seat at the bridal party, she breathes a deep sigh. Looking down at her dusty pink, lace boat neck bridesmaid dress, she feels exhausted. Worn out from choreographing everyone and over her mother's family behaviour; she looks around the table to find a full champagne flute sitting in front of her before embracing it firmly inside her fingers.

Swallowing a long pull, the golden effervescent liquid left in the glass beading vivaciously within her fingers, her moment of reverie is interrupted by the sound of the pitter patter of feet stopping behind her.

"Harriet!!!"

Turning hesitantly, she instantly finds her mother standing with a young man beside her.

"Harriet, this is David. The young man I was telling you about?!"

Nodding reluctantly, Harriet feels as if her head is going to explode and she exhales a deep sigh. Eyeing her mother sharply as she defiantly walks off towards her table, a less than enthusiastic Harriet smiles back up at David and watches as he places his hand out to her. Sitting up, she takes an elongated breath and nods before taking it and following him out onto the near empty dance floor.

As they circle in their spot, they notice the attention coming from her mother's table. Her fevered aunts with their hands covering their chests and sighing at her as David leads her across the floor.

"Harriet, it's okay. This is all just for show!"

Confused, she looks at him. "Wait, what?"

"Yeah, I mean you're a lovely girl and a knockout to boot, but you're kind of not my type!"

His eyes prompting her to follow his line of sight to a table where her male cousins have congregated. Shaking her head, she feels her body begin to fill with laughter.

"Right! But why did you agree –'

"Because I have a mother just like yours. A full blown Italian mamma who is not happy unless everyone is married and popping out children. If she's not happy, then she goes out her way to make everyone else's unhappy too!"

"Yeah. I know that feeling. So what do you suppose we should do???", a now animated Harriet replies.

"Well, it's a wedding. So if you're keen, how about we drink as much free alcohol as we can. Judge the delicious man candy on show before us and just have a good time!!!"

Smiling, she nods. "Sounds like a plan!"

Spinning, their view comes into contact with Nate's. "Tell me, Harriet, what's the deal with that one?"

Looking around, she follows his line of sight. "Which one?"

Discreetly pointing over towards him, David steers Harriet to look over at Nate as he watches on fervently.

"That one. The best man, Nate something or rather?"

Taking a deep breath, she looks away immediately. "Trouble. That's the deal with that one, nothing but trouble and . . . pain!!!"

"Oooooo!!!! I sense a story attached to that one. Spill!"

"Nothing to spill, David. He's just . . . not . . . well, anything. First off, he's uh . . . straight and secondly . . . he's a jerk!!!"

Not have any of it, David immediately becomes antsy. "Oooooo!!!! I love it when you talk nasty, Harriet. Ouch! Let me guess, he's your brother's best friend to whom you had a big ol' crush on and when he found out, he broke your heart and you moved to New York in order to get away from him and so that you didn't have to see him hanging around all the time!!!"

Smirking, she shakes her head at him. "Yep, that's exactly how it went!"

"Liar! So tell me about New York? You're a party planner?"

"Event planner but yes I do plan parties too. It's great, I love it. Actually, I've just been organising a wedding for the Forbes-Bennett's in Manhattan, that is up until I came home for Will's wedding."

Nodding happily at the news, he quizzes her. "Sounds delicious. Are they, Harriet? All that money and entitlement. Actually, I have a friend who went to boarding school with the young Bennett."

Curiously, she finds herself intrigued. Pulling her head to meet his inquisitive eyes, she asks. "Who, Damon Bennett?"

"Yes. That's the chap. Tell me, what does he look like these days or better yet what team does he play for?"

Giggling, she shakes her head. "He plays for the straight team, I met his girlfriend a couple of days ago."

"Bitch?"

"Opposite. Tall, blonde, beautiful. I think she's a dancer actually. Of course, you wouldn't have thought it by the dress she was wearing. Tight . . . strapless . . . hot pink thing. For a moment there, I thought Ken was going to show up, and they were going to escape in her pink convertible."

"Ouch?! You're tongue, Harriet. It's remarkable. *Remind me to never piss you off*!!!"

Smirking, meeting his eyes she nods in agreement. "Don't worry. You're growing on me, David. Who knows we might actually end up as friends."

As the music comes to a stop, he pulls back away from her to take her hand in his. Brushing her knuckles, he smiles back up at her.

"Thank you for the dance, Harriet. I'll let you get back to your duties, but I'd really love to do this again later!"

"Same here. See you in a little bit then . . . oh and David?"

"Yes?"

"Good luck tonight?!"

"You too!"

Walking back to her seat at the bridal table, she sees her glass has since been refilled. Wrapping her fingers around the glass's neck and empties it. Her now sister in law, looking on with intrigue, leans behind her friend to speak with Harriet.

"Harriet, what was that all about?"

Summoning a waiter for a refill, she waits until her glass is full before replying, "Just my mother trying to set me up with a gay man" and empties the glass.

Covering her mouth, Sophie can't help but laugh. "I'm so sorry, Harriet?!"

Shaking her head, "Its fine. Really!!! He's actually a really lovely guy despite well . . . well, you know!"

Nodding, Sophie smiles at Harriet before turning her attention back to her husband. Sitting back against the panels in her chair, she feels yet another set of eyes on her. Following her sixth sense, she looks to her left beyond the happy couple and feels a set of eyes glaring back at her. Noticing his chest as it rises and falls with every heartbeat, Nate finds himself battling with inner desires wanting desperately to throttle the man she had just been dancing with, to storm over to her and taking her in his hands. Never letting her go *ever*.

Unfortunately, Harriet can't reciprocate. Some might say she refuses. As she unlocks her eyes away from him, she looks back to the wedding program laid out in front of her. Reviewing the events the day and Nate's behaviour, her mind recalls her back to earlier that day when she walked down the aisle towards Will after Paige, remembering particularly how Will smiled happily as he waited for his bride to make her grand entrance. Especially remembering how his best man did nothing but look at his feet with contempt as she passed by. And how during the photo-shoot inside the hotel, Nate ignored her and refused to have his photo taken with her, shocking her family and most particularly, Will.

Sitting upright in her seat, she looks over in comparison to her brother and his new wife then at Nate. Feeling remarkably angry that Nate couldn't behave on today of all days. Taking a deep breath, she shakes him out of her mind for the last time. She's done. Finally had it and what's worse, up until that moment she'd been missing out on her brother's wedding, and it stops right now.

Picking up her glass, she takes a long pull and stands. Smiling, a smirk forms over her lips and as her cheeks blush a bright pink, she decides to walk off in search of David. To take him up on that offer of getting drunk and judging all the man candy, the event has to offer.

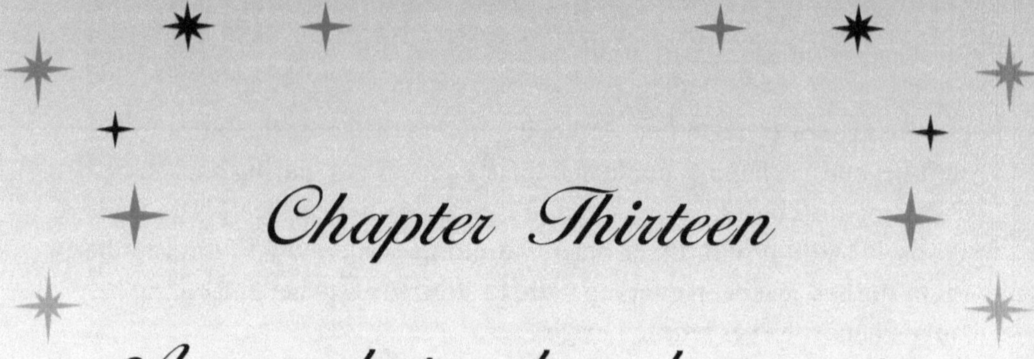

Chapter Thirteen

A somewhat awkward encounter

"Well, to begin with, it was a really horrible set up. It would never have worked!"

Stirring her coffee with a plastic spoon, Harriet giggles down at her cup. Taking a seat at the table, she discusses her brother's wedding with her colleagues in the break room of Enchanted Events.

Karen laughs back, "Well, that tends to happen when your mother sets you up!"

"I mean seriously! Kevin, he would've preferred to be on a date with you.", she replies back instantly.

Kevin shakes his head at her and huffs, clearly disappointed. "Well, I didn't get an invite!"

"Trust me you guys, if I was allowed you know you both would've been there. But in all honesty, the more we drank, the more it turned out to be a pretty great night. He definitely made the night enjoyable."

Unwrapping her sandwich from its cling wrap, she is about to take a bite when the intercom comes over the break room speaker.

"Harriet, you have a client waiting in your office"

Dropping her sandwich, she wraps it back up and stands. Placing her lunch in the fridge, she shakes her head briefly at Kevin and Karen before rolling her eyes. "Well, I guess I'll see you guys later then."

Taking her coffee in hand, she leaves for her office. Opening her door, she is startled by the sight of Damon Bennett sitting patiently awaiting her arrival. His eyes following her movements across the room from door to chair before she finally acknowledges his presence.

"So, are we thinking the same style of wedding as Harper's?"

Bringing bring up her client files on her computer, she scrolls to find Harper's file assuming that he will be wanting the same style of wedding like his sister's and begins to type up the details in a new client file.

"Sorry? What?! I mean no. I mean. Are you kidding? My mother would have a coronary if I married Lucy."

Looking up from her screen, she smirks. Watching as Damon has a momentary meltdown before shaking his head back at her.

"I'm just here and *only here* to drop off the cheque for Harper!"

Reaching over her desk, Harriet takes the cheque from Damon and starts typing out a receipt on her computer. She is about to press print when his voice pulls her attention away from the computer screen.

"So, how was your brother's wedding?"

Taking a deep breath, she assesses the perfectly postured Damon, waiting patiently for her response. Leaning back into her chair, she sighs. "Same as all family celebrations I guess."

"What your date didn't impress you???"

Irritated by his comment, she shuts down. "Okay. Well, it's been a pleasure seeing you again Mr Bennett, but I'm afraid I am rather busy. Your receipt will be available at the front desk!"

"Wait?! What???", Damon quickly interjects.

"I am busy and I especially don't like to be made fun of, so it was a pleasure seeing once again, but the door is over there Mr Bennett. Thank you for coming. Have a lovely day", she repeats.

"Do you always act this hot and cold towards your clients?"

Clearly slighted by his snide comments, she snaps. "Excuse me? No, I don't. And you were never my client. Your sister was. And I most certainly do not act hot and cold!!! And if I did it would certainly wouldn't be any of your business!!!"

"What? Well was that just now?", he snaps back.

Crossing her arms over her chest, her glacially annoyed eyes lock with his. "Seeing that you come from established breeding and obviously a far more providential lineage than mine, let me enlighten you. I don't appreciate it when people make fun of me. Especially when I have done nothing for the last year but plan the most magnificent wedding for your sister. I may not have the same entitlements or fortune as you, but I do have the right to defend myself. And on that note, it was a pleasure, but I am awfully busy and must be getting back to my work."

"For your information, I wasn't *making fun* of you. I just thought I'd be polite and ask you about your weekend!!!"

Retaliating irritably, she bites. "Why do you always act out quotation marks? Is there someone wrong with you?"

"What are you talking about? I don't always act them out!"

"I see you do it all the time!!!", Harriet shrieks.

"Oh really? When have you seen me do it? Hang on, if you've seen me do it then that means you've been watching me!"

Rolling her eyes, she marvels. "Don't be stupid!"

"Oh so now I'm stupid! There's nothing wrong with me? I think the question to ask is what's wrong with you?"

Rising from her seat, she marches over to her door. Before opening it, she sets him straight. "I believe I've taken up enough of your time today Mr Bennett. Good day!"

Just as confused as she is in that moment, he too searches for an explanation regarding their behaviour. "All I came to do is drop off the cheque and say hello. Maybe ask about your date? If I had known -"

"Yeah well, that's *clearly* none of your business."

Scratching his eyebrow, he sighs. "Clearly!!! I'm so sorry for interfering. I just thought, well that come down here and show our appreciation especially considering the hell my mother put you through with this wedding."

Taking hold of the door handle, she avoids his eyes and looks outside her office. "Well, while it's appreciated, it's also not necessary. I had a job to do, and it's now it's over. Your mother while harsh and most times cruel, I believe only wanted what's best for her only daughter's wedding. Apart from that, Mr Bennett. We're different people from different worlds. Thank you for coming down and handling the payment personally, it is appreciated. Lilly at the front desk will have your receipt ready."

Acknowledging defeat, he allows her to open the door for him to leave. "Fair enough. It was nice meeting you Miss Lancer."

Watching him briefly as he walks off towards the reception, she moves back to her desk to take a seat. Spinning around, she avoids her work choosing instead to look out her window. As her eyes climb higher,

higher than the New York skyline, she searches for the clear blue sky and white pillow like clouds she has always adored. But as karma would have it, in retribution for her earlier despicable behaviour, there are none.

Turning around from the window, she takes a deep breath. She looks at the work set before her. Knowing that she would need a stronger cup of coffee than the office houses, she picks up her handset and calls the front desk.

Harriet: Hey Lilly, could I trouble you for a favour?

Lily: Of course, anything Harriet

Harriet: You're about to leave for your break in ten, aren't you?

Lily: Yeah, just going up to the café. You want me to grab you a salted caramel frappe?

Harriet: Yeah Lilly, that would be absolutely great. I'll fix you up when you get back?

Lily: My treat. And I'll pick up some chocolate fudge brownies too. See you when I get back okay.

Harriet: Okay, my treat next time.

Lily: Sounds good to me.

Harriet: Thanks, Lilly.

Pulling a file from her inbox tray, she lays it open in front of her before clicking up a new client file document on her computer. Picking up her handset once again, she selects The Plaza Hotel's number from her address book.

Plaza Hotel, Stewart speaking . . .

Harriet: Hi Stew, its Harriet. Is Marco in?

Sure is, one moment . . .

Harriet: Thanks, Stew.

Plaza Hotel, Functions Department, you speaking with Marco . . .

Harriet: Hi Marco, its Harriet.

Hello Harriet, what can I do for you today?

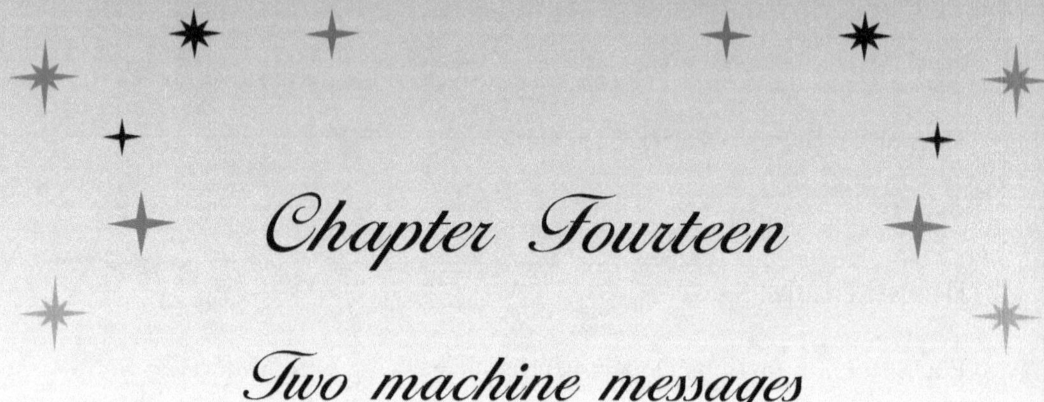

Chapter Fourteen

Two machine messages

and a Date

Arriving home later that evening, Harriet drops her things in her somewhat small foyer and immediately heads to her kitchen in search of a cold glass of wine. Filling a glass, she takes the bottle and enters her lounge to sit, hitting the answering machine button on the way. She has almost drained her first glass as the first message plays out.

First message - Today at 9:30 am Hi Harriet, it's David. I was just ringing to tell you that I had a fabulous time with you at your brother's wedding and I'd love to catch up for a drink or better yet, some shopping next time I'm in New York.

Emptying the glass now, she begins to pour another when she is interrupted by the sound of knocking at her front door. Standing she goes to answer it as the message plays in the background.

Second message - Today at 11 am Harriet it's your mother. Just checking to see that David called you . . .

Harriet, he seems like a very nice boy maybe you should give him a chance. You know, you two looked very cute together.

Opening her front door, she finds Damon standing on her landing. Startled, she breathes. "What the *hell*!!!"

"Please don't be mad. The girl at the front desk gave me your address", he replies at the same time.

"I'll kill her!!!"

Now Harriet, you're not getting any younger, so maybe you should at least give David a chance, I mean you never

know, he may be the one . . . You have no more messages

An embarrassed Harriet looks immediately to her feet while a cautious Damon remains awkwardly fixed in her doorway as the words of her mother, 'you're not getting any younger', seem to hover over her before dissolving in the cool New York night air. It's crispness finding a way to finagle its way into her two-story brownstone through means of her open front door.

"So, Mr Bennett, it's been nice seeing you again but -"

Stepping across her threshold, he peers inside inquisitively. "Wait, aren't you going to ask me in?"

"Err, well. Did you want to come in?"

Smirking, he confidently steps inside. "Well okay then!".

Following her past her small foyer, he can see a staircase obviously leading to the second story on his right and a short hallway to his front. Looking to the wall on his left, the wall that separates the hall from the lounge, he can see photos hung up of her family and friends. To his right, the wall hiding the stairs, he sees more photos. Only these are moments stuck in time, cascading from her childhood to days of recent, the latest addition being a photo of her with family at her brother's wedding in Hartford.

Watching her beautiful dark chocolate hair bouncing away as it disappears from the hallway and into the lounge. Its glow emanating from the warm apartment lighting shining upon it, beaming waves of luminance throughout her delicate tendrils and emphasising her presence in the room as she takes her position on the couch.

"Would you like a glass of wine? Or beer?", she asks softly.

"Uh, a beer would be good. Thanks."

Standing, she disappears through a swinging door only to return with a beer in her hand. Before handing it over, she pops the lid on the side of the bookcase and takes her seat back on the lounge, collecting her glass from the coffee table on the way.

Taking a seat on the chair opposite her, he smiles. "Mmmm . . . Impressive."

Puzzled, she looks at him. "What is?"

"Your bottle top handy work there."

Shrugging her shoulder, she grins. "Oh, uh. I have an older brother. Taught me everything he knows."

Taking sips of their drinks, they inadvertently avoid each other's eyes as they sit awkwardly in silence. Damon using the time to look around her home before Harriet can't help but ask, "So, not to be rude or anything but seriously why are you here?"

Smirking at her line of questioning, he can't help but laugh then mumble. "You rude???"

Unimpressed, she frowns. With furrowed eyebrows and an index finger drilling circles around the rim of her wine glass, she waits for him to give an actual answer and ignores his insult.

"Well, I just want to apologise -"

Agitated, she screams out, "Urghf!!!". Leaning forward, she slams her glass on the coffee table and empties the bottle into the glass, filling the glass to the very brim.

"What?!"

Glaring at him, she shakes her head. "For god sakes, would you stop apologising. Seriously, I don't care!"

"Oh okay. Fine!!!"

"Fine!!!", she snaps back as she crosses her arms and avoids his eyes.

Desperate to keep her talking and get to know her, he looks around the room for another topic of conversation. Stopping at her bookcase, he notices a photo of her family. Standing, he walks towards it and picks it up and notices on closer inspection that in the photo her mother is positioned on the left side of the group and Harriet on the right. Amused at the sight, he can't help but understand the similarities their mother's share.

"So your mother, she wants you to get married?", he asks softly.

Turning on her sofa, she nods. "Yes. No. Oh hell, I don't know. I think she thinks that I won't be happy until I'm married with children."

"Are you? Happy, that is?", he asks curiously.

Sniping sarcastically back, she grins. "I am normally."

"Normally???"

"Well, normally I stop getting harassed by wedding party members once the wedding is all over and done with!!!"

Damon smiles at her, his enjoyment at making her feel uncomfortable sends an un-nerving wave of discomfort throughout her body.

"What about this David fellow? What's he like? Does he have marriage potential?"

Grinning, she smirks at him and asks, intrigued. "Why? Do you want me to set you up with him? Because I could totally see that happening!"

To which he quickly refutes with, "What? I'm not gay?" and Harriet realises that she's hit a nerve. Running her hand lightly through her hair, she takes a deep breath and meets his eyes. "Then what's with all the questions, Damon???"

Smiling back at her, his elation at hearing her speak his name softens and spreads warmth across his chest. Opening up, he dares to show his vulnerability by being honest and declares to her. "Mmmm. I don't know. Maybe I like you!"

"No - ", she gasps.

"Wait?! I'm sorry but is that a bad thing???"

"One, I don't date clients and two, I'm not your type."

"I'm not a client, Harriet. You said so yourself today in your office."

"Okay then . . . what about your girlfriend???"

"We broke up."

"Oh really? So she finally realised her dream career was to marry a man named Ken and live happily ever after in their pink mansion and pink convertible???", she snipes spitefully.

Finding her comments maddening, he snipes back. "Seriously, what is wrong with you? Do you have something against blondes?"

"Again, why does there have to be something wrong with me? And no, I don't have something against blondes. No one can blame if anyone takes one look at her and immediately thinks that she lives in a pink house and drives a pink convertible.”

Shaking his head, he informs Harriet, “You know, for your information, she is a dancer with the American Ballet Company.”

“Well . . . good!!! I’m glad. I’m so happy for you both!”

Standing, she begins to move towards her front door. Feeling overly ashamed by her behaviour, she decides its time he left.

“I think . . . I think you should go.”

Nodding, he agrees. Placing his beer bottle on the table, he follows her. Stopping at the stairs, he admits as she unlocks her door. “We broke up. Let’s just say that someone might’ve mentioned that the relationship wasn’t leading to anything and that I needed to grow up.”

With guilt now flooding through her vein, she feels her cheeks flush with embarrassment. Mortified not only her misjudgment of him but also of her misjudgment of his former girlfriend, she turns slowly to meet his eyes.

“This someone. It wouldn’t be your mother would it?”

“No! As if I’d . . . yes!!!”, wiping his face in shame he grins before locking eyes with hers again, “Yeah . . . she might have said some things.”

Tucking her hair behind her ears, she feels a familiar pang of parental discomfort. Biting down on her lip, she can’t help but feel for him.

“Do you think . . . I mean, are you going to be okay?”

“Yeah. I mean I think I am. I just wish –’

“Wish what???”

"Well, that my mother acted like a mother sometimes and not like –'

"Like everything you do and say in your life wasn't a direct reflection on her?", she replies, instantaneously.

With their eyes locked, they both smile and nod in unison.

"I don't want to burst your bubble seeing as you're on a roll to the good life, but I don't think your mother likes me much. So I'm sorry but –'

"You're not even the least bit interested in at least going on a date???", Damon remarks immediately.

"I can't. I'm sorry. But I just couldn't."

Opening the door, she holds it wide for him to exit through. As she waits, her breath is shot by his guileless blue eyes staring at her, pinning her in the doorway. In passing, he tries one more time to coax her into a date with him. Placing one hand above her right shoulder and another by her waist, he draws her in.

"One date and if you don't ever want to see me again, I promise not to call and leave messages on your machine like

your mother does!", he pleads.

Defeated, she rests her forehead against the door frame and closes her eyes. Nodding, she accepts. "Ok fine?!"

"Excellent. Pick you up tomorrow night. 8 on the dot. You like Italian right?", he smirks.

"No. Of course not, I'm just half Italian for the fun of it!!!"

Smiling as he descends down her front steps towards his car, he smirks back at her. "Great, see you then!"

And as she watches Damon drive off down the street, she finds herself stuck in her doorway replaying in her mind what has just happened. Shifting, she steps inside and closes the door, turning the locks as she goes. Switching off the lights in her apartment, her mind still fuddled, she makes the walk upstairs to her bedroom.

Stepping into her walk in, she changes into her pyjamas before moving to her bed to peel back her doona and climbing into it. Shifting to turn off her lamp, she turns on her side to sight the night sky. As she slips away, further into a deep slumber brought on from one and a half bottles of wine, all she can see as her eyesight fades to black are the twinkle of stars from the night sky that seep through her bedroom window and into her dreams.

Chapter Fifteen

An unexpected recommendation

Harriet is walking into the offices of Enchanted Events, the very next morning when she takes a moment to pause at the front desk to collect her messages. Looking down at the reception desk, she sees Charlotte, a young intern studying business at Columbia who works as in their front office two days a week.

"Morning Charlotte."

As she hands over the messages, Harriet smiles. "Thank you. I'll be in my office."

Nodding, Charlotte looks over Harriet's shoulder to the couple and their daughter, sitting on the couches behind them. "You're 9 o'clock has arrived, should I wait ten minutes then send them in?"

"Sounds great, thanks Charlotte . . . Oh and Charlotte?"

Charlotte looks up from her computer screen, glances over to Harriet. "Yes?"

"Damon Bennett?"

Shrugging coyly at her, Charlotte knows exactly what Harriet is referring to and smiles back. "What? I thought it was sweet. He obviously likes you!!!"

Shaking her head in defeat, Harriet heads towards her office. Taking a seat behind her desk, she begins to prepare herself for the first appointment of the morning. She has barely readied herself, planner open and computer ready when a knock on her office door, finds her out of her chair and opening the door to the sight of Charlotte standing in the doorway with new clients.

"Mr and Mrs Fratelli . . . this is Harriet Lancer. Honestly, she's our best!!!"

Nodding, Charlotte steps away back to reception as Harriet smiles at them all, inviting them to take a seat and begin the appointment.

"Please, have a seat."

Sitting in her chair, she faces the middle-aged couple. "So Mr and Mrs Fratelli what can I do for you today?"

Mrs Fratelli is the first to speak. A well-mannered woman with a honey coloured layered bob to her neck, tucks her hair behind her ears, revealing a stunning pair of pearl earrings that match her exquisite freshwater pearl necklace which hangs from her neck.

"Well, my daughter is turning 17 next month", and as she takes her pearl necklace in her hands, Harriet senses this is an act of comfort for her as she looks nervously between her husband and Harriet. "And we'd like to throw her a party."

Smiling at the couple, she nods in understanding. "So, this is a 17th birthday party?"

As they look between each other, Harriet brings up her birthday planning file on her computer and begins steamrolling ideas.

"So does she have an idea of what she wants or if she'd like a theme?"

As her mother begins to speak, they are joined by their daughter, "Arabella, this is Harriet. She will be organising your party", and she takes a seat next to her mother.

Positioning herself towards Arabella, Harriet smiles at the young girl. "Good morning Arabella, so I understand you're turning 17. That's an amazing milestone. Have you had your prom yet?"

"No, it's a week after the date we'd like to have the party."

"Wow. You're going to be a busy girl but don't worry, it will all be fine because you have me."

Writing the dates down in her planner, she looks to Arabella's parents. "Do you have any idea of function places or will you have this at your home?"

Mr Fratelli answers for the party, surprising the women in the room. "Actually, we were thinking of having it in our hometown. At the Sheraton Hartford South Hotel in Hartford."

"Yes, I know The Sheraton very well. I've attended more than one event there. That's my hometown."

Smiling, Mrs Fratelli nods. "Yes, we are aware. Actually, your mother was the one who suggested we come to see you!!!"

Shocked at this revelation, Harriet raises her eyebrows in shock as a grin forms over her lips. "My mother did? Wow?!"

Rubbing her forehead briefly, she looks to their daughter. "So Arabella, do you have any ideas on numbers coming or a guest list. A theme perhaps?"

"Well, we have to invite the family, and I'd probably invite most of my class. Themes??? Hmmm. I think I'd like to go with colours if that's okay?"

"Of course that's okay. You'll be the birthday girl. Ah, will there be males attending this party?"

Mr Fratelli closes his eyes and looking up as if to pray while his wife nods quietly. All while, an extremely happy Arabella beams at Harriet.

"Yes, of course!!! The guys in my class will be coming?!"

Adjusting her view to her planner, Harriet holds back her smirk by biting her lip as she writes down these extra details.

"Okay well, this is truly an excellent start to our planning! I think that'd be it for today. I'd like to make an appointment for next week so that we can decide on decorations and possibly a menu. I will call Miles, the Event Manager at the Sheraton now to get it booked because even though we have a month, we still need to get the date and location set in stone now. I'll give you my card, if you have any questions, please don't hesitate to call me."

Turning to Arabella, "I have plenty of couture shops on speed dial so if you need anything like dress fittings, hairstylists for your party or even your prom, either here in New York or in Hartford. I can get in touch with them and organise a meeting the next time you're in New York!"

Turning back to her parents, "And if you could get me a list of party invites as soon as you can, I could possibly get started on the save the date cards", looking back at Arabella, "Once you've decided your colour then we will get started on your invite design and hopefully have them out by the end of next week."

Looking at each other, thoroughly pleased, the Fratelli's all smile back at Harriet. As they stand and make their way to the door, Mrs Fratelli steps towards Harriet and hugs her gently, before whispering softly.

"Your mother was right. You are very good at your job!"

Pulling back, she nods quietly back. Not fond of hearing that her mother was right but overwhelmed by Mrs Fratelli's motherly gentleness towards her, Harriet feels her eyes begin to well up.

"So, we have you booked again on Friday, and if Arabella can decide on colours and maybe even a music list, we can hook into it."

"Thank you, Harriet!"

"It's truly my pleasure. Take care okay."

Smiling as they all disappear down the hall to the front reception, Harriet closes her door and takes to her seat. Picking up her handset, she begins to dial The Sheraton Hartford South Hotel.

Sheraton Hartford South Hotel, good morning, you're speaking with Leanne . . .

Yes, good morning Leanne. This is Harriet Lancer of Enchanted Events, New York. May I please speak with Miles?

Sure, he's just in his office. I'll patch you through. One moment . . .

Thank you, Leanne.

Turning in her chair to look out her window view, she listens to one of Vivaldi's Four Seasons being played as she is placed on hold until Miles picks up. Losing herself in the music, she closes her eyes and can't help but think back to when she was Arabella's age, and she was getting ready for her very own prom.

❋ ❋ ❋

Eleven years earlier . . .

Seated at her white antique duchess, a birthday gift that her father scoured the whole of Hartford for, an excited but nervous Harriet is getting ready for her prom. Anxious about her date, a nice guy named Chace who sat next to her in computer class for the last two years and made her laugh, she knew deep down that even in her wildest dreams there'd be no way on earth that she could ever have a guy like Patrick Swayze take her to the prom. Yet Chace asked, and he seemed like a nice guy whom she'd have fun with.

Standing, she assesses herself in the mirror. Her flowing lavender empire-styled floor-length gown with lilac sheath covering her bodice up to her neck which is dusted in diamantes and trails of sequins adorning the skirt. Brushing her 50's inspired curled do to her side, she lines her lips with a touch of gloss. Running her finger over her handy work, she slips on her silver heels and collects her clutch off her bed.

Reaching for the door handle, she hears her mother screaming at her for the entire neighbourhood to hear. "Harriet?! . . . Harriet?! Are you ready . . . please get a move on! Your uncle will be here at any moment with the car, and I still have to take photos!"

Shaking her head, she knows deep down it's all an act. She knows her mother really doesn't want to take photos. She just doesn't want to look inconsiderate in the eyes of everyone else. You see; she played no part in the coming of age experience. It was Harriet's Aunt Mara, who asked to make a dress for her and her Uncle Barto, that said he'd gladly drive her and her friends to the prom. Her godmother, Aunt Wanda took her shopping and bought her the jewellery, shoes, and bag to match the dress and also did her hair.

After standing for some time and having posed for photos; a photo in front of the olive garden, a photo in the backyard, with Mom and Harriet, Dad with Harriet, Harriet in front of the garden, Harriet sitting, Harriet with Mom and Dad, Harriet with her Uncle Sal, Harriet with her Aunt Wanda and finally Harriet with her Aunt and Uncle, Harriet is relieved to see the sight of her ride pulling in the driveway.

Before she can move an inch towards the car and see her friends who are waiting for her, everyone hears Gloria yell for Will to get off the couch and for Paige to come outside. As she waits for what she assumes is one last photo, Harriet senses another's presence behind her from next door.

Nate, who was walking out to his car, is stopped by the sight of Harriet standing in her parent's driveway. Perplexed, he gazes. Her brunette hair flowing down one side, showing the curves of her beautifully articulated neck and as he continues to stand, begging her to look his way. His somewhat happiness turns to pain at the sight of a young man exiting the limousine and moving towards her in a dapper grey tuxedo carrying a corsage in a little plastic box.

Feeling his eyes burning a hole in her back, she turns to look, extremely annoyed.

"Are you right there? Don't you have anything better to do than to stare?"

Glancing down to his feet, he leans against his fully restored black Trans Am. Brushing his shaggy brown locks out of his face, he scratches his eyebrow as he smiles, again down at his feet.

"No. I mean yes!!! I mean, well of course I do!!! I have places to be, girls to see!!!"

Shaking her head, she fixes herself as Chace edges closer towards her, but not before snapping back at Nate.

"Oh, well right then. Well, you should be off then!!! -'

'Don't you worry, I will be!!!"

"Well!!! Good then!", she finishes.

Watching as her date places the corsage on her hand and smiles; Nate peels himself off his car and jumps in it, slamming the door as he goes.

Jumping at the sound of the car door, Harriet and Chace take a deep breath and make to move away from him. As she meets her friends, Nate can't help but watch them. Harriet testing the dancing quality of her dress, by twirling around with her friends to the point where Chace dispatches himself from his mates to catch her mid-twirl and dip her. His chest tightening, Nate continues to watch on as Harriet blushes out a smile that emanates her face.

His 'Harriet' trance is interrupted by the sight of her family as they all come tramping out of the house. Overly delighted at the prospect of taking one last photo, Gloria beings positioning everyone into place before realising that Harriet is standing at the car with her friends, ready to go.

"Harriet! Harriet! Please come on. One more photo" and realising that she won't be able to take the photo, she sees Nate. Sitting in his car doing nothing that she yells for him to come to take the photo, "Nate, come here and take the photo please!"

Mumbling, his attempts in refusal are squashed. "Sorry Mrs L, Will and I were just -'

'Please just one Nate, and then you and Will can go do whatever!!!"

"Sure. Okay, Mrs L!"

As soon as the camera flashes, everyone disperses. Paige and her mother disappear inside, Will has hopped the fence while Harriet has hugged her father, thanked her aunts and uncles and met her friends at the car. Sitting in his driver's seat, Nate watches from as she disappears into the limousine and continues to watch it as it departs down the street.

Later that night, once the glitz and the glamour had lost its allure, Harriet and her friends attend the after-party that quarterback Austin Thomas boasted about during the entity of their prom. They are standing at the back of the house and Chace is handing Harriet a red cup when Katy Evans approaches Harriet.

"Harriet!"

Rolling her eyes, Harriet looks up from her cup at her. "You called, Katy?"

"I think I just saw your brother in there with Austin. Talking football or something or other!"

"Uh, thanks for that, Katy. I uh, really needed to know that."

Yelling, "No problem", Katy moves towards another group of people she knows. It is when she is emptying her third red cup that Will and Nate finally show outside to source the keg and talent pool. Chace, handing Harriet another cup, stills as her brother and his best friend come strolling up to meet him. Will, looking from Chace to Harriet and back to Chace, is surprised at the vision of his younger and much more responsible sibling, drinking beer from her cup.

"Well well well. What do we have here?"

Rolling her eyes, Harriet turns her back on her brother to face her friends. Smirking, Will shakes his head as he heads in the direction of the keg whilst Nate takes a moment to look around at the small area in which Harriet and friends have been partying, paying particular attention to the copious amount of red cups surrounding them on the ground.

With Harriet's back to him and Chace's friends at the keg, Nate moves towards Chace who's standing at the keg.

"How many drinks has she had?"

"Who? Harriet?" replies Chace.

"No. Britney Spears. Who do you think? Idiot!"

"I don't know. Three or four, I guess."

"Full or half-full?"

"I don't know man, geez!!!', as Chace looks him up and down, 'why are you even here? This is a high school party!!!"

Smirking, his eyes building with fury, Nate closes the gap that separates them and gets in Chace's face. "I'm sorry, but you seem to have forgotten that I asked you a question. Now . . . how many full red cup drinks has she had?"

Timidly, Chace splutters loudly as he answers Nate's question. "Four. . . . she's on her fourth!!!"

Hearing the commotion, Harriet and her friends all turn around to see Nate pestering Chace. Infuriated, she shoots Nate a look before sculling the rest of her drink, throwing the empty cup and taking off inside the house. Hesitating for a second, Nate immediately runs off into the house in search of her, and his search is stopped by the sight of her storming down the street.

Racing to meet up with her, he grabs at her hand before stopping her and takes a deep breath.

"Go home, Nate!!!"

"Wait up!!! You've had four of those beers. You shouldn't be out here by yourself."

Facing him, she snaps. "Why are even here? You know I have a brother. You saw him, he was at the party!!!"

She begins walking again, pulling herself free off his hold. Following, he meets her stride and grabs at her wrist.

"Harriet, would you just stop -'

"You're not my brother, and you're not my boyfriend! For god's sake, Nate! Go home!!!"

"I can't -'

"Why???"

"You know why, Harriet."

"Fine. Whatever, Nate. I'm leaving!" and turns. Yanking back to face him, he snaps. "Harriet! Would you just wait!"

"Why???"

"You can't walk home, we're on the other side of Hartford!"

Rolling her eyes, she steps back. "Just watch me!"

Feeling beaten, he nods before running back to his car. Meeting her, he idles in his car beside her as she attempts to walk home. Enjoying the sight of Harriet trying to find her way out of the housing development where the party was, Nate giggles until she finally finds the exit. Looking to her left, she sees a pitch black road leading nowhere and to her right Nate idling in his car. Accepting defeat, she takes a deep breath, and without a word, she opens the passenger's side door and gets in.

When Nate pulls into his driveway, he turns off the ignition, and they sit awkwardly in uncomfortable silence, that is at least until Nate decides to exit the car and he's stopped by Harriet's soft voice.

"Why were you really there tonight, Nate? Why weren't you out doing . . . I don't know???"

"Why do you think I was there, Harriet?"

Shaking her head, she looks down at her lap. "I don't know, Nate. I just don't know anymore. It's like I don't know **you** *anymore."*

Turning to face her, he reaches over and takes her hand in his. "Yes, you do."

"No, I really don't! Why are you still here? Living in Hartford? Why haven't you gone off to college? You could go to any school you want, you don't have to go to Yale just because of family tradition -'

"Maybe I've decided that I don't want to college!"

"So what, you're just going to stay here then??? And do exactly what now???"

"I'm going to be running my father's auto shop and expand the business. My parents will move, and I'll stay here in the house. Eventually, I'll fix it up slowly and then when the time is right, I'll sell it."

Nodding, she slowly pulls her hand from his. "You'd really sell it?"

Meeting each other's eyes, he nods back. "Yeah, I mean. Everyone grows up, moves on."

She turns to open the door and is pulling at the handle when she hears him again. "You looked beautiful today!"

Glancing over her shoulder, her eyebrows crinkling and her chest pounds rapidly. "I did?"

Smiling, his warm eyes reassuring her, "You did."

Smiling back, she bites down on her lower lip. Feeling her cheek blush, a shade of rosy pink flushes across her face.

"You asked me why I was there. Well. The thing is that . . . I've never wanted to be where you weren't!"

Running his hands over his steering wheel, his fingers trace the stitching of black leather wheel cover. Just like when they were kids, he finds himself opening up to her like he used to.

"Today, when I was waiting for Will, I saw you. I watched how that guy placed his hand on your lower back. When he placed that flower on your wrist, it ate me up. Then you disappeared into the car with him, and suddenly, I couldn't breathe. Will and I were hanging out at Josie's Pub when he heard about the Thomas party, and he said we should go visit the freshman. When we walked out, I saw that guy filling you a red cup and snickering with his friends. It began all again. I couldn't breathe. I just wanted to rip his head off."

"Nate, why didn't you ever tell me that you felt this way?"

"A lot of reasons. Your brother is an important one. Mostly because we stopped talking to each other."

Nodding, she takes a deep breathe but not before turning around to lean over and kiss him. Startled at first, Nate hesitates. It is when she laces her fingers through his shaggy chocolate mane that his arms lock around her and he pulls her deeper towards him. Closing the distance between him, so they are chest to chest, he reaches out to wind his seat down with his free hand. Descending, they remain lip-locked desperately pawing at each other until they fall asleep in each other's arms.

Waking as sunlight cracks through the windscreen, Harriet frees herself from Nate's hold and exits the car quietly. Opening his eyes at the sight of Harriet quietly closing the door, she smiles. Leaning in to softly brush his lips, she whispers. "Promise me, we'll find some time to meet up later".

Nodding, he brushes a tress away from her face. Cupping her chin, they kiss once more. "Yes, I promise!"

Pulling away from the car, she smiles back at him as she hops the fence. Disappearing down the side of the Lancer house and through her bedroom window.

Exiting his car, an elated Nate can't wipe the grin off his face. Walking into his home, his smile deteriorates at the sound of his mother's news.

"Nate? Is that you?"

"Yeah, Mom."

"Nate, your Grandmother died in her sleep last night."

"What???.'

"Your father has already left, and I told him we'd leave as soon as possible. He's already organised the shop so pack a few things. We might be in New York for a few weeks."

"But . . . I'

'Nate, this is not a negotiation!!! Go and pack a few things. We're leaving in an hour!!!"

❊   ❊   ❊

Hearing a break in the music, Vivaldi's Four Seasons is cut as she hears a dial-tone ring and the hotel's function manager pick up after three rings.

Sheraton Hartford South Hotel, Functions, Miles speaking . . .

Hi Miles, Harriet Lancer.

Good Morning Harriet. Its lovely to hear from you. Did you enjoy the wedding??? . . .

Yes, I did. It was beautiful, thank you so much for everything. Will and Sophie really appreciated it.

No problem whatsoever. So, what can I do for you today??? . . .

Oh, Miles, you know me so well. New client, birthday/graduation party. Do you any dates free later this month or early July???

I'll just check my calendar, one moment . . .

Thanks, Miles.

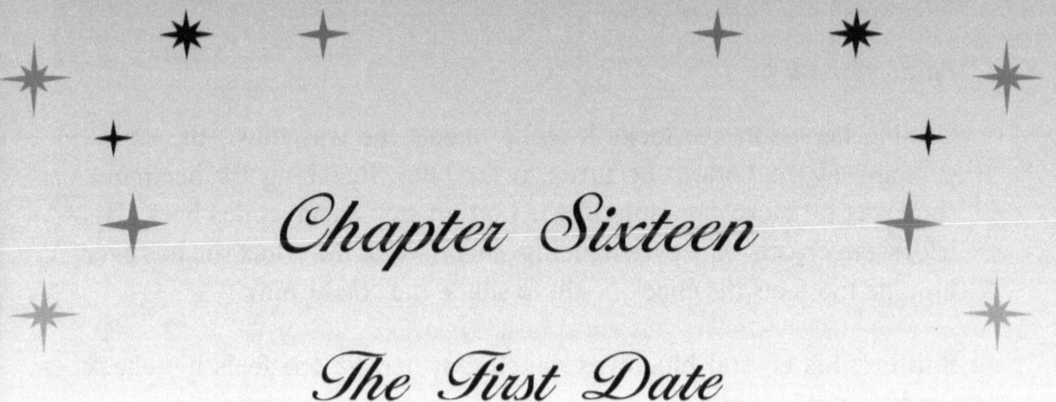

Chapter Sixteen

The First Date

Damon arrived that night at exactly 7:55 pm. Unsure of his plans for the evening or where exactly he was taking her Harriet chose to wear her dark rinse jeans with her favourite deep plum coloured lace peplum top, her brown bomber style jacket and gold gladiator flats.

Leaving her hair down straight, she would later come it find that it would naturally wind itself into a wave throughout the evening, syncing itself in line with the night air as it blew through. Before leaving her room and awkwardly awaiting his arrival, she decorated her ears and neck with quaint sized diamond stud earrings and a simple diamond pendant necklace.

Sitting on the couch, Harriet is waiting nervously for his arrival watching her clock as the hands click by. Her nervous thoughts are interrupted by the sound of a knock at the door. Standing, she grabs for her clutch before opening the door to meet a strikingly handsome Damon, waiting patiently for her on the landing.

"Hello Harriet"

Stuck, she's immediately rendered speechless. Her cheeks now flushed, she stammers. "Hi, I mean, Hello Damon."

"Are you ready to go?"

Nodding, she smiles. "Sure"

Closing her door, she locks it as he makes his way down the stairs, stopping at the bottom he turns to face her. Reaching for her hand, she takes it before stepping off the bottom step as he smiles back. His iridescent crystal blue eyes dancing, surprised at the effect she has over him, he too feels his cheek begin to shade the colour pink.

Smiling, his crystal blue eyes dancing at her, he too feels his cheek shading a colour pink.

With her hand still in his, he leads her towards a silver BMW sedan. Opening the door for her, he smiles.

"You look beautiful, Harriet!"

"Thank you, Damon. You look quite handsome yourself. Different than -'

'Than you thought I'd dress?', looking down at his own attire. A brown leather jacket, blue dress shirt, jeans, and brown boots. Glancing back at her, he playfully chuckles, 'I dress like this whenever I get the chance, Miss Lancer, you just don't see it!"

"You know, you can call me Harriet."

"I know."

Closing her door, she watches as he walks around to take his place behind the steering wheel and start the car.

"I didn't mean to insinuate that all you wear is -'

Silencing her, he places his hand gently over hers. His comforting touch igniting sparks throughout her entire body. Watching as the hairs on her arms rise to stand like blades of grass follow the sun, she swallows a breath.

Running his fingers over the indents of her knuckles, he warms and smiles. "It's fine, Harriet. Really, we'll just have to fix it."

"What do you mean?"

Looking into his rear-view mirror, he indicates before pulling out into the street and peering back at her.

"The clothes you see me in. We'll just have to change that and we will!"

Amused, she finds laughing at his words as she relaxes into the smooth, soft leather car seat. Peeking a look at him, her thoughts are overwhelmed with warmth and comfort. Glancing back to the site in front of her, street lights and park views, her thoughts take her to the night sky. Spotting a star, she looks on as it fights to continue shining despite the thinly veiled cloud willing it to stay behind it. Smiling, her nerves begin to ease and finally for the first time since they met, Harriet begins to find herself warming to Damon.

❋　❋　❋

Pulling into a side street in East Village, Damon stops the car. Repeating his earlier behaviour, he opens her car door and reaches for her hand as he helps her out. Linking her arm through his, he walks her through some lively nightlife scenery before stopping at an Italian restaurant in the street. Charming and surprisingly intimate, Harriet would have never in her wildest dreams have spotted the restaurant unless she was looking for it or that Damon would bring her to such a place.

Placing his hand softly on her back, he shows Harriet to their table. Pulling her seat out for her, he waits patiently for her to take her seat before taking a seat of his own. Watching with anticipation, she observes as Damon speaks with the waiter and orders a bottle of white wine and hands her a menu.

When the bottle arrives, she continues her surveillance. Watching as he expertly pops the cork and fills their glasses. Taking her glass, she entwines her fingers around the glass's neck and takes a sip. Feeling his eyes now on her, he smirks.

"So Harriet, how was your brother's wedding, really?"

"Fine."

Picking up his napkin, he drapes it over his lap. "That good huh?"

Shrugging her shoulders, she simpers back. "Yeah. Honestly, it was just another family function."

"Do you have a big family?"

Reluctantly, with her forehead crinkled and eyebrows cocked, she replies. "You really want to know this stuff?"

Meeting each other's eyes, she notices how the ambient glow from the restaurant's lighting fluorescents his golden hair. Her eyes trail down to his now powder blue eyes and rest down on her hand, watching as his hand comes into view as it reaches over and lightly brushes over it.

"Sure, I do. As you saw during Harper's wedding preparations, Harper and I are it. We have cousins, but most of them live in Europe. My grandmother, my father's mother, is still alive but she resides in London. But now Harper's married so . . ."

"Okay', nodding her head, she takes a moment to descriptively mull over her families story before starting. "Well. Ugh, my mother is Italian, so her side of the family is quite large, but my fathers is small. His mother was Italian, but his father was American. They all grew up in and settled in Hartford. They met in high school and got married young. His brother, my uncle Joseph is a builder, and he built our house. Most of my uncles are all tradesmen – electricians, plumbers, painters except for Sal, my Aunt Wanda's husband. He lives here in New York, and he's a Tailor."

Pausing, to take a pull from her glass she continues. "I have two siblings. A brother and sister. Will, my brother, was a linebacker for the New York Jets but he tore his ACL badly four years ago. It was a rough time, mainly due to that it was the second time it happened. When the Doctors suggested he retire, he lost it. Football was his life, you know. But luckily, he was offered a specialist position with the Jets. Not long after, he met Sophie and they recently just got married. Sophie's a para-legal who grew up in Stars Hollow, a small town not far from Hartford. They just bought a house and much to mother's delight and encouragement will probably start sprouting children."

Chuckling into his glass, he nods amazingly, knowing what that feels like. When you stop becoming a person in the eyes of your parents and instead become a baby breading machine. Nothing other accomplishment matters, as long as there are heirs to continue the family lineage.

"My younger sister Paige is still in high school. She's a senior and quite the athlete. She has already been accepted to Ole Miss and will be attending next fall."

"What? That's it?', disappointed that he hadn't heard her story, he urges her to continue, 'Well, what about you?"

"Me???"

"Yeah. How did you get from Hartford Connecticut to working at Enchanted Events and living in your own brownstone in Tribeca?"

Cocking an eyebrow, intrigued, she asks him. "Really??? You really want to know all this???"

Nodding back at her warmly, he encourages her to continue. "Yes, really!"

"Ah, well I was never an athlete like my siblings. I guess you'd say I'm more of a bookworm. I got excellent grades and growing up I wanted nothing more than to go to Dartmouth. These's dreams were thwarted time and time again by my mother. She used to say that I should just find a job, meet a guy and settle in Hartford. It didn't change anything though. Just made me even more determined to see the back of Hartford."

"She sounds like my mother!"

Smirking, she meets his eyes and smiles. "Funnily enough, I couldn't help but see the similarities between her and your mother during the planning of Harper's wedding."

"So . . . what'd you do?"

"Well, I worked my ass off. Studied harder than anyone. Worked two jobs, one during the week at the library and the other, helping in my father's office. I got into Dartmouth with a full scholarship and won the school's academics bursary. I bought a car and then two weeks before the term started, I left."

Momentarily interrupted by the waitress as she takes their food orders, Damon politely waits for her to leave before continuing.

"So, you majored in?"

"Business and Digital Innovation. I know it sounds silly but what can I say, I love working with technology and computers."

"No. I would never say that's silly. At the rate the world is moving, technological innovation and development are going to take over the world. So how'd you go from Business to Events?"

Slightly shocked at his comments, she stumbles. "Um, well. During my first year at college, my Aunt Wanda offered me a front desk job at her hair salon in Manhattan, so I came here and stayed with my Aunt and Uncle. On my second week, one of my Aunt's clients came in, Elizabeth Cadott, the owner of Enchanted Events. As she sat in my Aunt's chair, they were talking about a fall/winter internship they were trying to fill and immediately Wanda starts talking her ear off about me. Before I knew it, I found myself smack bang in the middle of an internship on Lexington Avenue at a party planning company. When the internship ended, I went back to Dartmouth, and Elizabeth asked me if I'd like to come back during the summer. She personally attended my graduation ceremony to offer me a junior position, and with that, I moved here and lived with my aunt and uncle. It wasn't long before I found myself moving up the ranks. Then my Uncle Sal decides he wanted to buy a two-story brownstone apartment in Tribeca, to fix up and rent out. Only after he bought it, I found out that he bought it for me to live in and rent off of him. So he fixed it up, and I moved in."

Looking up from her glass, she meets his astonished eyes. "What? Too much???"

"No, not at all. Why didn't you just say no?"

"What?"

"Tell your Uncle no."

Reaching down, she takes hold of her necklace. Fingering the pendant delicately. "He's my godfather. Wanda couldn't have children, and since the day I was born, they have treated me as if I was their own. I have never asked them for anything yet somehow everything I ever wanted, they've made true for me. I try to give back as much as I can, but sometimes I'm not sure if I'm worth it."

"Except you are. And amazingly gifted. Harper's wedding, all of it. It was incredible. I know Harper was blown away and my mother well -"

Tickled at his comments, she bites down embarrassingly on her lip before meeting his eyes. Blushing, she looks down to the table as their food arrives in front of them.

"So . . . do you want to get married?"

Mid-bite, she coughs before spluttering out. "What?!"

"Oh, I'm sorry. I just meant that after helping plan numerous of couple's special day, I just thought I'd ask."

Blinks softly, she shrugs. "One day. I mean, I like to think I will. I guess, I just haven't found the right one yet."

Her response startles him and looking up from his plate, he finds himself momentarily caught. His heartstrings pulling at the sight of her lustrous hair, its length hanging past her neck and ending above her chest, casting a web over his heart. Enraptured by her beauty, he can't help but fight back visions of her straddling his lap, his fingers laced through her hair as he pecks at her neck before trapping her soft, delectable lips amongst his.

When she asks, "What about you? Do you want to? Or will your mother organise yours?", his train of thought crashes. Flushed, he adjusts the collar of his shirt feeling overwhelmingly bothered.

"Ugh, yes I do, and no, she won't be. If she does, I will emancipate from her and never speak to her again!"

"That's a shame. She does have good taste . . . for Satan."

Shaking his head at the reference, he agrees. "Satan??? I'll have to remember that one. I hope, well I like to think that she just wants me to be happy. Surely that's what all parents want, right?"

"Oh, I hope so. If not, I think you're pretty much screwed!"

Tickled, yet again, by the sound of his laughter, Harriet's cheeks beam a brighter shade of pink. It's shade almost neon. Picking up her fork, she takes a mouthful of her pasta and asks, "So Damon, now that you know all there is to know about me. Why don't you share a little more about you?"

✳   ✳   ✳

When they finished eating at the restaurant, Damon stood and taking her hand, linked her arm through his as he led her to the car. Pulling out of the carpark, he takes the FDR to head towards Central Park, thinking maybe a nice walk through Central Park and perhaps coffee would be a perfect end to the night. After finding a park on Fifth Avenue, he eyes a free horse and carriage and turning off the car's ignition, he jumps out and opens her door before pulling her towards the carriage.

"Damon, I -"

Taking her arm firming in his grip, he smiles reassuringly at her. "Harriet, it's okay. I won't let go."

Paying the driver, he motions for Harriet to step up and follows taking a seat beside her. Leaning back into the seat, they make themselves comfortable with his hand laced through hers, they glance around the night sky of New York City. Hearing her laughter, he inquires. "What's so funny?"

"Not funny!!! Amazing!!!"

"Sorry???"

"It's just. Well, all the time I've lived here in New York, I've never taken a carriage ride."

Glancing down, his hand running softly along her jaw, he admits. "Me either."

"Really?"

"Really!!!', lacing his fingers throughout hers once more, 'this is my first!"

Placing his arm around her shoulder, she nestles up close to him. Looking in the opposite direction to hide her blushes, she reflects on his moves throughout the night. Opening doors, holding her hand, pulling her seat out at the restaurant, linking her arm in his to latest of lacing his fingers in hers too now, the placing of his arm around her.

As Damon softly strokes her shoulder, she leans further into him to rest her head under his chin as he crooks his head down. His chin resting softly on her forehead.

"Harriet?"

"Hmmm???"

"I've never felt this way about anyone. I mean, I know we've just met but I -"

Glancing upwards through her eyelashes, her rosy cheeks flush as she too, admits. "I know. I feel it too."

"You do?"

"Yes. I do!"

Meeting each other's eyes, pure lust swells between them causing Harriet to pull feverishly at her lip. Her appetite is hungry once again and surprisingly not for food. As the carriage turns for the last time, heading back along Fifth Avenue off of East 65th, Harriet and Damon are pretty much sitting in each other's laps.

And when the carriage ride was over, Damon drove Harriet back home to Tribeca, proceeding to open the car door and then walk her to her apartment door. When she stood on her landing and took her to unlock the door, for the first time that night he truly found himself in a jam. Caught between being the impeccable gentleman he was brought up to be and wanting to crassly ravage her right there on that door stoop.

Taking the high road, he instead chooses to remain every bit the gentleman. Reaching for her hand, he brushes a soft kiss against her knuckles, locking his eyes with hers and grins.

"I'd very much like to do this again, Harriet and soon."

Elated, she nods happily back at him as he begins to walk back to his car, grinning eagerly. Turning she opens her door and stops. Her mind screaming at her to turn around and chase after him. Closing the door, she spins and heads his way only to find him there, standing before her. Feeling his nose rub hers, Harriet lifts her hands to his neck as Damon inches his lips closer to hers to kiss her fervently. His soft lips pulling her in, she feels the warmth of his chest touch hers as he engulfs her into his embrace. When a cool breeze from the night air wafts past them, she winds her free hands higher, one at his neck and the other through his hair.

When the kiss eventually slows, he gently pulls back. Leaning down to kiss her forehead softly before meeting her eyes. Watching as he moves off towards his car, she grabs hold of the doorknob for support for fear of her legs giving way. Climbing her stairs, she enters her bedroom and changes into her pyjamas. Peeling back her duvet, she slides into the middle of her queen bed and relaxes. Hearing her phone ping, she picks it up.

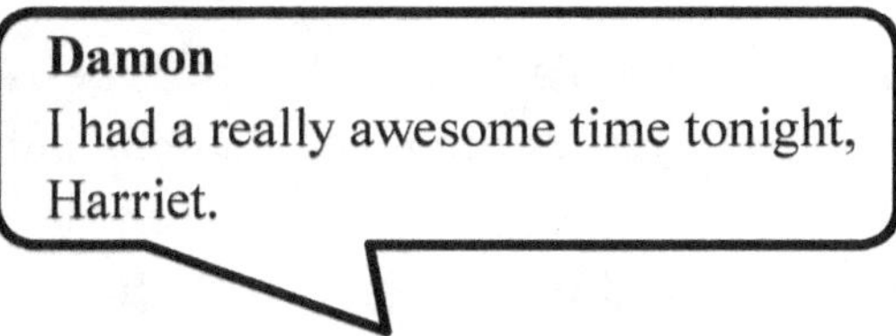

Smiling, she texts back.

Happy at the prospect of seeing him again, she quickly types back.

Clicking her phone off, she places it on her bedside table. Turning on her side, she closes her eyes. Feeling the Sandman lulling her into the deepest of sleep, thoughts of Damon materialise and begin to take shape in her mind. She misjudged him. Yes, he hails from a privileged and well-entitled family, but he also has his scars. Deep down he has the kindest of hearts and judging by the events of the night, they clearly are both affected by each other.

Just like Baby and Johnny had disliked each other at first. He had taken her for a spoilt rich girl, and she just misjudged him for being an egotistic middle-class worker. But as they spent time together and got to know each other, the pent-up undeniable attraction they had on each other caused them to fall. To fall head over heels in love with each other, that is.

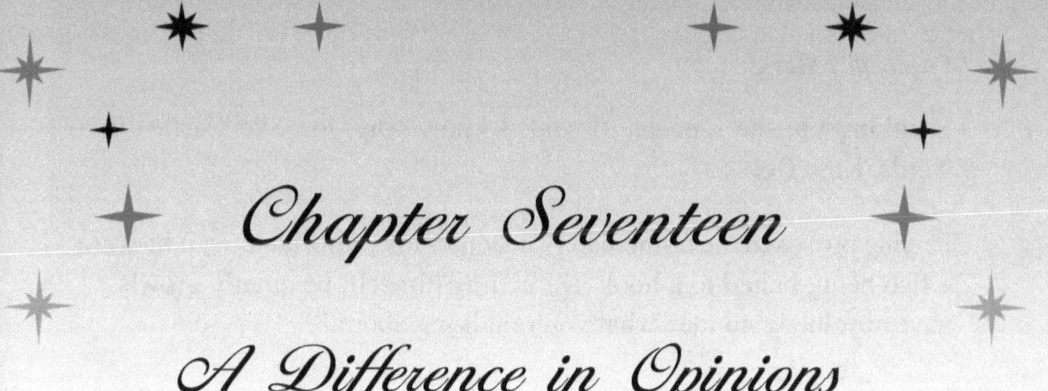

Chapter Seventeen

A Difference in Opinions

With her fork poised over a plate of honey chicken and fried rice, Harriet is snacking on the Chinese that Damon brought home for dinner while flicking through work on her computer. Grabbing a cold beer from the fridge as he moves towards her, his wet hair curling at the bottom of his neck from his shower, he leans down over her and places a soft kiss on her forehead.

Smiling as she feels his lips leave her, she feels Damon take her hand in his. "Come on honey. You work hard enough. That will still be there tomorrow. Let's go unwind on the couch."

Picking up her plate and glass of white wine, Damon leads her to the couch. Placing her feet up on the coffee table, he covers his and her lap with a blanket. Swallowing a mouthful, he places his beer next to her glass and picks up the remote. Turning on the TV, he flicks through the channels and stops when he sees Castle. Glancing up from her plate, she curiously grins at him.

"Damon, you watch Castle???"

"Yeah. Kind of, I guess."

Noticing his strong concentration on Stana Katic, a hint of jealousy rises in her voice. As she glances down at her food, she mumbles. "Oh, I know why you like Castle!!!"

"What???"

Speaking up, she repeats. "I said. I know why you like Castle. Two words. Kate Beckett."

Feeling provoked, he immediately becomes uncomfortable, as if he were a fish being baited to a hook. Defending himself, he quietly growls. "I have absolutely no idea what you're talking about!!!"

When the screen changes to a close of Nathan Fillon's character Castle appears, Harriet's mouth twitches and a smile forms over her lips. "Well, I find Nathan Fillon absolutely charming. He's really funny. I really like that in a guy. Maybe you could take notes???"

"What??? I'm funny!!!"

Shaking her head, she takes another mouthful of food as he continues to defend himself. "What??? Harriet, I am!!!"

Dropping her fork into her food, she places her plate on the table in front of her and explodes in laughter. Watching Damon sit bothered opposite her, she can't help but smirk as she notices his mouth slowly twitch as if he too was fighting back a smile.

Resigning her laughter, she reaches over to softly kiss his cheek then his mouth. Giving up the ghost, he knows that he can't possibly remain annoyed with her. So he relaxes and wrapping his arm around her shoulder, he nestles into her.

"So, your brother and I talked today."

"Really??? What about?", she replies curiously.

"Not much really. Just plans for the Buck's Night."

Rolling her eyes, "Hmmm –"

"Harriet, he's your brother. He's extending an olive branch."

"Hmmm, okay. First of all, nice pun. Second of all, when Will talks about planning a Bucks Night. Well, I for one would be worried."

Intrigued, he cocks his head down at her. "Worried about what? What could possibly go wrong?"

"Just trust me on this okay. After the trouble that he and Nate got into on their night out, he was lucky that he's allowed entry into the Sheraton. I had to sweet talk Miles Layne into letting him have their wedding there."

"Why? What they'd do???"

Taking a deep breath, she brushes the frustration from her face and explains, "It was all Nate's fault. He took Will and my cousins to a bar where they got rip-roaring drunk before entering a titty bar. Will was arrested for indecent exposure after peeing on the building and while he was being cuffed, he vomited all over the officer and tried to evade arrest by streaking down the street."

"Wow, really?"

Nodding, chuckling as she does it, "Yes. So just think about it before you agree to anything okay."

Shaking his head, he smirks. "Oh yeah. I will."

"Harriet?"

"Yeah –"

"My mother called me today."

"And -"

"She is renovating the apartment, and she wants me to clear out my old room. She knows that I am no longer living in Manhattan so I was just wondering –"

"If you could store your things here in the spare room?" she replies, meeting his uncertain eyes.

"Yes."

Smirking, she cocks an eyebrow. "You know, you don't have to ask. You can just tell me this stuff."

"I know, it's just"

'It's just, what –"

"Well, this is your place."

"And –"

"Well, when I moved in and started putting my things in places, you went around fixing them up!!!"

"Because they were untidy, Damon!"

"Yes, but –"

"But nothing, Damon. Yes, this is my place, and yes, you are now living in it with me, but something you should know about me is that I don't like a mess. I didn't have nannies and maids growing up, picking up after me and cleaning my mess –"

He huffs, "Oh, I knew you'd throw that back in my face!", clearly annoyed.

"What??? It's true!"

"Harriet, all I'm asking to is to put some things around the house that make it look like, I live here too."

"You do live here!!! You know how I know. I'm always picking up after you, that's how I know!!!"

"Thank-you. Thank you for making me so welcome in my own home."

"You want to feel welcome? Then how about you pick up the vacuum cleaner every now and again and clean the place. Or wash the dishes? Or -'

"Fine! You know what, I shouldn't have said anything!", he spits before moving away from her to stand and walk out of the lounge.

Turning around he walks back to pick up his keys from the hallway table. Hearing the jingling of keys being picked up, she looks behind her and asks.

"Where are you going?"

"Out for a drive. I need some space. Don't wait up", he snaps.

"Oh, so you don't win the argument, so you're leaving? What you can't stay and sort things out like a normal person? Typical."

Angrily, he sneers. "Typical what? Typical Bennett's? Typical of *my* people? Typical of *my class*?"

"Yes!"

"Right!!! ", he spats before he prowls out of the brownstone to his car and drives off. Standing, Harriet walks to her front bay window and watches.

Both amazed and fathomed by their argument, she remains perched on the window seat, confused. Looking around her home, she realises that she is in fact right. There aren't any remnants around that say that Damon lived there too. Other than the photos of them as a couple positioned around, the home has remained femininely decorated. Sitting there, watching the time as it clicks by on her living room clock, it also dawns on her that she hadn't been that cruel to another man she loved since Nate.

Glancing over at her bookshelf, her eyes search for the photo of them at her eighteenth. Closing her eyes, she recalls the events of her eighteenth birthday and when her life would never be the same.

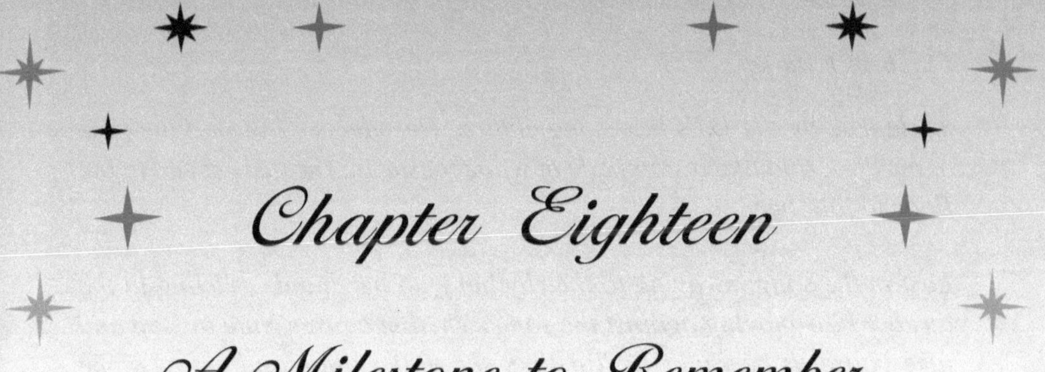

Chapter Eighteen

A Milestone to Remember

Ten years earlier . . .

Harriet had returned home from Dartmouth for a few days before the summer break and was about to celebrate her coming of age. Her father and Godparents have hired out a function room at Sheraton Hartford South Hotel, and all her family and friends were going. She was most especially excited to show off her college boyfriend Ryan whom she'd been dating for six months. They met a frat party and have been hanging out ever since.

The night passes on by, and Harriet is having an amazing time at the party. Her dark brown hair is waved and hanging loosely around her face; she is wearing jeans with a blush lace top with a deep brown aviator jacket. She is having a ball, drinking and having a really good time to hide her disappointment about Ryan.

He called earlier that day, told her it was too soon to meet her family. They'd only been dating for six months after all. Angry that he thought so little of their relationship, she snapped and told him maybe he shouldn't even bother coming. Disappointed and hurt that their relationship may have ended, she tries her best to enjoy the night, and the alcohol is certainly helping her do that.

When her cake is brought out by her Uncle, her guests sing "Happy Birthday", and as they finish, she blows the candles out. Closing her eyes are tight as she can she makes a wish, a wish that conveniently is made true by the DJ's next song choice. He selects "I've had the time of my life", and like a stampede of wildebeests, all the girls speed to the floor to join her.

Lost in the song; swaying to the rhythm with her hands twirling in the air, her hair moving against the song's rhythm causes Nate to stop and take pause as he walks in. Turning, she notices him and waves as he begins to move toward the nearest table and put his things down only to walk straight back onto the dance floor to take her hands in his and twirl her around.

When the song finishes and they're all standing there waiting for the next song. Nate looks at Harriet. As he watches her, he realises that he is still as madly in love with her since that day on the swings when they discussed clouds and Halley Sawyer having to get her hair cut. Then he remembers the last time they spoke and that she now has a boyfriend. On that realisation, he drops her hands gently and walks off the dance floor.

She watches him walk away, disappointed but her disappointment doesn't last long as "Girls Just Wanna Have Fun" is blasted over the speakers and her friends circle in around her. When the party ended that night, feeling jazzed Harriet and her friends made the decision to head out to some clubs uptown in Hartford. Seeing as a few of her friend's boyfriends are going to go, after some persuasion from Will, Nate decides he'll go too.

As the night becomes early morning, numbers from the party begin to dwindle until it is only Nate and Harriet are left in a smoky pub, with no more than maybe five patrons still there.

When a fellow patron selects "It must have been love" on the jukebox, Harriet meets Nate's eyes, whose standing holding his hand out, ushering her to join him into a slow dance with him. Taking their place in the middle of the floor, she takes his hands and margins her frame against him. Swaying against him, she feels his touch as he takes a piece of Harriet's hair and twirls around his finger. With the reminders that she has a boyfriend and after not speaking for six months swirling around in his head, he swallows back a hurt thought that there is no possible way that she still could feel anything for him.

"Nate –'

"Hmmm?"

"Nate, I'm really sorry for -'

"No, Harriet. Please don't."

'But -'

Brushing his fingers over hers, he adjusts his cheek against hers. With a soft whisper, he leans closer to her ear to put her mind at ease. "I was lost. My life was going in different directions, and I had to grow up earlier than I thought I would. I don't regret what happened but I do regret not calling you. By the time, I had gotten home from New York, you were leaving for college. The look on your face as you drove past, I couldn't . . . uh and then Will told me that you met someone, well that . . . it ate me. But deep down, I have always known how you felt about me."

Pulling back to meet his eyes, she can feel her heart pounding inside her chest over his honesty. "You . . . you have?"

Nodding, he brushes his knuckles lightly over her cheek as he smiles softly at her. " Harriet . . . you know . . . you were never just another person to talk to for me. Surely deep down you know that right? Yes, I've felt overprotective of you and at times, I act how your brother should but you know I would intentionally hurt you because –'

"Because???'

"I am in love with you! I have been in love with you since that day in the playground when we sat on the swings, and you yelled at me for putting chewing gum in Halley Sawyer's hair."

Shaking her head, she smiles. Her eyes brightened by his honesty, spurring up wanting feelings within her chest. Feelings she thought she had to put to rest when they had last spoken. Knowing that he probably get the opportunity like this again, Nate takes his chance to show Harriet how he still feels by slowly positioning his face near hers. Noticing his movement, she welcomes Nate in to kiss her. Placing one of his hands firmly on her back and one on her neck, gradually moving them upwards to rest in the dark locks of her hair and below her ears, their wanting lips meet and the warmth of his mouth on hers causes an electric spark to run throughout her entire body and her hungry heart to grab a tighter grip of him.

Ending the kiss, Nate pulls break to search her eyes. Looking for some sign, a glimmer of hope that she might want him as much as he wants her, right here right now in this moment. Taking her hand, he leads her out of the bar and keeps walking until they meet a secluded alleyway behind the street's row of bar and restaurants. Stopping, he releases her hand only to push her gently against the brick wall.

When her back has met the wall, he glances down as she looks up to meet his eyes. Her soft pink lips, pleading at him to be kissed once more, are caught between her bottom lip and her front two top incisors. Pulling her hips against his with a sharp tug as their lips lock once more, Harriet takes her leg and wraps it around his thigh, and Nate's hand leaves her neck to run his fingertips slowly along the length of her thigh to rest on her bottom.

Exhaling as Nate's lips leave hers to run down against her jaw, Harriet bites her lip softly to contain her merriment, and it is when Nate's hands find themselves moving up the insides of her lace peplum top, that Harriet puts a stop to their fun.

"No Nate, not here . . . not in this alleyway!"

Nate pulls back and nods. Their foreheads meeting, they both stop to take a breath and process events of the night and their friendship. Taking her hand, he leads her out onto the street and proceeds to hale down a cab. Opening the door for her, he ushers her in as he jumps in behind her.

No more than ten minutes later, they arrive back at his place. Unlocking the front door, Nate leads Harriet into his house, and as they move further into the home, she can't help but glance over at her own childhood home through the kitchen windows. Gripping Harriet's hand firmly, he pulls her towards his bedroom, and once inside she glances around the room, fixed against the door she remains nervous and unsure of initiate things with him again. She has wanted this for so long, to be alone with him like this and have the boy who stole her first real kiss and her heart, touch her like he has. The boy who came to her rescue after Halley Sawyer thought she had the last laugh. The boy who showed up at her prom after-party to make sure she had a lift home and because he wanted her to save her from falling into the hands of a guy who bragged about his intentions for her.

Taking a seat at the edge of his bed, she patiently waits for Nate to meet her, watching as he proceeds to take his jacket off and then take his seat beside. Feeling nervous himself, his heart thumping so loudly as if it were to take flight and escape from inside his chest. Turning himself to face her, he reaches over to cup her chin in his hand and look into her eyes.

Glancing up from the floor, Harriet meets his eyes and allows Nate to pull her closer towards him by her chin and taste her lips. Soft and tender nips at first then growing ferociously, its intensity heating up as she feels one of Nate's hands moving down her chest, hovering momentarily on her breasts before moving down to the hem of her top and pull it up over her head onto the floor.

Responding to his touch, she uses her hands to find the hem of his shirt. Gathering his shirt in her fingertips, she pulls off his shirt and throws it on the ground where hers currently sit. Standing, she moves to take a seat in his lap. Her legs wrapping themselves around his back, her fingertips brushing softly against his shoulder blades as he proceeds to kiss the length of her neck and rest on her chest.

Standing up, Harriet firmly attached to his waist; he places her gently down at the head of the bed. Placing her gently down on his pillows, he brushes her cheek and smiles down at her.

"Hi"

Smiling sweetly up at him, she mumbles back, "Hi."

Taking one of her hands that is resting on his shoulders, he lifts it to trail soft kisses from her palm to wrist then finally on her lips. As Nate climbs slowly over the length of her, her legs still wrapped around his thigh, Harriet takes her free hand to reach down to his belt and flip its buckle, flinging the belt out into the darkness of the room. Removing his jeans, Harriet sees the mist of blue fabric fly from the bed and land softly on the carpet.

On hearing her own zip coming undone, a sudden sensation flashes through her as the room starts to spin around them. Closing her eyes, she aims to control the fuzziness that is slowly beginning to consume her mind, an after-effect that she no doubt earned from her alcoholic efforts for the night. As the room goes dark, she feels her eyelids growing heavy luring her to meet the darkness too, she senses Nate's touch as he enters her. Opening her eyes, she locks them with his. When he finishes moving inside her, an exhausted Nate collapses in the space beside her. Turning on her side, her back against his front, a wearied Harriet falls into a deep sleep. A very profound sleep where she dreams of watching cotton candy clouds on her childhood trampoline.

❄   ❄   ❄

It isn't until around lunch-time the next day that Harriet awakes in Nate's bed. Looking around, she tries to recognise where she is.

Looking over, she sees the bed is empty and with a pounding head, she can only recall pieces of the night before. Rising from the bed, she searches for her clothes. Pulling on her underwear and jeans, she is clipping her bra together when she hears Nate walking towards the room.

As she searches for her purse and puts her top at the same time, Harriet is seated fully clothed at the end of his bed with her face fully invested on her phone screen when Nate arrives.

"Morning sun....shine.', puzzled by her behaviour, 'Where are you going?"

Awkwardly she blurts out. "I'm sorry Nate, but I've got to get going. I have ten missed calls from the family and Will's just texted me to say we're having lunch."

Disappointed, a somewhat hurt Nate nods, "Fair enough."

Standing, she takes a few steps before turning around to meet his eyes. "Maybe I could come over later, so we could talk? Would that . . . that be okay?"

Watching her; glancing at the distance between them now, in contrast to their behaviour last night, he looks away from her and nods down at the floor. "Sure"

Leaning down, she places her hand on Nate's cheek and wills him to meet her eyes. Softly meeting his lips, she tenderly grazes her lips against him before departing the room. Stuck in his seat, paralysed by the state that Harriet has left him, the befuddled yet mesmerising effect she has always had him, he looks to his window to where he can see Harriet enter her backyard through the gate that connects their houses and disappear inside her bedroom window.

*　*　*

As the day passes and stars fill the night sky, Nate's hopes from hearing from Harriet begin to dwindle. Making himself comfortable in the lounge, he fixes himself in front of his television with his phone by his side until he falls asleep only to wake later that night to move to his bed. The following morning, when his alarm goes off and alerts him to get ready for work, he unlocks his phone to find a message from Harriet.

"Nate, sorry I couldn't make it over to talk last night. When I got home, I had to go out to lunch with all the family. Lunch turned into supper then dinner, and when we got home, Ryan showed up. Before what happened, before coming home for the party; Ryan and I were supposed to be heading off on a road trip to Washington for the rest of summer. I'll try to come see you if I can get away from the family and Ryan before we leave for Washington."

Only Harriet never came.

Chapter Nineteen

Two months and counting

With less than two months to their wedding day, Damon and Harriet decide to make one last drive to Hartford before the wedding to check final numbers and catch up with family. Things had been a little frosty between them since their argument that night with Harriet realising that she had been too hard on him and Damon realising how much Harriet does for him. They always knew things were to going to be difficult but with two months until the wedding, let's just say that things weren't going all that smoothly.

Pulling his car into her parent's driveway, he takes a look around the street and smirks. "Wow honey, I forgot how nice your little house is!"

Getting out of the car, she moves towards the boot as he meets her. "Little? Oh, that's right. Compared to your house at the Hamptons, this would be what? Your foyer? Your bedroom???"

Smirking, he just shakes his head at her. "Ha! You're so funny."

"I know . . . but be honest now . . . you secretly love my humour!"

Leaning down to kiss her nose, he smiles. "True, so very true!"

Unpacking the car, her parents walk out to meet them. Gloria immediately plants a hug and kisses on Damon while Frank just walks straight to his daughter and pulls her into his arms for a hug. Releasing her, he bends down to grab and help Harriet with the bags. Frank quickly disappears inside, then her mother goes in while Damon waits for Harriet, takes the bags that she was carrying and moves behind her as they walk into the house. Once settled, Harriet's mother ushers them into the lounge where she's baked goodies for them to eat. Settling into the couch, Damon's eyes ogle the array of goodies, cakes, and slices on display in front of them.

Pouring a cup of tea, Gloria hands a cup to her husband before turning to Harriet. "So how's the wedding planning coming, Harriet?"

"All set. I just have to speak to Sal about final measurements for Dad and Will and then Nate about the cars."

Damon puts his hand on her thigh, "Oh honey I'll do that." She smiles at him and nods in appreciation.

"Thanks that'd be great. Dad, Sal says you need a new suit, and no, you can't wear that awful one that you wore to Will's wedding."

Protesting, "Why? What was wrong with it? It's fine. I've had it since I was 18", Frank whines.

Giggling at her father, she remarks. "That was the 70's dad. Panels on the elbows and houndstooth aren't in style for weddings anymore."

Frank sighs, knowing he can't win but would do anything for her, he smiles "Okay. Fine. Anything for you love."

Pouring herself a coffee, Harriet settles back into the couch next to Damon when her mother begins rattling off about things happening in Hartford. For instance, subjects like Mr's Twitch's cat ruined her roses by peeing on them and how Nate's dog has been escaping and chewing up things in the backyard.

Harriet, who is not the least bit interested replies with, "Oh really Mom. How unfortunate", before rolling her eyes at her father.

Her mother keeps on yapping away. "Actually, talking about Nate, you should see this girl he's dating . . . I think you may have gone to school with her . . . Halley something???"

"Halley Sawyer?"

"That's her name . . . So anyway, I was out trimming the hedge the other day when I see this leggy blonde thing standing in his backyard, having a smoke and then Nate comes out and tells me that he and this Halley have been dating for a few months."

Harriet, whose now sitting up intrigued by the story. "They're still together. Wow. Didn't think it'd last that long."

Damon who has stopped eating to notice how tense Harriet is getting, leans into her and whispers "Honey, are you ok?"

Harriet taking her hand over her chest, she shrugs it off. "Yeah. Just tired from all the driving. Might just go outside for a bit."

Harriet excuses herself and walks to the backyard. Her trampoline calls to her, begging to be sat on as it still stands upright and untouched. She slowly pulls herself up onto the trampoline and closes her eyes. As her sanctuary or a place to escape, she tries to block out all the stress and white noise.

Just the night before, Damon and Harriet made the decision to go out for dinner, and as Damon was making the reservation, his father overheard and invited himself. Upon hearing about the dinner, Harper and Glenn asked to come along too. Harriet had absolutely no qualms about, but when Damon's mother got wind of the dinner plans, she told Robert that she wasn't feeling well.

This seemed to be a recurring excuse for his mother. Every time Damon or Harriet suggested to do something together, Beverly wouldn't attend unless Harriet was unable to and if they did happen to be at an event together, Beverly barely spoke two words to her.

Beverly's dislike for Harriet pretty much began during Harper's wedding. Beverly complained (more than once) to Harriet's bosses that she was rude and unprofessional. Luckily enough, Will's wedding was on the same weekend, and as soon as she found out, she let Elizabeth know and took time off to come home for it.

The latest drama between Beverly and herself that truly took the tip of the iceberg was that Harper had recently confided in Harriet first when she found out she was pregnant. In most families, I guess a daughter would always tell her partner or mother before anyone else but Harper, who has become very close with Harriet and already thinks of her as a sister, told Harriet because she would treasure the moment and most likely have her support.

But truthfully, Harriet knew Harper didn't tell her mother because like her own mother; she could just imagine the reaction.

Beverly wouldn't exactly be happy about the news like the rest of her family. No, she'd be thinking instead of people calling her a grandmother (*when she considers herself to be too young to be called a grandmother*) and that the baby will take all (*if any*) attention away from her.

Eyes closed, she is almost in a happy and stress-free place when she hears a car drive up in front of Nate's garage. Opening the garage back door, he walks into his backyard towards his shed. She then hears, Halley talking to the dog and wishing she was invisible hides her face under her hands and hopes that neither Nate nor Halley can see her.

Halley is walking back into the house when spots Harriet lying on the trampoline. "Harriet?"

Harriet looks up with her elbows positioning her back. She lies back down and looks up at the sky. Rolling her eyes, she gets off the trampoline to go to the side picket fence.

"Hello Halley"

Halley, who is now at the fence as well, looks at her up and down. "Harriet, look at you. Can't believe how pretty you are."

Feeling awkward, Harriet looks down at her feet and smiles briefly at her comment. "Gee thanks, Halley. You haven't changed a bit since I last saw you."

Twitching her nose a little, like she's a witch (*that she is?!*) is somewhat offended by Harriet's comment. "So what are you doing in town?"

Damon, who is bringing his plate to the kitchen sink, sees Harriet talking with someone over the fence and decides that he'll go out too.

"Um. Nothing much. I'm just back for wedding stuff", replies Harriet.

Chuffs out a little snort now like she's a chimney (*which is probably true because it would explain the colour of her heart*), "Oh really, who's getting married now?"

Harriet quickly snipes back, "I am!"

Halley becomes dead quiet. Speechless, her mouth remains open, and she digests Harriet's words. "Oh really . . . that's great . . . Um, yeah I think I remember Nate saying that."

Harriet takes a deep breath, "Yeah I think the last time I saw you was on the night of my engagement party."

"Oh yeah, I remember now. You made your fiancé dance to that Dirty Dancing song", she giggles.

Slowly take another deep breath, "Yes. . . . *Yes.* That's what happened."

Becoming silent, Harriet wants to walk away and escape inside, but her plan is thwarted by the sight of Damon, who is walking out to join them. Walking directly up behind Harriet, he shifts her hair off her shoulder and kisses her neck. Watching this exchange, Halley's eyes pop out of her head as he looks up to see Harriet has company and smiles at Halley.

"Oh sorry . . . excuse me . . . Damon Bennett. Harriet's fiancé. We met about a year ago."

Halley smiles back, "Nice meeting you again Damon, I'm Halley." Flashing him with her flirty eyes, Harriet watches and feels sick.

Damon looks curiously at them both. "So how do you know Harriet?"

"Oh, we went to school together", replies Harriet.

Damon looks at Harriet "Really?"

Halley snorts. But unfortunately, to everyone's discomfort, the snort becomes a giggle to finally eventuate into a cackle until all Harriet can do is picture Halley, on top of a broomstick with a giant wart on the end of her nose.

"Yes. She was crazy for Patrick Swayze back then. Always writing Mrs Johnny Castle all over her books and then re-enacting the dance at lunchtimes."

Damon smiles politely and nods. "Yes, I do believe you mentioned that to me on the night of our engagement party."

Glancing at Harriet, he notices her face is red, mouth tight-lipped and livid that Halley is definitely taking the piss at her. Nate, who has been standing near his shed, the entire time and has heard Halley, comes over to join them when Harriet decides she's tolerated enough from and surprisingly, she gets mean.

"Yeah, I did. It was a phase. We all have our phases, I'm pretty sure that it was around the same time that you had a fetish for chewing gum. Hey . . . didn't you have to get a haircut because you got chewing gum in it?"

Halley, whose face was once glowing from her trip down memory lane, stops smiling and goes awkwardly quiet.

Taking Damon by the hand, she turns to Halley and says, "Well good seeing you again Halley, but Damon and I have wedding stuff to do. Take care", before ushering him back inside.

Once inside her room, Damon closes her door as Harriet collapses on her bed. Damon standing at the foot of her bed, puzzled by her behaviour.

"That wasn't very nice Harriet!!!"

Leaning up on her elbows, "What?"

He sits on the foot of the bed with his back facing her, "You didn't have to be mean?"

Harriet snaps at him. "Damon, what are you talking about? She was making fun of me?"

Looking over his shoulder, he glances at her. "Yeah she was, but you didn't have to be cruel."

Harriet sits fully up and is getting angry. "Just whose side are you on?"

Unsure of her anger, precisely from where it's coming from or exactly who it's directed at, he remains confused but responds.

"Yours?"

She lies back down on her bed, turning her body so that her back faces him. "That's funny because it doesn't sound like it."

Getting up, he takes a deep breath, walks over to her at the head of the bed and crouches down. He takes her hand and looks into her eyes. "Harriet? If I was rude and insulted everyone that gave me hell in my life, I wouldn't be allowed back in Manhattan."

She just rolls her eyes. "No, you'd just walk out or leave the building, mid-sentence or argument!"

"Direct hit, fine. I deserved that but all I'm saying, honey, is that you have to stop letting people getting to you. So, she made fun of you . . . big deal! You clearly have won the battle!!!"

Crinkling her face, she replies, confused. "What are you're talking about?"

"Harriet, she clearly hasn't left Hartford, and she's 28 and unmarried." She smiles then nods in agreement. "True"

He smiles down at her and leans in for a kiss. Taking her by the hips, he pulls her into his lap, and they snuggle up into other, lip-locked strewn across the bed. Their moment of privacy is short-lived by the sound of Harriet's mother's voice.

"Damon; Will and Sophie have arrived. Mr Lancer is helping me, would you mind helping them unload love?"

Damon looks at Harriet, and with shared thoughts, they giggle before Harriet rests her forehead against his. Eventually, Damon pulls away and jumps up off the bed towards the door. "Sure Mrs L. I can do that."

Smiling, she watches him walk off before taking a pillow and hiding her face under it. Looking up out her window through a crack of light peering from under her pillow, she looks for the clouds. Her dreaming is cut short at the explosion of Nate and Halley arguing. Rolling off her bed, she crawls onto the floor and sits with her back against the wall, listening in on their fight.

'God, Halley would you just accept responsibility for it.'
'She insulted me, Nate, she should apologise!!!
Why do you always take her side?'
'I don't always take her side. When have I taken her side?'
'Gee, let's see. Um, maybe when you put chewing gum in my hair?'

'Oh come on!!! That was years ago -'
'Yeah well, it wasn't that long ago, and my
hair has never been the same!!!'

'Well next time, you want to take the piss out
of someone, take it out on me okay -'
'Why are you always defending her???'
'She's like family Halley. You should apologise -'
'Huh!!! No way in hell. She's got a perfect life,
why does she need me to apologise!!!'
'Halley, just apologise to her for crying out loud -'
'Nate, just who do you think you're dating???'
'Last time I looked . . . you –'
'Funny cos it doesn't seem like it!!!' she snaps
before slamming the door shut.

Sitting on her knees, Harriet leans over to look at Nate. He is walking around his backyard punching his fists angrily into the air and

shouting silently at the sky. Giggling, she continues to watch as he calms himself and take a deep breath and disappearing into his house. Returning to her room, she leans back against the wall and closes her eyes.

As the darkness pulls her eyelids down deeper, she can't help but reminded of the last time that she was inside that house.

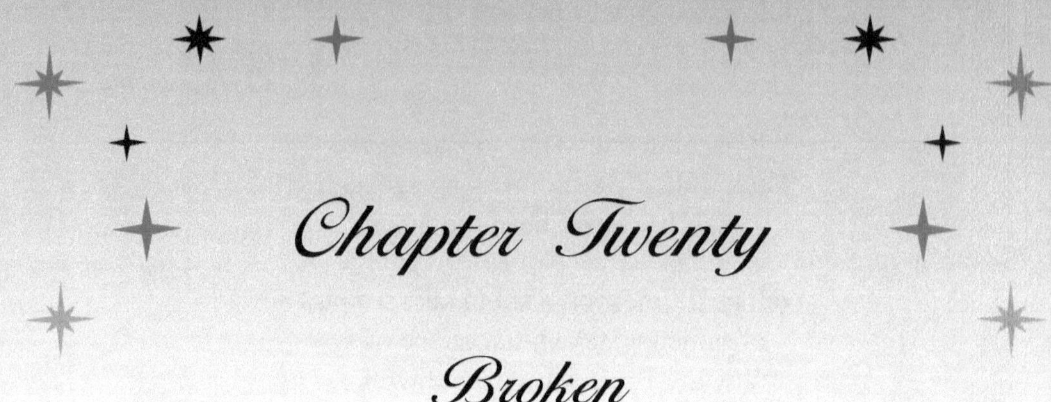

Chapter Twenty

Broken

Ten years earlier . . .

One early Saturday morning in September, Harriet is standing in her childhood kitchen, sipping back a coffee. She had just returned from a three-month road trip with Ryan and is about to make the drive back to Dartmouth for her sophomore year.

Before departing, her father suggested he stay until she left, but her mother reminded everyone that Harriet is quite capable of driving back to college, that they had a brunch to go to and that Paige needs to be dropped off at training.

"Dad, I'm fine . . . seriously you can go."

Her father stands in the kitchen watching her, pulls her into him and hugs. Patting her on the back, he smiles. "You sure honey?"

She pulls back and looks at him "Yeah Dad, I'm fine."

"I worry about you. And I miss you. I always miss you."

She smiles, looking down at her feet then looks up at her father, through her eyelashes "I miss you too, Dad."

Gloria walks out from the back of the house. Paige following her, "Come on Frank, we'll be late."

Frank kisses Harriet's forehead. "Call me when you arrive okay". Harriet nods. Gloria looks over at her daughter. "Behave, drive carefully, and we'll see you at Thanksgiving."

Paige walks over to her sister and they hug. "Take me with you" she whispers into Harriet's ear. They pull apart, and Harriet smiles.

In a low voice so only Paige can hear, "You'll be out before you know it. They smile at each other "Besides, you can't leave Dad alone with her. He'd go insane."

Giggling at each other, Gloria looks at them then at her watch. "Come on. We'll be late."

Frank and Paige look to Harriet, "Bye" and Harriet smiles back as they leave out the front door, "Bye."

Standing outside her car door, she leans against her car. Knowing that she needs to talk to Nate and thankfully no-one is around to see it happen. She takes a deep breath and wills herself off the car to move towards his front door.

In the past three months, Nate hadn't heard from Harriet. That was until the first Saturday morning of September, when he hears a knock on the door and yells towards the front of the house, that he's coming. As he reaches the lounge room, he hears Harriet's voice and then slowly paces himself before opening the door.

Awkwardly standing on the landing, she knocks again on the door. "Hello Nate, are you there."

Nate stopping at the door, he leans his head against it. "Why?"

"Nate, I'm so sorry for just showing up here with no notice or phone call, but I need to talk to you."

He opens the door, and he sees her standing there. She is twitching uncomfortably on the spot. Her eyes watching him intently, waiting for him to invite her in. He stands back with the door wide open, and she steps inside. Looking around the room. His house hasn't changed one bit, and as she stands in his lounge, she becomes nervous and begins to hesitate her decision to speak with him.

Nate walks into the lounge and takes a seat on his sofa. An uncomfortable silence fills the room. He sits there, watching her and as he watches her, he positions a finger on this mouth like he's prophesying a theory. She sits down on the couch slowly and killing the silence, he speaks.

"Three months and nothing? Is this payback? Are you trying to hurt me?"

Unsure of what to say, she just manages to mumble out. "I'm sorry I just thought -"

Nate angrily spits out "Are you and Ryan still together?"

Turning white, she feels goose bumps spread across her body. "Well yes but -"

"Then why?. . ."

As tears form in her eyes, Harriet blurts out "Because I'm pregnant that's why!!!"

✳   ✳   ✳

She had begun to feel sick a couple of weeks ago during her road trip with Ryan and thought nothing of it. She had pinned it down to, in her mind, to the confined space of Ryan's car and the fact that they had been on the road trip for two and a half months. They were road tripping around the east coast. It wasn't until they arrived at their last stop in Washington when Ryan suggested see a doctor for her severe case of car sickness.

Upon finding a clinic and speaking with a doctor, she left the clinic in shock that the doctor suggested she take a pregnancy test.

That night in the hotel room as Ryan slept, she locked herself in the bathroom to pee on a stick and sat perched on the bathtub edge.

Whilst she waited, the prescribed ten minutes, her life flashed before her. What she would do if she were pregnant, would she keep the baby, would she abort it? Could she give it up for adoption? If she told her family, would they understand? But mostly . . . would she tell the father?

Finally, she looks down at the stick and her nightmare materialises. The stick had turned blue.

Swallowing back a hurtful sob, she knew that by the time she was back home in Hartford that she would have to make a decision on what to do. She remained tight-lipped the entire drive home. Not mentioning her drama to anyone. Anyone except for Nate.

✻ ✻ ✻

Back in his lounge, a completely stunned Nate blurts out, "What?"

Harriet looks away from him, not wanting to see his face as she wipes tears off her face, "You heard me."

Nate gobsmacked. Wiping his mouth, astonished at her. "Is it?"

"Yes –"

"Are you sure? I mean how do you know it's not Ryan's?"

She shakes her head, her honest eyes look back at him. "It's not. Ryan and I haven't. You were well my -"

Nate cuts her off, "You're first?!"

Harriet nods slowly. Avoiding her eyes, he looks around the room. Searching for a question, looking for an answer

"Are you going to keep -"

"No . . . no, I'm not!", she immediately snaps as he fires back immediately, "Why not?"

Tears filling her eyes, she looks down at her feet. "Nate, I'm 18. I have my whole life ahead of me. I can't do it. It wouldn't be fair on me. I mean on both of us."

He gets up and walks over to sit on the coffee table directly in front of her. He looks into her eyes, takes her hands in his. "Yeah, but shouldn't it a decision we both should make? I mean, Harriet I think I could handle this."

Avoiding having to look at him and say, what's breaking her up inside to say to him. "Nate I don't want this -'

"But don't I -"

Taking her hands back, she stands up and walks to the opposite side of the room. Rubbing over her forehead, a confused, unsure, and heartbroken, Harriet is in pieces. When she finally blurts out the only thing she can piece together in her head to make him see reason, to make this whole situation seem plausible. Paining, she aches. Knowing that whatever she will say from here on in, will affect their relationship for the rest of their lives.

"Do you have to carry the baby for 9 months and then push it out of you!!! Do you have the money to pay for hospital bills, clothes and food for two other people besides yourself!!! Nate, I'm not blind and especially not stupid. I am very well aware that you and your father are really trying to get somewhere with the repair shop -'

Reluctantly, she reflects back to herself to drive her point home. Reminding herself of how hard she's worked to get into college. How much money and time went into studying, applications, and tests to score a scholarship. Her wishes, her hopes, her dreams of getting out of Hartford . . . for good.

"I'm sorry but I'm not quitting college and giving up my scholarship because I stupidly got drunk and slept with the boy next door. I begin an internship next summer with an Event Management firm that I've already committed to, I just can't . . . I'm . . . I'm sorry!!!"

Harriet stops. Stopped by an exasperated Nate, who puts his hand up to signal her silence.

"Don't . . . just . . . don't! . . .", pausing, he buries his face in the palms of his hands and turns his back on her. "You're right. I mean, how you could ever have meant for this to happen. Of course, you have your whole life ahead of you. What was I thinking?"

Her eyes glistening, she pleads with him to see reason. "Nate, be logical?!"

"Me? Be logical. Like you. Looking at the facts of the situation . . . So when?"

"I'm going in a couple of days before classes start next week and I run out of time."

"Can I? -"

Wiping her tears, she looks away from him. "I'd prefer it if you didn't!"

Shaking his head, choking back a hurt laugh. "Right. I'm just the donor, not the decision maker?!"

Standing, she decides it's time to leave and makes for the front door. Coming undone, she reaches her car and jumps in. Turning the ignition over, she takes off, and as she wipes away the tears flowing from her broken self, she sees the back of Hartford.

Nate, on the other hand, remains fixed in his spot. Stuck in his living room, he replays his morning before finally hearing her tyres burning rubber as they zoom off towards Hanover and disappear out of his life.

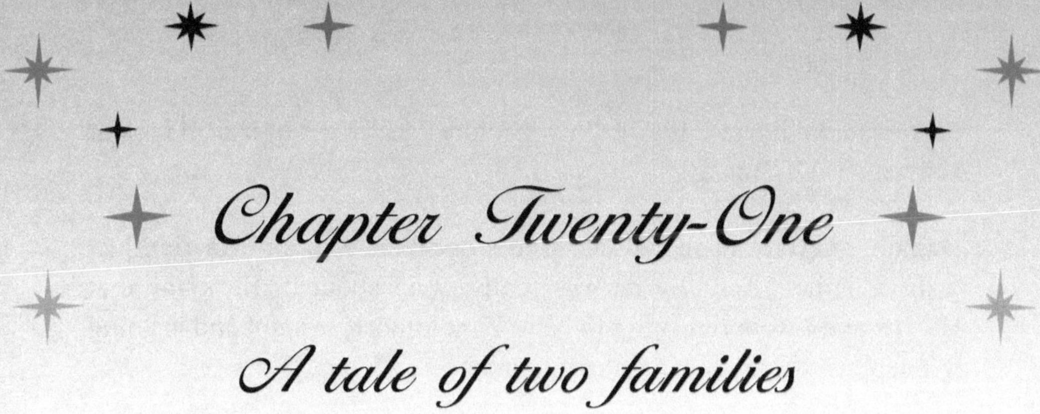

Chapter Twenty-One

A tale of two families

Later that evening in Hartford; Damon and Harriet are sitting at the table having dinner with Harriet's family. Listening to Harriet's mother fawn over her son and his wife with questions about the renovations they're making on their home in Stars Hollow. Taking a long pull of his beer before glancing over at Harriet to see her lost in a daze.

Covering her hand with his, he attempts to pull her back into the world of the living. "Harriet! Woohoo. Harriet, earth to Harriet?"

She looks around realising where she is, noticing that she hasn't been paying any attention.

She glances over at him, embarrassed, "Sorry Damon. My mind was a million miles away."

He smiles, takes her hand, "Along as I was there with you."

She smiles sweetly at him, "Yeah. You were". Knowing it's a lie, she covers it up by continuing to smile at him.

Will looks over at them. "So Damon, Harriet mentioned that you were possibly going to ask Nate about renting cars for the wedding?"

Damon looks up from his plate, over at Will. "Uh yeah, I have an appointment with him tomorrow."

Surprised, Will raises his eyebrows before sneaking a quizzical look at Harriet. "On a Sunday?"

Damon, unaware of the awkwardness between Will and Harriet, just grins a smile. "Actually he was really great about it. He knew that Harriet and I were returning to New York tomorrow night and is going to open his office for a couple of hours."

Will nods. "Well, I'll go with you if that's okay". Damon looks at him "Well, yeah that'd be great."

Watching them, she can't help but notice the easiness between her brother and her soon-to-be husband when Will looks to Harriet and asks, "Was there anything you needed doing, anything I can help out with?"

Damon looks over at Harriet. "Um, not really. It's pretty much all been organised but thanks anyway."

Gloria intervenes. "Oh Will, you don't have to bother with that stuff".

Harriet glances away from Will, rolls her eyes and looks down into her plate. Will slightly raises his voice. "No Mom, I want to help out!"

Gloria looks at him unimpressed and then glances away towards the kitchen. Will glances over at Harriet; she looks up and smiles appreciatively.

Taking a bite of his food, to fill the uncomfortable silence, Will looks to Damon. "So Damon, what's your family like?"

Harriet smiles and glances over at him. "Um, they're different", she giggles.

Will, watching them both, smiles. "What?"

All eyes are now on him, well rather her family's eyes; Harriet is just shaking her head, giggling into her plate. Her father speaks up from his food. "Surely they can't be any worse than us".

Gloria shoots her husband a dirty look as Frank just rolls his eyes before looking at Damon. "No, really! Damon, what's your family like?"

Damon looks over at Harriet, she shrugs and smiles back at him. He touches her hand again, takes a deep breath then looks up at her family through his eyelashes. "Well, um. I grew up in the upper east side of Manhattan. Ah, we have a house in the Hamptons."

Feeling embarrassed, he looks over at Harriet, she nods him to keep going. "They were going to find out at some point, may as well as let them know."

He continues, "My family are fifth generation Manhattan-bred Bennett's. My mother is a stuck up High Society matriarch, and like my grandfather's and father, I was brought up and bred for Wall Street" Chuckling, he confides, "My nanny raised my sister and me until I was shipped off to an elite boarding school then off to college at Harvard. I returned home to Manhattan only to take my place in my father's office."

He looks around the table. Her family is all quiet and well, rather stunned.

"I'm no saint. After college, I rebelled a fair bit." He looks over at Will. "Dated the wrong girls to get back at my mother, crashed a couple of Bentleys." As Will's jaw drops, shocked at what he's hearing, Damon feels the heat from her family's shock and looks down into his plate.

Unsure of what to say next, so he looks over the table to Harriet's left hand. "It wasn't until I attended my sister's wedding that I met the amazingly beautiful woman I've ever met." He smiles across at her "She was the planner and well a feisty one at that!"

Harriet giggles at him. "Ughf!!! Was not. You were being a snob". Damon flashes his gorgeous smile back at her, "Fair enough".

Reaching over, they take each other hands. Unaware that all her family are now watching them and smiling, even her mother, they realise they're being watched and sit back in their chairs and giggle.

Finishing their dinner, they all begin clearing their plates. Sophie looks over to Harriet. "We've got this, you two go hang out". Harriet smiles warmly at her, "Thanks, Sophie."

She takes Damon's hand and guides him outside. He looks at her, wondering what they're doing, has to ask. "What are we doing?"

Stepping onto the patio, she turns to kiss him, and as she pulls her lips off his, she whispers. "Just come with me."

Pulling herself up onto the trampoline, she stands and lies down in the middle of it and then motions for him to jump on as well.

Once he's on the tramp, they look up at the sky. Harriet glances at him. She smiles, happy that she gets to share this piece of her childhood with him.

"Growing up, this was my place of solace. Whenever my mother would be off her rails or I'd be stressed about school, I'd just come out here for peace and quiet, to watch the stars."

He smiles. He takes her hand in his and watches her. She is looking above at the night sky, searching for the brightest star and to make a wish on it. "It's beautiful . . . I never had something like this. You were really are lucky."

Harriet sighs. "I know. It's just. Sometimes, I don't know."

Damon turns himself into her before taking her hand and kisses it softly, "I know. It's called growing up". Harriet smiles and turns to look at him.

Nate, who is washing up in the kitchen, can see her and Damon through the window lying on the tramp, pointing at stars.

He turns to look at Halley, whose still in a bad mood from their fight earlier in the day. She is sitting on the couch watching television with its volume turned up loudly.

Damon and Harriet remain on the trampoline when Will pokes his head out the back door. "Damon, Dad and I are heading down to the pub for a couple of cold ones. Want to come?"

Damon looks at Harriet, "Go on, you know you want to". Kissing her softly, he departs and jumps off the trampoline.

Seeing Damon leave, Nate sees this as a perfect opportunity to slip out and apologise for Halley's behaviour earlier. Honestly, the apology would just be a pretence and an excuse to talk to her. Despite their history, despite their differences; he'd never pass up the opportunity to speak to her even if it was an argue or fight, at least they were speaking.

Harriet's eyes are closed when she hears someone voiceover at the fence.

"It's a beautiful night for watching stars!"

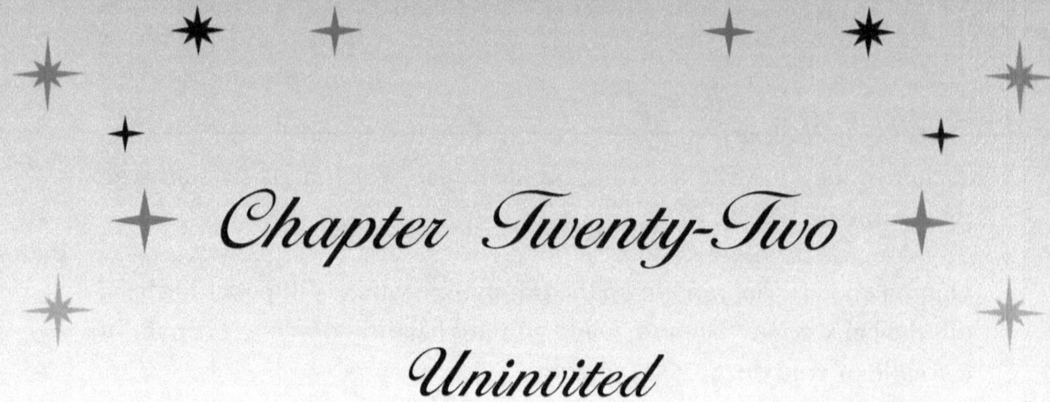

Chapter Twenty-Two

Uninvited

Sitting up, Harriet sees Nate at the fence.

"Sorry. I didn't mean to scare you, I um . . . I just wanted to apologise. You know, for earlier today. Halley's well . . . Halley . . . and you know she was always jealous of you!"

Climbing off the trampoline, she stands to lean against it and folds her arms. Annoyed, possibly disgusted but most of all confused as to why he's dating Halley. Of all the stupid blonde bimbos, he decides to date her.

"Nate, *why* are you dating her?"

"What do you mean, *why* am I dating her?!"

"Well . . . I just thought you never liked her?"

Smirking, his jaw tightens as he shakes his head in dismay. "I may have had disliked her at school but she's kind of hot so why can't I date her?"

Exasperated, she just shakes her head. "Okay. Fine. Whatever. Forget I asked!" and she makes towards to the back door. She about is disappear inside the house when she stopped by his soft dulcet voice lulling her back to him.

"Harriet -'

Her hand fixed upon the door handle, she remains at a standstill.

"You're not *jealous,* are you?"

Turning in her spot to face him, she locks her now infuriated eyes with his. Moving off the back steps to the fence, she seeks to put Nate back in his place.

"Why *would I* be jealous Nate?"

"Gee, I don't know maybe I'm dating someone!"

"*Who cares* if you're dating someone? Good on you!!!"

"Oh well, when you put it like that."

Shaking her head towards the night sky, she rolls her eyes. "You know what ... whatever Nate. I'm going back inside to -'

"It really doesn't bother you?"

Shrugging her shoulders, she bites her lip. "Nope. Why would it?"

"Well whatever, she's my plus one!"

"Plus one for what?"

"You know, the wedding!"

"Who's wedding? Wait?! You don't mean *my* wedding', smirking at him, she shakes her head, *'you must be joking*!!!!"

Watches as his jaw muscle flexes and tightens, he snaps. "No Harriet, I'm most definitely am not!!!"

"Nate . . . I'm sorry but you're not invited."

"What? -'

"You heard me. You're not invited!"

"What do you mean I'm not invited?"

"Easy. You won't be coming to the wedding because you haven't been invited!!!"

"But aren't you using the vintage car collection from my shop?"

"Ah, Damon and I haven't decided yet and at this rate, probably not. I, we just haven't got round to telling you!"

"Then why am I opening my office on a Sunday, for your fiancé to come in and look at cars tomorrow?", he snaps furiously.

Taking a moment, she thinks of Damon and how they might come of use to him. "Damon was thinking of hiring some cars for his buck's party. As for the wedding, I was going to go with a company from New York."

Looking to her feet, she avoids his eyes. "Look, I'm sorry Nate, I truly am but . . . I just . . . can't do this anymore. This is exhausting."

"What is?"

"This', ushering her index finger between himself and her, 'It's not fair to either of us. It's not fair to Damon. We're not friends so let's just stop with the pretending."

"Pretending? Who's pretending?"

"Nate!!! Please just stop!!! Stop fighting me on this. Just stop!!! I can't do it anymore!!!" she states. Turning her back on him, she moves back to the house. Only her escape is foiled by an angry Nate who has now jumped the fence and is pinning her against the garage wall. Slapping his hands off her upper arms, Harriet tries to fight him off.

"Nate . . . What are you doing? Let me go! Get your hands off of me . . . for god's sake!!! What's your problem!!!"

Letting her go, he steps back only to pace back and forth in front of her. "Unbelievable -'

"Yes, you are!!!"

"No, you?!"

"Wait . . . What?', pointing at him angrily, her index finger poking at his chest as she closes the distance between them, 'I know, you just didn't!"

Snapping up her finger, roughly in his hand. He pulls her closer into him, their lips mere millimetres away from each other.

"After all *we've been through. After all these years* and *I'm not invited* to your wedding?!"

Glancing away from him, she feels her eyes beginning to well up with tears. "No, no you're not."

Disappointed, he steps back, letting go of her finger, astonished. "Well', taking a deep frustrated breathe, he scratches his eyebrow before wiping his face, 'I guess that clears that up then. And here, I thought we were friends?!"

In her softest, most honest voice, she speaks, and her dulcet voice sends shivers to his somewhat now broken heart. "Nate, we were never friends. Deep down . . . you . . . you must know that!"

Tightening his jaw, its muscles pulses through his cheek as he gruffly nods in acceptance. "Right -"

Stepping towards her slowly, he kisses her lightly on the cheek. It wouldn't have meant anything to her or that's to say, it wouldn't have affected her if it were just a simple peck on the cheek. But the fact, that he seemed to let his lips linger on her cheek for longer than he probably should of have, well in all honesty; made the situation all that more awkward.

When he did finally step away from her, he locked eyes with her and taking her hand in his to place it on his chest, a destroyed Nate utters before departure, "I hope you and Damon will be very happy!"

Stunned, Harriet just stands there watching as he disappears over the fence and inside his home. Feeling like her legs had stumbled into wet cement, and she's lost all composure, she leans her head against the garage as her eyes trail upwards towards her stars, splattered across the night sky as if the gods had just thrown salt over their shoulders for good luck. If only she could use some of that good luck right now to walk away from her past unscathed. But she knew better than that, and you can't walk away from your past unscathed especially when you wear the battle scars on your body. Serving as a constant reminder of what had occurred and what was lost.

Slowly regaining feeling, she breaks free of the garage wall and makes the short walk to the back door to her bedroom. Lying on her bed, she fans out a star on top of her doona. Looking up to her ceiling, she sees Patrick looking back down at her and imagining herself to be in conversation with him, her mind fights to find an understanding for the events of the night.

Am I mad? Why am I letting Nate affect me so much? Why does he have this power over me?

Patrick: Because you're letting him get to you.

Why can't he just forget anything ever happened and just let it go?

Patrick: Because you're happy and he's not. Because you got out of Hartford and he didn't. Because he's still hurting over what happened. Because even though, he doesn't admit it, he clearly is still in love with you. More importantly, Harriet and this is the one thought that should be above any other – is the fact that you and Damon are getting married in two months. I mean, what are you thinking? You're in love with Damon, you're marrying Damon. Why are you wasting precious time on Nate when -

When I should be spending all my precious time on Damon?

Patrick: No and well yes. What I was going to say was, yes to spending time with Damon and no to figuring out this what you truly want. Are you truly ready for marriage, for kids, for this life with Damon? I mean, will his Mother always be like this? We both know your mother will never change. Just think about it okay. It's okay to take some time to think about these things.

Sitting up, she rubs her forehead. Standing up, she walks into her walk-in closet and changes into her pyjamas only to return her bed to peel back the covers and climb in. Curling up into her blanket and pillows, she takes a few deep breathes to calm her body and mind before falling into a what-will-be restless sleep.

❋   ❋   ❋

Damon was standing on the front porch, waiting for Mr Lancer to change so that they can go off and have a few drinks at the pub, a few streets over, when he heard Harriet's name being spoken by a male's voice that doesn't belong to any of her family members or himself.

"Harriet - you're not jealous, are you?"

Walking to the end of the porch, he leans around to see Harriet approach the fence, looking like he's just insulted her. Unfortunately for Damon, he is all too well aware of that tone in her voice.

"Why would I be jealous Nate?"
"Gee, I don't know maybe I'm dating someone!!!"
"Who cares if you're dating someone? Good on you?!"

"Oh well, when you put it like that?!"
"You know what ... whatever Nate. I'm going back inside to -'
"It really doesn't bother you?"
"Nope. Why would it?"
"Well whatever, she's my plus one!"
"Plus one for what?"
"You know, the wedding!"
"Who's wedding? Wait!? You don't mean my
wedding . . . you must be joking!!!!"

And as Damon hears this, he creeps from the front verandah to lean against the garage door.

"No Harriet, I'm most definitely am not!!!"

And with a deep strained breathe, he hears Harriet's voice break up. *"Nate . . . I'm sorry but you're not invited."*
"What? —"
"You heard me. You're not invited."
"What do you mean I'm not invited?"
"Easy. You won't be coming to the wedding
because you haven't been invited!"
"But aren't you using the vintage car collection from my shop?"
"Ah, Damon and I haven't decided yet and at this rate,
probably not. I, we just haven't got round to telling you!"
"Then why am I opening my office on a Sunday, for your
fiancé to come in and look at cars tomorrow?"
"Damon was thinking of hiring some cars for his buck's
party. As for the wedding, I was going to go with a company
from New York. Look, I'm sorry Nate, I truly am but . . .
I just . . . can't do this anymore. This is exhausting."
"What is?"
"This. It's not fair to either of us. It's not fair to Damon.
We're not friends so let's just stop with the pretending."
"Pretending? Who's pretending?"
"Nate!!! Please just stop!!! Stop fighting me on
this. Just stop!!! I can't do it anymore!!!"

Fixed against the door, he continues to listen in as he hears Nate jump the fence and pin his fiancé against the back wall of the garage. Hearing her slapping his hands off her upper arms, Damon's hands ball themselves into fists, his body pulsating as he listens as Harriet fights him off.

"Nate . . . What are you doing? Let me go! Get your hands
off of me . . . for god's sake!!! What's your problem!!!"
"Unbelievable –"
"Yes, you are!!!"
"No, you?!"
"Wait . . . What? I know, you just didn't!"
"After all we've been through. After all these years
and I'm not invited to your wedding?!"
"No . . . You're not."
"Well . . . I guess that clears that up then. And
here, I thought we were friends?!"

Thinking their conversation is over, Damon makes to move off the door but is stopped by her soft dulcet yet broken voice.

"Nate, we were never friends. Deep down . . .
you . . . you must know that!"
"Right -"

Scratching his eyebrow, a wave of disbelief overwhelms him. Peeling himself off the garage door, he makes his way back to the front steps but is stopped one last time, at the sight of Nate stepping closer to Harriet to plant a kiss on her cheek. It wouldn't have bothered him if it just a simple peck on the cheek but watching Nate place a lingering kiss on his fiancé, tells him that there's more to their story. A story she has never shared with him.

"I hope you and Damon will be very happy", is the last thing he hears as Nate disappears over the fence and back inside his house.

He is pulled from his thoughts by the sound of Will's voice. "You ready Damon?"

Unable to speak, he just nods. Maybe a beer (or five hundred) will erase the memory of tonight. As he takes a seat in Will's car and Will makes to turn over the ignition, Will just has to look at Damon to sense that something is bothering him. Is it when the car door opens, and Harriet's father jumps in the back, that Will turns to look at them both to say, *"Okay, let's go."*

✳   ✳   ✳

Taking an exasperated breath, Harriet closes her eyes. Turning on her side, she snuggles up in her blanket when she feels a cold tear spill down her cheek

Closing her eyes, Harriet snuggles up in her blanket, pulling it all around her as tight as possible. As hard as she can, she tries to erase the night (or the events of the night). Turning on her side, she looks through her window for some inspiration but deep down she knows that this is one mess that she made herself and one she'd have to solve.

Turning back to lie straight on her back, Harriet's eyes well with tears. Confused as to what exactly she's tearing up about, she

tries to make herself forget and get some sleep. But as she feels her eyelids fall, her mind can't help but reiterate Nate's words.

> *Well, I guess that clears that up then, and*
> *here I was thinking we were friends.*

Turning on her side once more, she snuggles deeper into her pillow. With Nate still clearly on her mind, she is reminded of yet another memory she shared with him.

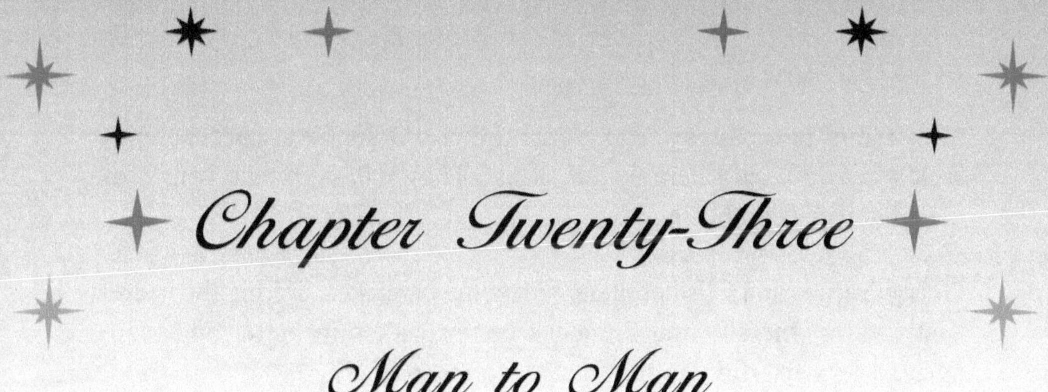

Chapter Twenty-Three

Man to Man

When Harriet wakes up in the morning, she notices that Damon isn't there. Getting up out of bed, she grabs her robe from the back of the door and walks out to the breakfast table where her father is reading his newspaper and having a coffee. Taking a seat at the table, she smiles at her father. "Morning, Dad"

Peering over his paper, he smiles gently at his daughter. "Morning love."

Dropping his paper, he pours a glass of juice and gets up of his chair to hand it to Harriet. As he hands it to her, he leans down and kisses her forehead then returns to his seat to continue reading the paper. Looking around as she nibbles on some toast, she wonders where Damon is.

"Dad, have you seen Damon?"

Her father, lifting his paper down, looks around the room. "Ah, no love. Well not since he drove off in the car with Will"

Harriet nods a sigh of relief. She couldn't help but think for a moment that her mother drove him back to New York.

"Ah, okay."

Noticing she's a little on edge, he drops his paper once more to look over at her. Pushing a plate towards her, he smiles.

"Have some pancakes sweetie. Your mother and Sophie are out shopping, so it's just you and I here for breakfast. They will help take your mind off whatever is bothering you."

Harriet smiles and fills her plate with some pancakes. Taking the nearest seat to him, she sits and drenches her pancakes in butter and maple syrup. "So what did you boys get up to last night?"

Looking at his daughter, he grins. "Uh love, we just had some beers."

"Just some beers hey -"

"Yeah love. Damon asked about Nate though, which I found strange."

Harriet who has just swallowed a mouthful of pancake stops chewing then looks to her father. "What? -"

"Yeah. He kept asking Will questions about him."

Putting her knife and fork down, she awkwardly glances sideways at her father. "What kind of questions?"

"I don't know sweetie, I stopped listening. Not that I blame him for wanting to know."

Rubbing her temple, her eyebrows crinkle at the thought of why Damon would be asking questions about Nate.

"Blame him? For what, Dad?"

"I don't know love. Maybe he finds it strange like I always have, that that boy is always around!"

"Dad, he's Will's best friend!!!"

"I know, love but still —"

"Still what Dad?"

"Well, I've always felt for the boy. Being stuck in that house, alone while his parents were off working and building that business. I didn't mind that he was over here because well, I was happy that at least someone was looking out for him. But, and I say this with all the love in the world my dear, but he seems to be very protective of you. More than one should, that's all."

Smiling sheepishly over at her father, a smirk forms across her lips. Standing, she meets him and kisses him on the cheek.

"You know, that there will never be anyone that I love more in this world than you, don't you Dad?"

Nodding, he smiles as she leans down to hug him. "With the exception of that young man of yours. I like him. He's a keeper, Harriet."

"Thanks, Dad, I do too!"

Finishing her breakfast, she stands to take her plate into the kitchen and place it in the sink before running off to have a shower.

After her shower, she dresses and decides to go check out the markets in Hartford. Anything to get her mind off of Nate and now Damon's behaviour.

"You're phone buzzed, while you were in the shower."

Picking up her bag, she rifles through it until she finds her phone. Checking it, she sees Harper tried to call.

Rubbing her forehead, she looks down at her phone's screen and breathes a deep sigh.

"Was it important? I should've answered, but I didn't want to go through your things. Sorry love"

"Yeah, Dad. I just had a missed call from Harper. Damon's mother is probably having a whinge."

"Is everything okay???"

Rubbing her forehead, she looks up from her phone screen, to smile at him. "I think. I just want all this wedding drama to be over and done with!"

He smiles at her. "I know honey. It will be all over and done with soon."

Looking up from the paper, seeing her handbag draped over her shoulder and car keys in hand, he asks her. "Are you off then for a bit, love?"

Smiling at her father, she nods. "Yeah, Dad. I wanted to do a couple of things in town. I'll see you in a bit okay."

❋   ❋   ❋

Meanwhile, Will and Damon pull up in front of Michaels Mechanics. Last night, whilst they were at the Pub having a few beers, Will suggested that he should come with Damon, seeing as he had also been wanting to catch up with Nate and that Damon had been stewing over Nate, considering the questions he had been asking the night before.

Stepping out of Will's car, Damon takes a look around at Nate's mechanic and repair shop. To his left, is a building front with window to floor glass windows, displaying the latest car parts and accessory from the country and international wide brands known to all potential customers and car enthusiasts.

To his frontal view, is a huge five-door industrial garage with a huge "Michael's Mechanics" painted in red above the doors to advertise the space. Seeing as it is a Sunday and the shop isn't open, there is only one garage door open and taking up its space, is a red Ferrari which assumes is for either Will or himself to test drive. Most likely . . . Will.

Peering out the glass window of his office, Nate sees they have arrived. Coming out of the office, he ushers them inside.

Will and Nate pat each other on the back. "Will, good to see you."

Will grins and scratches his chin. "Yeah, it's been a while."

"How's Sophie?"

Will looks at him, happiness fills his face as he spills his news to Nate. "Um, we haven't told our folks yet, but she's pregnant."

Nate smiles and hugs his mate, "Congratulations" but then can't help but smirk at the thought of Will as a parent.

"This is going to be fun!"

Noticing Damon, standing to the right of Will, he introduces them to each other. "Oh sorry, Nate this is Damon. Harriet's fiancé."

Nate nods and extends his hand to shake Damon's hand. "Great to meet you."

Damon looks down at him with a quizzical look. Standing straight and reserved, much like his mother would if she were meeting Nate, he coldly hands his hand over to shake hands with Nate.

"Really?"

"Well yeah. It's all Mrs L can talk about it."

Damon surprised at this knowledge; mumbles, "Mrs L talks about me? That's funny because Harriet would say the opposite."

Will, sensing a pending awkwardness between them, intervenes. "I'm pretty sure he means the wedding and Harriet getting married."

Damon, knowing this is all a lie, nods in acceptance. "Oh right" as Nate ushers them to take a seat.

"So I'm guessing we're here to talk about the vintage collection. Damon was pretty keen to see the bridal car, Nate."

Nate, unsure of what to say. Looks between them, confused. "Oh? Well um, I thought Harriet had changed her mind."

Curious as to what he might mean, Damon, asks, "When did she do that?"

Looking between them, Will senses an impending argument on the horizon and chooses to slip away while he still can. "Ah, I might just go for a look at some of your cars for myself."

"Okay Will. The red Ferrari was just brought in yesterday', fetching the keys off his table, he throws him at Will, 'take it for a spin, just make sure you bring in back in one piece, okay?"

Will nods and quickly walks off out of the office. Damon waits until Will has left the office before he speaks. "Nate, do you mind. Can I speak frankly with you for a moment."

"Sure! Soooo . . . what's on your mind?"

"Well, I was just wondering. What you and Harriet were arguing about last night?"

Nate avoids his eyes, looking out his window he tries desperately to shake Damon's stares off of him. Facing him, he shakes his hand away, brushing it off like it was nothing.

"Oh um, it's nothing. She was telling me that she didn't have enough in her budget for the cars."

"Then why did you have to jump the fence last night and pin her against the house? I mean, are you really that upset about the collection not being used? Because I am happy to pay for any late grievances that she's caused. I mean, she soon will be my wife!"

A shocked Nate is speechless, and he continues to sit in his stuck in his seat, listening on as Damon continues on, making his intentions very clear.

"Because that's all it was? Right? Just an argument about the cars? Not anything else."

An astonished Nate just nods.

"Okay, well. I don't know what Harriet is thinking, but we'll need three cars. We can't fit everyone into my BMW, so if you can put together an invoice for costs, maintenance and servicing whatever, and send it to my office', taking out his wallet, he hands Nate his card, ' this is my card."

As he stands to make his way out of the office, he stops in the doorway to look back at Nate.

"Nate -"

Slightly angered yet humoured by Damon's proud demeanour, glances from Damon's card to look at him.

"Nothing is going on between you and Harriet is there? Something that I should know about before we get married?"

Nate shakes his head. "No."

"Okay well. I guess I'll just see you at the wedding."

"Ah, no mate —"

"But we'll need you to manage the cars, and it wouldn't be right if you didn't stay for the wedding. Plus, aren't your like family? Like another brother or something?"

Stalling for an answer and excuse, Nate thinks of a lie he can sell to Damon. "Ah, I can get a couple of the guys to drive the cars. I was already planning a getaway with Halley that weekend anyway so."

Surprised, Damon responds. His eyebrows crinkled and head cocked to his side. "The weekend that we're getting married?"

Stifling back a laugh, Nate scratches his eyebrow. "Yeah. Halley wants to get away. Not too fussed on being in town when Harriet gets married."

"Oh ok. Well. Thanks again and it ah, was nice meeting you", knowing that he personally wouldn't care if Nate didn't attend the wedding, Damon just nods and disappears out of the office.

✳   ✳   ✳

After spending most of her day; following up wedding planning, talking on the phone with Harper and updating her work planner, Harriet finally pulls into her parent's driveway. Seeing that her mother's car is not in the open garage; she assumes that Will,

Sophie and her mother are still all out doing, well whatever it is they were doing.

Walking inside the house, she sees her father asleep in his armchair. Not wanting to disturb him, she moves quietly past him and dumps her things in her room on the bed. Her eyes moving around the room, she scans her room. Picking up a photo frame from her bookshelf, she giggles at the silly poses that she and her friends were doing at age fifteen. The hairstyles, the clothes. Those goddam denim overalls that she used to wear everywhere and her hair always in plaits, at least until her senior years.

Taking a seat near her window, she smirks at her younger self and shakes her head. Dropping the frame on the window seat beside, she looks out her window and is stopped by the movement coming from the top of her trampoline. As she looks harder at the figure lying there, she recognises Damon's sandy brown hair and exits her room in a heartbeat to meet him at the tramp.

"Damon -"

Turning on his side, he turns his back on her.

"Damon . . . what's wrong?"

Reaching to touch his back, he shudders at her touch and makes to move further away from her.

"Damon???"

"So remind me, Harriet, when did decide that we weren't asking Nate for the use of his vintage car collection?"

"Um, well. . . I've been going over the budget and costs and I simply can't afford Nate's hire and insurance fee."

"What do you mean that you simply can't afford it?"

"Simple. I can't afford it on *my* budget!"

"Harriet, are you paying for the wedding???"

"Yes —"

"And you didn't think to tell me this? If I had known —"

"You would have what, Damon? Hmm??? I can't talk about money with you. We've never been able to talk about money with each other. You're swimming in it, you grew up surrounded by it and me? Well, I had to work two after-school jobs and study my ass off to just so I could go to college!"

"Harriet, if you needed money, for our wedding, you should have just asked!!!"

Harriet scoffs sarcastically, turning away from him to lean against the trampoline edge. Crossing her arms, she angrily spits out over her shoulder at him.

"Oh right sure. I can just see your mothers face now and the comments she'll be making on the day about how she had to pay for the - ', making quotation marks with her index and middle fingers, remembering Beverly's comments during Harper's wedding planning, she imitates his mother's upturned nose and society voice, 'Way below par decorations and entree selection."

Annoyed at the snipe directed at his mother, he leans over to grab her arm and pull her against the tramp to face him. "Harriet!!! Stop avoiding the subject by taking this out on my mother. She's not that bad!!!"

Harriet snaps back at him. "Not that bad? Your mother is Satan!!!!"

"And you're not -"

"What does that mean?"

"Well Harriet, you come off as this know it all, fully rounded person but sometimes, you're actions -"

"Oh really??? You want to go there, do you? The poster boy for teenage angst, rebellion and parental hate. Whose deeply misunderstood, just wants to be loved and be a part of a real family???', stopping herself, she immediately realises what she's just said to him. Damn her mouth and its inability to filter her words.

"What? Oh please don't stop on my account, you're on a roll. Please keep going -"

Shaking her head, she refuses to continue.

"Well, at least I know now how you really feel."

Taking a step back, she attempts to move away from the trampoline and escape. Unfortunately for her, Damon notices her escape attempt and cuts it short. "Harriet, do you even want to marry me? Because lately, I swear I look at you, and at times, I don't even know who you are!"

Remaining speechless, she stands frozen in her spot. Her mind, rummaging over his words *'do you even want to marry me?'*

"Harriet?! I asked you a question?!"

"What?!"

"I asked you a question. Do you even want to marry me? Are you sure there's no one else, like let's say a certain next door neighbour, that you would rather be with? Because if so, tell me now so I can walk away before it's too late!"

"Of course I want to marry you. *I love you.*"

"Then why is Nate jumping fences and pinning you against garage walls like he's in love with you, Harriet?"

"I'm not doing this – ', retreating she turns to head inside when Damon jumps off the trampoline, grabbing at her wrist and pinning her against a tree. Frightened, she attempts to pull her wrist out of his hand. "Damon, you're *hurting* me!!!"

"Harriet, I know something is going on between you and Nate!"

"Nothing is going on. Please, Damon, you're hurting my arm!"

"Harriet, why would Nate be organising other men to drive your bridal car, refusing to come to our wedding when he's pretty much an older brother to you but won't because he and Halley are going away that weekend? Why would someone be acting like that?"

Staring her down and trapping her against the trunk of the tree, he refuses to release her wrist until she answers him.

"Harriet, either you give me some kind of explanation or truth now, or I'm -"

Finding her voice, she snaps at him. "You'll what? Exactly what is it Damon that you'll do? Because you're behaviour right now makes want to -"

"Do what? Call our wedding off?"

"Honestly, yes! If you're in love with another man, then yes Harriet. That's exactly what I'll do!"

Releasing his grip on her wrist, he backs away from her. Looking down at his shaking hands, he immediately hates himself and his behaviour just now. Falling back onto the gazebo stairs, he runs his shaking hands through his hair. Completely flummoxed, he looks to her for answers.

"I'm sorry, Harriet."

Lost he looks down into his palms, searching with his eyes for an explanation as to his sudden rage and behaviour somewhat towards her but mostly towards Nate, "I . . . just. I don't know what's come over me. I . . . um . . . I heard you fighting with Nate last night and I -"

He wipes his face. His eyes glittering, panic throbbing through his body, he brings his hands within eye-sight again. They are still shaking. "I didn't know what to think. I . . . I . . . don't know what to think. You told me that you were never that way with him? I mean why is this guy so invested in you Harriet? And don't say he's like another brother to you because clearly, he isn't!"

Placing her head back against the trunk of the tree, she takes a deep breath. Falling down to the ground, she takes a deep breath and runs her hand lightly over the blades of grass as she searches for an opening to an explanation she can give her fiancé about the boy whom she fell in love with at age nine.

"Nate was always more than just my brother's friend and next door neighbour. We have a history!"

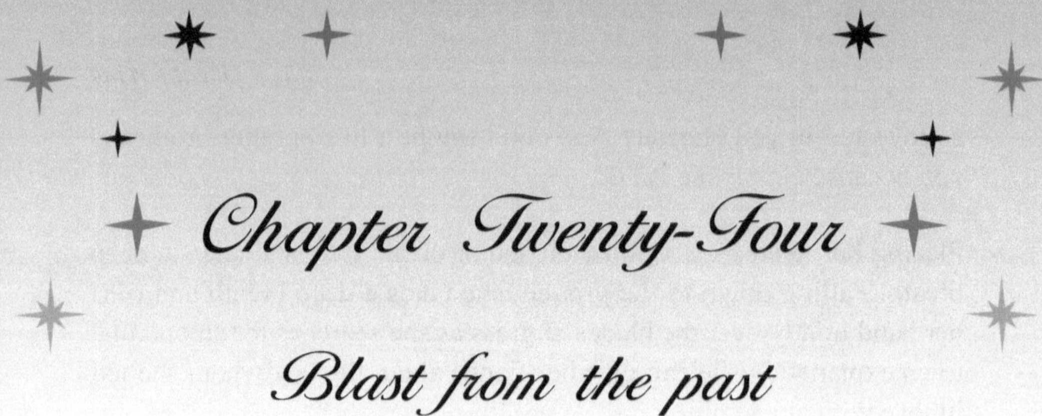

Chapter Twenty-Four

Blast from the past

Sitting under a gazebo in her parent's backyard, Damon's ears are ringing.

'Nate was always more than just my brother's friend and next door neighbour. We have a history.'

Her words are now etched on his brain.

Needing a few moments to register her sudden honesty, he wipes his face in disbelief before prompting her to spill everything.

"From the start. *Don't leave anything out*, Harriet. I want to know all of it!!!"

Picking up a blade of grass, she weaves it between her fingers as she begins the story that is her and Nate.

"The reason why Halley Sawyer mysteriously got chewing gum in her hair and had to have all her locks cut off was because I came home one day from school upset because Halley had gotten up in front of our whole class and humiliated me by telling everyone that I loved Patrick Swayze and wrote Mrs Patrick Swayze all over my books. She then went and told the whole class how I practised the dance at lunchtime all by myself and that someone like Patrick Swayze would never be interested in someone like me because I was too fat to ever be someone's dance partner!"

Rubbing her forehead, she looks to her trampoline, remembering what happened next. "Instead of getting angry, I walked straight out of the classroom and came home. I laid there on that tramp until Nate came home, saw me curled up in a ball, crying. When my dad found out from Will, he let me stay home for a couple of days. When I did go eventually go back, I found out that Halley mysteriously got chewing gum stuck in her hair, Nate somehow ended up getting detention for like a month, and Halley and her friends never made fun of me ever again."

Damon is looking up from his feet to look at her asks. "That's it?"

Looking down at her hands, knotting and unknotting them, she shakes her head and nervously continues.

"During my final years of high school; when I wasn't studying or working, I would occasionally go out to parties with my friends. At times, it was as if a flare had lit up the sky *'Harriet is at a party . . . She must need saving'* because Nate was always there. Sometimes with friends, sometimes with a date. But always watching over me and never saying anything. The night of my prom, I remember Will had come home, and they were heading out somewhere. I was asked to the prom by my lab partner and arranged for a group of us to go. I knew that my lab partner liked me so at the after-party when Nate and Will showed up, Nate and he got into this huge fight about how much alcohol I had drunk that night because clearly, he had other intentions on his mind. So anyway, I stormed off, and Nate followed me. We got into this huge fight which resulted in me kissing him. He drove me home, and after talking all night, we fell asleep in each other's arm, and he promised to call. Only I found out later that his grandmother died in her sleep that night and he was pulled to New York to attend to family duties. He was gone for almost a month, and in all that time, he hadn't called, and I left for Dartmouth the day he returned home."

Watching her unravel, he softens. Unable to fathom why she would think that, he can't help but ask. "Did he ever talk to you about what happened?"

Harriet closes her eyes and nods her head repeatedly. Biting her lower lip, she continues. "No, well not until my 18th birthday."

"Okay . . . so then what happened?"

"Damon, are you sure you want to hear this because I've never asked about your history with girls?"

Crossing his arms, he nods at the deck. "Harriet, I said I wanted to know everything!!!"

She opens her eyes and looks over at him. His arrogance is rearing its ugly head, she wondered when it'd appear. Shaking the thought off, she levels with him. "You know, I never asked once how you meet Lucy or what you got up to at Harvard!!!"

Damon glances over at her, point blank. No emotion, just straight out. "Don't change the subject. I want to know Harriet."

Taking a deep breath, she continues. "About six months later, I came home for the summer and my 18th. Dad had organised a party. Will invited Nate, and by the time he showed up, I had had a lot to drink. I didn't have anything to eat, but I also think I kind of drank too much because Ryan and I fought over the phone before the party. Somehow, everyone seemed to fade away, and it became all about Nate and I. He kissed me, and we ended up back at his place. I woke that morning to missed calls from Ryan and my family so I told Nate that I'd call him later because I had to go home."

Damon smirks with a cheeky grin. "So you two hooked up? Seriously that's it? That's why you're unpleasant with each other???"

Looking sideways at him, she reluctantly bites at her lower lip.

"There's more????"

Harriet nods slowly. Closing her eyes, shutting them ever so tightly so she can't see his face when she confesses to him her most guarded secret. A secret that no other person alive knows of other than Nate, she takes a long deep hurtful sigh. The kind of sigh that you know that your heart is going to break into a million pieces just from hearing it.

Tears brimming her eye ducts, she looks away from Damon's anxious eyes. The memory alone reminds her of the painful experience, one that haunted her for so long that she had to seek medication to deaden her mind from its experience from Student Free Clinic to help her sleep through the night. Her roommate, despite being the best of friends with her at the time, eventually had to seek other accommodation because of Harriet's recurring nightmares and inability to sleep through an entire night.

"A few months later when I was getting ready to head back to college, I found out I was pregnant."

Astonished, Damon straightens in his spot. Locking eyes with her, he inaudibly whispers to the air with shock, "Pregnant?"

Nodding, she gazes down to her open palms resting on her knees. Leaning down, she places her forehead on them.

"Harriet, do have a child with Nate?"

"No."

"You got rid of it?"

Watching on as she shakes her head against her palms, he feels himself growing more and more agitated as the story continues.

"Then what . . . *Harriet???* What happened?!"

"**Alright!!!**", she eventually spits. "I was going to. *Okay!!!* I found out that I was pregnant during the summer road trip around the East Coast with Ryan and his family. I told Nate before I left to go back to college of my plans, but when I got back to Hanover, I chickened out. I hate hospitals . . . I hate needles even more. So after about a week of thinking of nothing but the issue, I woke up bleeding in the middle of the night and by the time I reached the hospital, I had suffered a miscarriage."

Placing a hand over his mouth in shock, Damon can't help but ask, "Does he know?"

She shakes her head. Her eyebrows furrowing at him intensely. "And he doesn't need to know Damon!!!"

"Harriet, that's not fair! He should at least know –"

Having had enough, she finally snaps. Watching as she storms over towards him with her finger pointed over at Nate's home, her emotions reaching boiling point consume her body. All the unspoken thoughts, the raw and brutal niggling judgements that she's had hanging over her all these years coming to the surface and like a short fuse on a stick of dynamite, she explodes.

"Do *you* know *what* he said when I told him I was pregnant? He said that we could keep it. That we could get married and live in that house! I worked my ass off to get into Dartmouth!!! I was on a no-expense paid business scholarship. Enchanted Events had offered me a second internship starting Spring Break, and another for the Winter Break after that. They even offered me the opportunity to get my Event Management diploma. I wasn't going to drop out and become a washout here in Hartford. I had *I have* worked too hard to become a stay at home mom at age 18, Damon!"

Utterly confused, he questions Nate's family's business. "How do you know that Harriet? I don't know him that well but I doubt he'd let you become a washout. Besides, isn't his family company doing well?"

"Yeah, now they are. But they weren't ten years ago; they were still building the business. A baby would've just . . . would've just set everyone back. But it's not just that, it was a lot of other things as well —"

"Like what Harriet?"

"Well, I wasn't sure if I was even in love with him. A lot of stuff was happening so fast; I hadn't had the time to think about how I felt. What if I what I felt was just a childish crush? We were so young. He was building his life here; I was heading towards living and working in New York. I couldn't do that to him; I couldn't do that to myself."

Damon sighs and shrugs. "Well. I asked you to tell me the truth. So I guess -"

"Damon . . . *What would you have done?* You weren't there. You don't know how it was. I already felt so alone in this house. The punchline to my mother's cruel jokes. I worked so hard for so long to get out of here."

Looking away from her, he looks to Nate's house. With anger slowly encompassing his entire body, he tries to remain calm. Their history was so different yet so similar. They've both made mistakes, they both made decisions in their lives that have hurt people but did it to survive this life.

"I don't know what I would've done."

Biting down on her lower lip, she nods at the ground. Disappointed, she releases a hurtful sigh before moving away from him.

"I just . . . I just need some time okay. I'm sorry, Harriet. I know, I wanted to hear the truth and you told me, I just didn't think, I just need to process it okay!"

Swallowing another wounded breath, she wipes her pained face with her hands. Moving towards the house, she quietly distances herself away from him. Before she disappears inside, he feels the need to justify his reasoning to her.

"Harriet . . . come on. You'll have to forgive me for needing just a moment to understand it all. I mean all this stuff happened and well ', himself now taking a deep frustrated breath as he looks at her, 'honestly would you have told me all this if I never asked?"

Silently, she turns to meets his eyes only respond with a slow nod before disappearing inside the house. Taking a seat on her cupboard floor, he later finds her with tears are streaming down her cheeks with her hand clasped over her mouth to muffle the sound of her pain. Grieved at the sight, Damon takes a seat beside her before pulling her into his lap. As her tears moisten his shirt, he pats her hair softly and takes a lock of it within his fingers. Winding it around the length of his index finger, he searches for the right words to say to her. To comfort her. To stop her pain.

"I'm no saint. I know that okay. This was just unexpected. Please just promise me, that from this moment on, that we're honest with each other."

Taking his index finger and crooking it, he places under her chin to tilt it up until her eyes meet his. "And that if there's something you want, for the wedding or whatever, that you won't be afraid to come to ask me for. Harriet, I can't help that I grew up with money. It's a burden; I bear from growing up in the family that I did. But Harriet, I love you, and all I've ever wanted is you. That's all I've ever wanted since we met. Ever since I saw you in that purple cocktail dress at Harper's dress rehearsal!"

Smirking, she feels her stomach filling up with a wave of light. Meeting his eyes, she smiles. "I'm sorry about this -"

Pulling her wrist up to rest his chest, he takes a deep breath and looks down at it. Rubbing it gently in his hands, he feels like a fool. "You know that I would never intentionally hurt you right?"

Taking his hand, he reaches down to her wrist to brush a light kiss upon the angry red mark from his touch earlier.

"Harriet, I really am sorry."

Nodding, she purses her lips and takes a breath. "I know. I am too. I should've told you everything a long time ago."

Meeting each other's eyes, they both smirk. Looking around her closet, he sees the purple lace cocktail dress that he fell in love with at Harper's Dinner Rehearsal, reminding him that their rehearsal starts in a matter of hours.

"We'd better start getting ready. Dinner's at 7", leaning down to kiss her lightly on top of her hair.

Getting up, she offers her hand to help him up. Taking it, he stands and engulfs her into his arms for a soft hug.

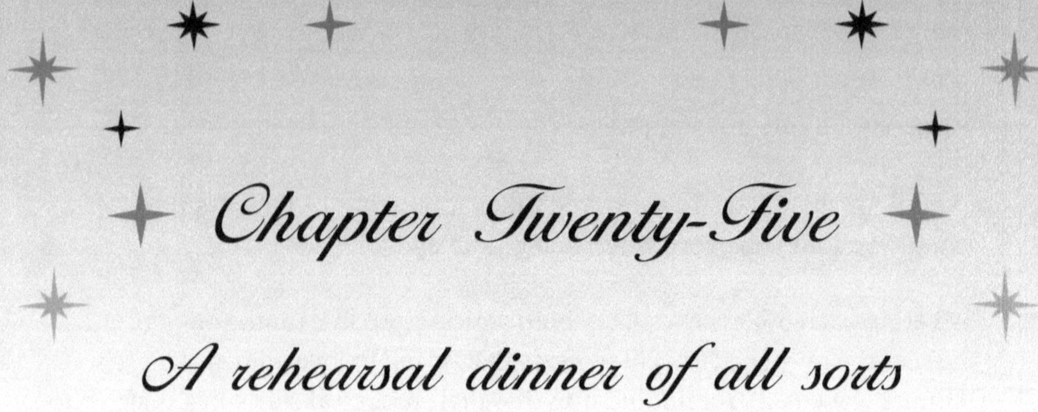

Chapter Twenty-Five

A rehearsal dinner of all sorts

That evening, Harriet and Damon held a rehearsal dinner at the Sheraton Hartford South Hotel. Even though their

wedding reception was going to be held at The Plaza in New York; the hotel function manager asked knowing she'd be in town if he could plan a dinner rehearsal for her. The purpose for dinner was more so, for the guests from Hartford or a part of Harriet's family that couldn't make it to the wedding.

Damon is putting his tie on when Harriet walks into her room, dressed in the purple lace cocktail dress she wore to

Harper's dinner rehearsal three years ago. His eyes trail the length of the dress as she moves around the room picking up bits and pieces to place inside her clutch purse.

When she takes a seat in front of her Duchess and begins rifling through her jewellery case, she notices that Damon has gone still and his tie, is still un-tied in the reflection of her duchess mirror. She smirks, placing earrings in her ears then swings her body around on the chair to face him. A grin breaks over her cheeks causing them to go blush bright pink at his staring.

"See something you like, Mr Bennett?"

His eyes slide up and down her body. "Yes. That dress!"

She giggles. "I had a feeling you'd remember this dress."

Walking towards her, she stands as he approaches. Taking her arms and hooking them around his neck, he kisses her softly as his hands trail the dress's zipper and lace down her back. She giggles in his mouth, and he breaks the kiss.

"Why Mr Bennett, I do believe you're being naughty."

He whips her around; her back is now tightly against him. Wrapping his arms around her chest, he kisses her neck.

She rubs his arms gently and kisses his cheek. "Your tie', she giggles as she sees his tie is awkwardly angled, 'Here, I'll do it."

She turns in his arms and ties it for him all while he is looking down, smirking at her. When she is finished, he pulls her into him.

"I love you, Harriet; you know that right -"

She giggles again. "Well, I hope so!"

He shakes his head at her, "So you ready to do this?"

Putting her necklace on, she turns to look him over her shoulder. "Yeah. Did your parents say if they could get away?"

"Harper and Glenn are coming. They're staying at the hotel. Dad wanted to come, but Mom is being -"

Harriet nods.

"What? No comment? No inkling of an insult?"

Looking at him, she just smiles. "No Damon. Not tonight"

He smiles and giggles back at her, "Hmm -"

Looking at him, with one hand on the door, she glances over her shoulder at him. "Come on, let's do this -"

Lacing her fingers through his, she grabs their coats and her clutch, and they leave her bedroom to join the others waiting for them in the lounge.

❋ ❋ ❋

Walking into the private room at the Sheraton South, which Miles prepared for their dinner; Harriet scans the room. She can see all her mother's family, Sal, and Wanda, Will with Sophie, Paige, Harper and Glenn. Also attending the dinner are Damon's groomsmen, friends from school and the Manhattan society.

Harriet also takes time to assess the room. Being a professional party planner, she can't help but take time to notice the little "intricacies around the room. Going with the same theme and style choices as their engagement party, purple chiffon and taffeta have been hung where appropriate to enchant the room. The staff has lined the ceiling, covering it with fairy lights that meet in the centre of the room under a beautifully lit chandelier.

Very much like the engagement party but with fewer people, there are three large rectangular tables situated in the middle of the

room forming the shape of a horseshoe. The tables are lined with white tablecloths, silver cutlery, and champagne flutes. Last but not least, each table is adorned with purple and pink roses. Their vases have been beautifully crafted with lace and pearls.

Placing her bag down on her chair in the middle of the centre table, she takes a glass of champagne from the waiter and walks back to the door to stand with her bridesmaids; Paige, Sophie and Karen when much to her surprise Damon's parents walk into the room.

Beverly, who is wearing a look best described as if a truck has just run over her; scans the room with narrowed eyes and postures herself with her nose up in the air and her look radiating immediate disapproval. Assuming these are his parents, Harriet's father begins to make the short walk over to them. Harriet who is watching holds her breath and calms herself for a less than a positive result.

Instead, to her amazement; Damon's father sees her and smiles. He walks straight up to her and pulls her in for a loving hug.

Kissing her the cheek, he smiles and then looks around the room to see her father walking their way.

"Good Evening, Mr Bennett. Thank you for coming"

Smiling at her, "Nonsense. Wouldn't miss it for the world. And Harriet, its Robert.' Looking over to Frank, "Is this your Father?"

Harriet nods and smiles. "Yes – ', gesturing to her father who has joined them. "This is my father Frank Lancer', gesturing to her mother who is at the tables and most likely rearranging seating arrangements. "And my mother Gloria is just over there."

Robert takes his hand and shakes Frank's hand. "Excellent. Lovely to finally meet you both. You have a remarkable daughter. I'm so please that Damon finally found someone to ground him." Harriet smiles as her future-father-in-law, declares "He is so lucky to have you, my dear."

She smiles again. Robert looks around the room and then back at his wife. "My wife, Beverly is over there' he looks towards Harriet's parents 'don't take too much notice of her. She always looks like that"

Harriet bites her lip to stifle a giggle.

Robert smiles at her. "Would anyone like a drink?". Frank nodding, "I loved one. I might come with you."

Robert nodding happily, "Of course, where's the bar?" and leaves with Mr Lancer. Sophie is has been standing behind Harriet with Paige, comes to stand next to Harriet. Smiling at Harriet, as they watch Robert and Frank walk off in search of the bar, is curious about Robert's insinuations.

"Harriet, what did he mean about Damon's mother?"

Harriet looks to Sophie and takes a deep breath. "You'll know soon enough. She's not such a nice lady. She has claws, Sophie, be careful and tread lightly."

Sophie's eyes grow wide but then soften as the truth comes to her mind. "Well Harriet, they obviously adore you despite his mother." Harriet smiles and nods. "Thanks, Sophie. Come on, let's go get this party started!!!"

Across the room, Harper and Glenn walk in towards Damon. Harper is waving at Harriet who is talking with her Aunt Wanda, smiles back her brother, patting his shoulder.

"I'm so happy for the both of you', turning Harriet's direction, 'I'm going to have a sister. I always wanted a sister."

Harriet excuses herself and makes the walk over to Damon, Harper and Glenn. Harriet reaching them pulls Harper into a hug.

"Hey, you made it. I'm so glad you're here."

Harper smiling. "I was just telling the men here, how happy I am that I'm getting a sister."

Harriet giggles and looks to Damon. Smirking at her, "I thought you did have a sister?"

Damon, who's been taking a sip of his drink is now widely alert and shooting glares at Harriet.

Harriet smiles back at Harper who is now giggling too, "He's so easy."

Damon takes Harriet into his arms. Her back against his chest. "Oh, am I now?", turning in his arms, she kisses him on the cheek.

"Yes. So very easy!"

Harper and Glenn, who are now standing together, smile at them as Frank joins them and requests they sit. "Hello', holding his hand out, 'I'm Harriet's father, Frank. Thank you for coming."

Harper smiles. "Hello Mr Lancer, I'm Harper, and this is my husband Glenn', turning to Glenn, 'I'm Damon's sister!"

Frank, his face lighting up as he claps his hands together. "Marvellous. Wonderful to meet you. We are all going to take our seats, would you like to come and join us. Your father is already here and your mother', looking around the room, 'Ah, she's here somewhere."

Harper nods. "Yes, I did here she has made an appearance', gently touching Frank's arm, 'I'm sorry about that."

They all giggle and make the walk to the tables to sit.

Harriet and Damon take their seats in the middle of the centre table. Glenn and Harper are seated to Damon's left with his parents and groomsmen. Taking a sip of her drink, Harriet continues to look around at the beauty of the room, when her thoughts are interrupted by Harper and Glenn, who are curious as to what Damon has organised for their honeymoon.

Glenn looks to Damon. "Damon, where are you two honeymooning?"

Harriet, who is giggling yet again but intrigued. "Yes, Damon. Where are we honeymooning?"

Damon takes her arm and pulls her closer to him. "I was thinking Paris."

He kisses her nose, and she smiles. "I've never been to Paris!"

Watching them, Harper whispers to Glenn and nestles back into his arm that's placed around the top of the chair. They smile looking at them both. She whispers to her husband, "My baby brother. He's finally found the one. I can't believe it!"

Damon looks over at Harper. "Father is mingling well." Their parents who haven't taken their seats yet, leave Damon and Harper to ponder as to their whereabouts. Harper smiles back. "Yes. I think he's quite taken with Harriet's Father and Uncle."

Harriet giggles. "Well, that's great', looking up at Damon, 'at least, that's one of your parents who is having a good time."

Rolling her eyes, Harper nods. "Yeah, I don't even know where she got to."

Placing a finger on her nose, he assures that he'll sort it out. Letting her go, he whispers. "I might just go find her and have a word before we begin here."

Harriet nods and smiles. Noticing the discomfort that her mother has caused, Harper reaches over and takes Harriet's hand reassuringly in hers. "Come on Harriet, let's go have a drink," and they walk off towards to the private bar in the room.

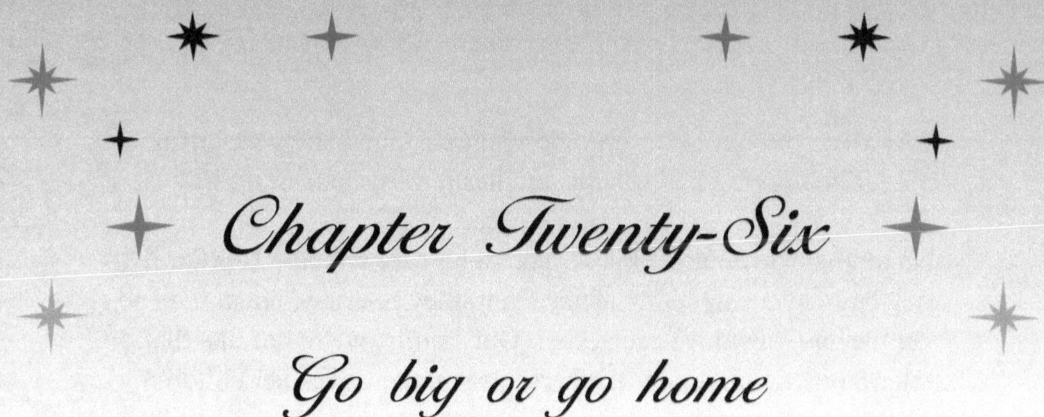

Chapter Twenty-Six

Go big or go home

A couple of hours have passed, and Harriet is seated at the table having a drink with Harper, Paige, and Sophie. Looking up from her glass of champagne, she looks around and sees that Damon is not in the room. He told her that he would find out where his mother wondered off to, but that was hours ago, and she thought he would've at least been back by now.

Glancing down at her watch and seeing the night approaching nine o'clock, she assumes that her father will want to start speeches soon and her mother's lot will want desserts to be served soon.

Putting her glass down, she says to the girls. "I'm going to go and find Damon. If Dad asks, tell him, I won't be long."

Harriet slips out of the room and walks towards the restaurant. She is about to walk past the general bar when she notices Beverly and Damon sitting in a booth. They are huddled over, having a quiet but hostile argument and neither seem to have noticed that Harriet has entered the room and stands behind the booth.

Resting against the wooden partition, she eavesdrops on their conversation and quickly catches on to the subject of the argument. Freezing in the spot, stunned that his mother had the audacity to show up and ruin their night, she can't help but stay and eavesdrop.

Damon, you cannot go through with this. She is all wrong
for you. She is not acceptable to our way of life!!!

Mother, you have no idea. She's amazing, and she's beautiful.
She's loving and caring, and her family is amazing!!!!
Oh please!
No mother!!! You don't know. You don't care either!!! Her family,
they truly love each other. They fight, they're crazy, but at the end
of the day, they love each other. Our family, we're not like that.
Her mother, you're not like hers. Her mother loves her children.
Damon, that's enough. You're being rude and disrespectful.
No Mother!!!
Damon, listen. You need to talk to Lucy. You need to know something
Oh please, don't start this again!!!
Damon, I'm serious. She's still in love with
you. At least, she has a talent

Feeling like her ears are going to explode, Harriet exits the bar, having heard enough and figuring that Damon will enlighten her with the conversation later on. But instead of instantly returning to the party; she walks the opposite direction of the private room and instead towards the alfresco patio, needing a moment alone, just to be by herself.

Reaching the railing, she leans against it and takes a deep breath. Looking out at the view of the grounds, she rubs her forehead

and is startled when feels someone presence next to her.

"Harriet"

She turns to see Nate. Eyebrows crinkled, confused at his presence, she asks. "What are you doing here?"

"Halley and I were having dinner when I saw you storm out of the bar."

"Of course, you did!!!"

Slightly infuriated by her comment. "And what's supposed to mean -"

"Don't worry about it. Pretend you didn't hear me." She turns away from him and looks up at the stars. Her stars.

Instead of leaving, he remains standing next to her. "Aren't you, I mean, isn't it your rehearsal dinner tonight?"

"Yeah -"

He looks around. "Well, why are you out here?"

"Just needed a minute."

He laughs and shakes his head. "I'd think that it was a sign, not to go through with it."

She straightens, whipping her head to glare at him. The combination of Damon's mother and Nate's unwanted presence finally overwhelms her, and she snaps. "I'm sorry. I must have forgotten that I take what you think into consideration when it comes to my relationship and wedding. Nate, you have no idea. Damon and I adore each other, and we're getting married next month so I'd appreciate it if you'd keep your thoughts to yourself. You lost the right to comment on my life a long time ago!"

She turns on her heels, about to walk from him when he curls his hand around her upper arm. Pulling her close to him, "Don't marry him. Please, just don't marry him!"

Releasing her arm from his, a painful look spreads across her face as she looks back at him. "Why?"

Her frantic almost shrilling reply sends a chill through him. It was the first time they've touched each other in ten years. Finally, seeing her as he should. No longer a girl but a fully grown woman with her own life. Agony strikes his chest and stomach and like a dagger to his soul, its as if all the butterflies he once had finally shrivelled up and died. He realises that she grew up and he had been a coward, but most importantly, he had loved her. He was still in love with her.

She is like the wind to him. She is everywhere and everything around him and when she wasn't, her passion and essence was eing carried to him. Through the trees, over the fence, written across the stars at night. Straight into his head. Straight into his heart.

"Harriet, please. Just please don't marry *him*!"

"Why shouldn't I marry him, Nate?"

Tears begin to well in her eyes. Grabbing him by the shoulders, as panic rises in her voice. "Why don't I deserve a happily ever after?".

She sighs a deep hurtful sob.

"What's so wrong with me that I don't deserve to be happy and with a man who adores me?"

Stuck, Nate takes her arms off his shoulders. Unsure of what to say to her. His once knightly demeanour has slipped, and he finds he's retreating into his old cowardly ways.

Assessing him, her eyes attempt to make contact with his. "Is it because of what happened? You think I don't deserve to be happy? I don't deserve at least a chance? Yeah. That's what I thought. You never could be honest with me. It must kill you to have to declare how you really feel, how does Halley bare it?"

Looking to the ground, she shakes her head in disgust until finally, she glances back at him. "Go home, Nate. Find Halley and from now on this, you and me, we don't know each other okay. I can't do this anymore. I deserve better than this. I love Damon, and I can't do this anymore. After 19 years, I'm done. I'm exhausted and well and truly over it!!!"

Straightening up, she wipes her face. Taking a deep breath and heads back towards the room.

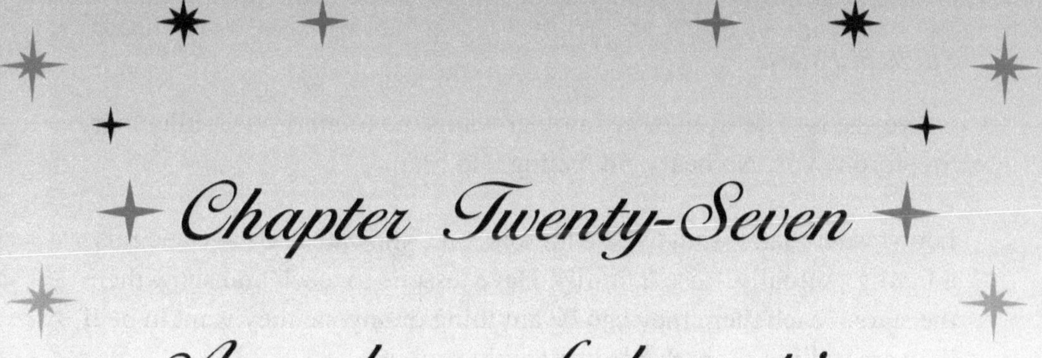

Chapter Twenty-Seven

An exchange of pleasantries

☆ Damon ☆

I can't believe my mother. I mean, *how dare* she show up to Harriet and I's rehearsal dinner. Then pull me out into the bar, to talk to me about my nuptials with Harriet.

I sit there, looking at my mother. She is ranting on about what society will think (blah blah blah!!!)

Now, she's talking about Lucy and how I have to speak to her. How crazy is that? I mean, considering she was the one who suggested to me in the first place, that I needed to ditch her.

Lucy is a talented ballet dancer, now living in Chicago and making a name for herself, so of course, my mother wants to make ties to that industry now. What she doesn't realise is that if we stayed together, Lucy wouldn't have pursued her career. At Harper's wedding, all she could talk about what how we should get married and have children. How she had accepted that she wasn't the most talented ballet dancer at ABC, New York.

Only I didn't feel the same. I never did. Well until, I met a feisty event planner with glamourous brunette hair, sparkling brown eyes and luscious curves. From the moment, she walked into my life I haven't been able to think of my life without her. She's refreshing and different. She has dreams, and she's passionate. She's worked her ass off to get where she is. The women my mother wants me to marry are ridiculous. Stepford wives. No heart, no feeling. No brain.

I don't want that. I want to be with someone who wants to have and raise a family. Actually, raise a family. Have lessons to teach and show them the stars. Teach them they can be anything or anyone they want to be if they are willing to work hard and truly want it.

Why can't Mother see, that's what I want. I want Harriet. Why can't she see that?

Her family is amazing; I've never known that kind of love and support. Sure, she has a tough relationship with her mother, who doesn't but the end of the day; I know they love each other. I want to be a part of that. I am apart of that.

I've had enough. I can't sit across from my mother and listen to her carry on like a bitter hag. Harriet is probably wondering where I am. Standing up, I leave my mother's presence and walk back towards the function room.

As I leave the room, I see Harriet in her beautiful purple lace dress. Her dark brown moving with the wind as she stares up at the

stars in the sky, the place where her mind goes to escape from her thoughts.

Then I notice Nate.

He is standing behind her watching. His eyes follow her train of thought, and as he approaches her, a smile brightens his face as if the slightest glimpse of her. Standing there, watching him watching my fiancé; I can't help but feel rage overcome me.

My once relaxed hands are forming into fists.

Of course, he'd be here. Anywhere the Lancer's go, he's there tagging along or following Harriet around like a lovesick puppy.

I creep closer towards the doorway, watching their interaction with each other.

His hand on her upper arm, he is pulling her closer to him but she is not welcoming in him, and then I hear Harriet.

"I'm sorry. I must have forgotten that I take what you think into consideration when it comes to my relationship and wedding.

Nate, you have no idea. Damon and I adore each other, and we're getting married next month, so I'd appreciate it if you'd keep your thoughts to yourself. You lost the right to comment on my life a long time ago."

Obviously, done with him and wanting to get back inside to me, he leans in closer to her. Blocking her escape.

"Harriet, please. Just please don't marry him!"

Angrily she persecutes him. I watch as her voice gains momentum. I am familiar with that tone. I hate that tone.

"Why shouldn't I marry him, Nate?"

I am surprised though when I think I see her eyes glistening. Maybe it's my imagination, but surely she is not wasting any more

tears on this asshole, but I am outsmarted by my faith when I see her grab him by the shoulders and the panic that is rising in her voice.

"Why don't I deserve a happily ever after?"

She sighs a deep hurtful sob. *I really can't watch this.*

"What's so wrong with me that I don't deserve to be happy and with a man who adores me?"

Oh no. *I'm such a fricken twat.* She's not trying to find out how he feels about her. She's asking him for forgiveness, *I think.*

"Is it because of what happened? You think I don't deserve to be happy; I don't deserve at least a chance?"

He is just standing there. *What a gutless coward.* He's not saying anything. Maybe he doesn't love her as much as I thought he did.

"Yeah. That's what I thought. You never could be honest with me. It must kill you to have to declare how you really feel. How does Halley bare it?"

Looking to the ground, she shakes her head in disgust until finally, she glances back at him. She's done. I can tell.

"Go home, Nate. Find Halley and from now on this, you and me, we don't know each other okay. I can't do this anymore. I deserve better than this. I love Damon, and I can't do this anymore. After 19 years, I'm done. I'm exhausted and well and truly over it!!!"

Then off she goes. Righting herself as she leaves to return to the room. Probably thinking well that's precious time that I've wasted and will never get back again. She doesn't see me as I move behind a door out of her vision.

I step back into view and turn to make my way back before I do though; I stop to look back at Nate. He's annoyed and angry.

Watching him as he turns and makes his way back inside stopping when he sees me perched against the door, watching him.

"Damon, hey. How's it going, mate?"

Looking at him, I shake my head. "I'm not your mate -"

Nate's eyes narrow and then immediately become cautious.

"What was that?" I demand from him, only he replies too coolly. "What was what?"

He's playing the dumb card.

Gesturing to the outside patio, I snap. "That thing that just happened with Harriet."

Fidgeting in his spot, I watch as Nate remains speechless. Yeah, he's the coward I thought him to be.

"Nate. Stop. Whatever it is. Just stop. We're getting married in less than a month."

Anger flashes in Nate's eyes. "You don't deserve her!"

"Oh, and you do?"

Cockiness becomes Nate as he smiles smugly back at me. "She will come to her senses soon, and when she does, I will be there to hold her hand."

"Wow. You really think highly of yourself don't you?"

Nate shakes his head. "No. I just know your kind of people. Quick to judge and okay to snub everyday people."

Looking at him, I watch as a scowl spreads across his face and I shake my head in disgust, tired of his antics.

"I love her Nate. I would never hurt her."

"You say that now, but what happens a couple of years down the track when you realise you might have made a mistake and she was better off with someone else?", he growls.

"Nate. Back off. I get your angry. I would be too if the woman I was still in love with after all these years was marrying someone else, but you have to stop this. It's done. We're happy. We'll be married in a week, and we're going to live long happy lives together."

Nate snaps at him. Trying to shut down the reminder of those feelings from ever seeing the light of day. "I never said I was in love with her."

"Then *why* are you *here* then. Meeting with her private at her wedding dinner rehearsal. Grabbing her arm and whispering to her behind closed doors? Why do any of it, *if you're not in love with her?*"

"She just . . . she deserves better", he cowers.

"Well, I'll take that into consideration. Thank you for your kind wishes and concerns on Harriet's wellbeing, but we have a rehearsal dinner to be getting back to."

Turning my back, I move towards the function room in search of Harriet. Once inside the room, I pan across the room until her seated between Sophie, Paige and Harper with a drink in hand, smiling from ear to ear, all giggling like school girls. My need for reassurance, to hold her in my arms, overwhelms me and I move towards them.

And as if by magic, she meets my eyes and smiles, it's the smile that is painted across her face when she is most happy. I am almost there when without words, she stands and meet me mid-journey. Wrapping her arms around my body, she rests her head on my chest and grabs hold of me tightly.

Whatever doubt had been brewing in my mind regarding Nate seemingly disappears as I force the ill thoughts of Nate and Harriet out of my mind. Reaching down at her, I place her hand mine and kiss its palm softly. I continue to smile as I go on to gently cup her chin and run my fingers against her jaw before locking eyes with hers. She smiles sweetly before kissing my neck and placing her head back on my chest.

Standing there, we become lost in our own private serendipitous moment that is, until Harriet's father taps a glass with a spoon gathering everyone's attention as he prepares to make a speech.

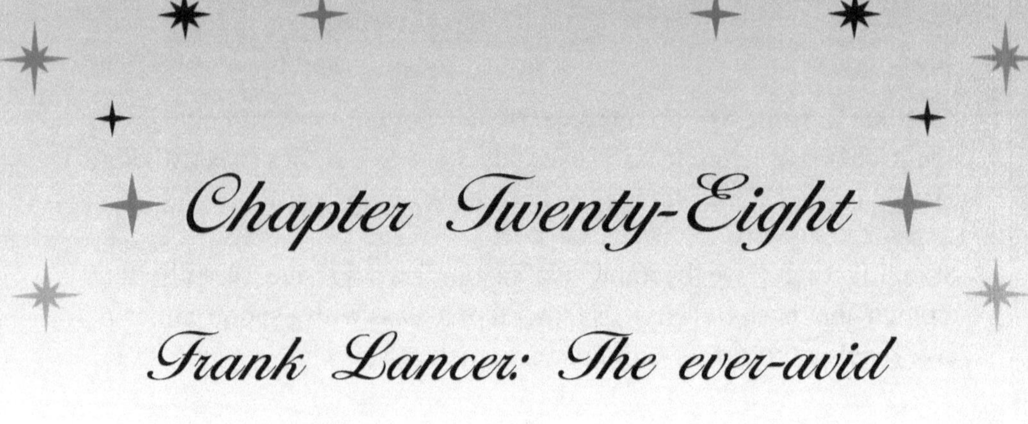

I know my family thinks I purposely don't pay attention, but they're wrong. The truth is, I see and hear everything. So, when I saw that boy from next door hanging around outside my Harriet's dinner rehearsal, I knew something was up. Don't get me wrong; he's a good kid. He is. Despite his absent-minded parents, he turned out into quite a well-adjusted young man with a good eye for business.

Yet there is one thing that unnerves me about him, and it's his interest in my daughter. For instance, I never said anything when she came home in tears at age nine because some silly girl humiliated her only to later find out that Nate got a month's detention for doing something to the girl. I never said anything the night I came home to find that my wife and daughter got into a fight and Harriet disappeared only to reappear on the back of his bike later that night. I didn't say anything when I saw her get out of his car the morning after her prom and I certainly never said a word to anyone after seeing her jump the fence the morning after her eighteenth birthday.

I know it might sound irresponsible and unfatherly of me, but I trust my daughter. I know that something happened between them and when she is ready, she'll tell me. But I also can understand why she hasn't said anything. She is my daughter after all, and she knows that we have a family full of drama queens.

So when I saw that boy outside the room, I found myself wanting to know why he was there. He wasn't invited, and I almost felt sorry for the boy. He was like the older brother to her that Will wasn't growing up. I don't blame Will though. My wife is a force to be reckoned with and loves her son. I think this got to Will's head and he definitely played on it.

As I watched Damon walk back into the room and approach us, his father and I, for a drink I excused myself and went in search of Nate. Departing the room, I see Nate heading towards the front doors of the hotel.

Calling out to him, I yelled. "Nate"

Turning he looks back to me, "Mr Lancer?"

Stopping, I take a moment to recover and leaning over slightly, I take a steady breath. Meeting his eyes, I start.

"Nate, you know you are almost like a son to me, and I care about you. I do. I only want for you to be happy."

"Yes, sir. Thank you."

"Well, why do I get the impression that you're not?"

"Not what, sir?"

"Happy?"

"Oh???"

"Nate, I'm not blind. I know my family thinks I am, but I'm not. Or deaf. I know things, and I also know that when a man shows up uninvited to a party, he's not invited to, to speak with or catch a glimpse of a woman that isn't his. Well, that tells me that something is bothering you. It's making you unhappy."

Watching him, I look on as he nods gravely back at me.

"Son, I know you love my daughter, and I also know that you want only the best for her."

Nate nods in agreement back at me, but as Harriet's father, I feel the need to say the words that I will later hate myself for.

"My Harriet is happy, Nate. I only want her happiness. I've only ever wanted to see her happy. And right now, she is happier than I've ever seen her. I'm asking, as her father, please don't do anything to ruin this for her. Please think about it before you do something that could hurt her and ruin her happiness. Maybe she was yours once but right now, she is Damon's, and that boy is set on making her life a joyous one. So have a think about it, will you, son?"

Nate nods silently, his face lifeless and grim. Turning around slowly, he moves towards the doors and disappears through them.

Standing, I watch him. That poor broken man that I have just warned off. I feel about as small as a grain of sand right now. I know it was an awful thing to say, but for the sake of my daughter's happiness, it needed to be said. He'll be okay. He'll let it go and hopefully find someone to move on with.

Turning around myself, I head back into the room. Reaching the bar, I go to order a drink but am interrupted as Robert immediately hands me a drink as I watch my son walks towards me with the microphone in hand. Well, drink up. I guess it's speech time!!!

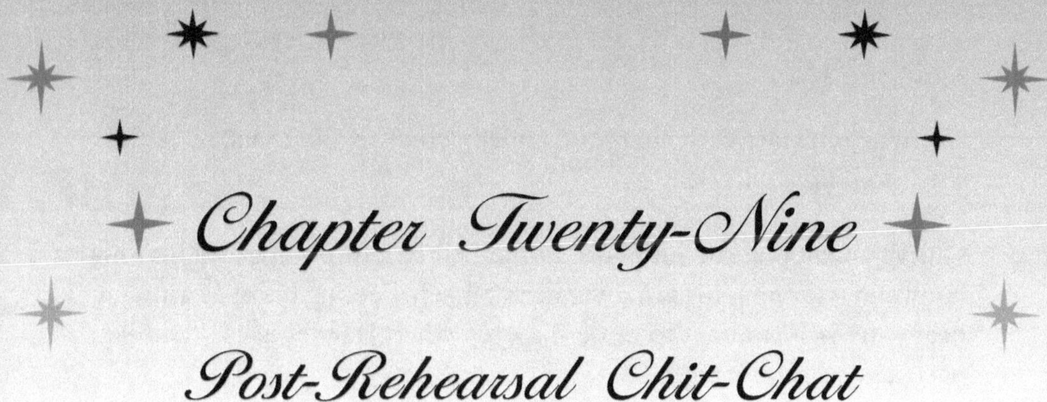

Chapter Twenty-Nine

Post-Rehearsal Chit-Chat

Returning home from the Sheraton, an extremely tired Harriet walks straight to her room to change into her pyjamas. Dead on her feet and her head swirling from copious amounts of champagne, she looks around her room. Sitting on her bed, she looks to her bedside table to where two paperback novels sit. Picking one up, she runs her fingers over its spine and reads its title.

"Ah. Anne of Green Gables. Anne Shirley and Gilbert Blythe."

She smiles. Remembering Anne's escapades, picturing their characters in her head. Picking up the other book, she didn't even have to look to know which book this was. It's cover rattier than any other due to use. Flipping through its pages, she stops a page that has been earmarked for quotes and smiling; she reads the quote.

"To be fond of dancing was a certain step towards falling in love – Jane Austen."

Leaning back into her bed, she makes herself comfortable and opens the book. Looking to her right, she wonders where Damon escaped to and unbeknown to her, he has been outside in the Lancer's backyard, sitting on her trampoline eyeing down Nate's house and recreating the night's event in his mind.

Rubbing his forehead, he feels like his head is going to explode but instead, a yawn escapes from his body. Standing up, he returns to the house to join Harriet in her room. Quietly entering the room, he notices she is still up.

Quickly changing, he joins her in the bed before pulling her into his body and wrapping his arm over her stomach. Feeling his eyes growing heavy, he is just about to close his eyes when Harriet asks. "Did you have a good time tonight?"

Leaning down into her neck, "Yes I did. . . . I was surprised to see Nate there though."

Tensing in his arms, she shakes her head. "So was I. I didn't invite him. I think Will might've told him."

"Does he always just show up?", Damon snaps.

Turning around to face Damon, she notes. "Kind of. It's annoying actually. I wish someone would give him a clue at times you know."

"So you don't think it has anything to do with you?"

Cocking an eyebrow, her eyes narrow as she snipes back. "If you have something to say, Damon, I'd rather you just say it!!!"

"You know what I meant Harriet. The guy seems to show up whenever you're around, it's just well, suspicious that's all!"

She sits up in the bed, pushing him off her and sits upright against the bed's head. "Well, Damon, for your information; he's had years to make the situation right. To pick up the phone and talk to me. I've wasted too much time worrying about how he feels and what happened between us. I'm over it. He needs to get a clue. I'm not interested. I'm in love and engaged to this amazing guy who I thought knew me well enough to trust my own heart."

Feeling foolish, he remains quiet.

"You know the weekend of Harper's wedding when I came back here to attend my Will's wedding; he abused me for coming home. He knew that I was planning it too. I mean, I get that he was angry at me but telling me I shouldn't have come home to go to my only brother's wedding. What kind of heartless prick says that to someone?"

Sitting up in the bed, Damon joins her by placing his arm around her shoulder to pull her into him. Rubbing his hand against her shoulder, he tries to reassure her that everything will be okay. "Don't worry about it, Harriet. I'm sure he'll get over it and find someone."

"So did you and your mother have a nice chat tonight?", she impishly smiles.

Meeting her eyes, he smirks. "Usual pleasantries. Told her to go to hell."

Leaning in, Damon kisses his fiancé softly before softly yawning. Watching his yawn brings on a yawn and she motions for them to move back into the bed. Reaching over to her lamp, she switches off, and they are met with darkness as it fills the room. Turning to face Damon, she whispers *Night* before nestling her head against his chest. Kissing her nose, he smiles before resting his head on her crown and whispering *Night* back.

It doesn't take long for Harriet to feel Damon's chest humming away peacefully in a dead sleep but her, the ability to fall soundly isn't coming as easily. Her mind, an ever-growing minefield consumed by thoughts from the night's events that she just can't seem to shake. Closing her eyes, she attempts to sleep as her mind replays the low points of the night before she falls into a deep sleep herself.

Don't marry him. Please just don't marry him . . . Not him . . . Please just don't marry him.

Damon, you cannot go through with this. She is all wrong for you. She is not acceptable to our way of life.

Damon, listen. You need to talk to Lucy. You need to know something . . . Oh please, don't start this again?

Damon, I'm serious. She's still in love with you. At least, she has a talent.

Why shouldn't I marry him, Nate . . . Why don't I deserve a happily ever after?

What's so wrong with me that I don't deserve to be happy and with a man who adores me?

H & D
You are cordially invited to attend
the marriage of

Harriet Arabella Lancer
and
Damon Thomas Bennett

Saturday 23rd June
2pm
The Cathedral Church
of Saint John Devine

1047 Amsterdam Avenue
112th Street
New York

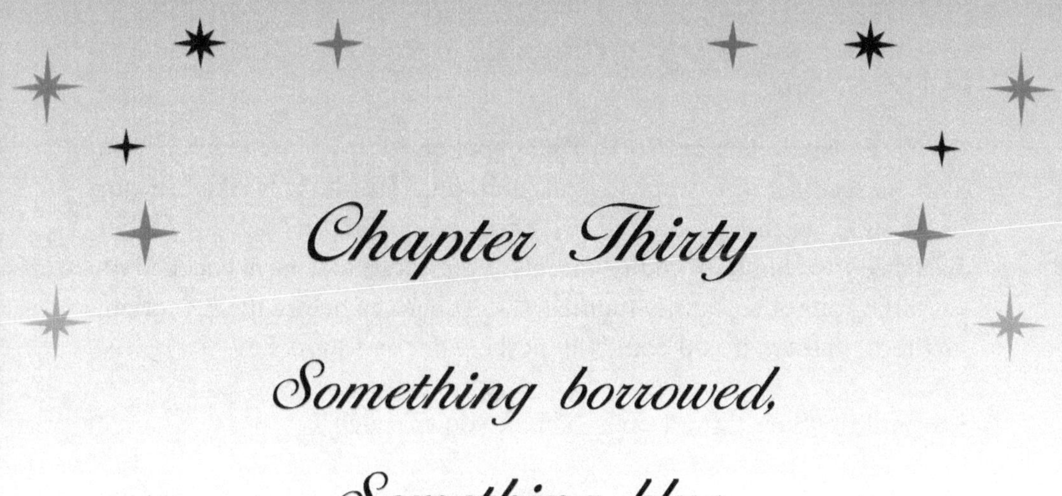

Chapter Thirty

Something borrowed,

Something blue

Waking in her bed the morning of her wedding, Harriet realises it's the first time she's slept alone in almost four years.

Feeling calm and rested, she jumps out of her bed and makes it. Grabbing her robe off her vintage French satin-lined bedroom chair, she jumps into the shower quickly so that she can meet up with Sophie, Karen and Paige at her parent's suite at The Plaza.

As soon as she is dressed and dries her hair off, she takes her luggage that she packed the night before and puts them up on the

bed. Double checking that she has everything she needs, she zips them up and takes them down the stairs and leaves them in front of her front door. Going around the apartment, she checks her windows are locked and that her lights are turned off. Leaving the apartment, she locks her door and packs the luggage into her car.

Pulling up in front of the hotel, she parks her car out front for the valet and grabs her things. Walking inside, she makes for the concierge's desk.

"Miss Lancer, good morning."

"Good Morning Lewis, how's your day going so far?"

"Busy as usual Harriet. So I've just spoken with Louis, the function room is ready if you want to look and your family is booked in our finest suites at the discounted price we spoke about as per our earlier discussion. So far, only you're parents and bridesmaids have checked in. I assume your other family members will check in before the reception. Just remind them if you could about the valet parking, okay."

She smiles. "Sure thing Lewis. Thank you so much."

"Anything for you Harriet," he comments as he hands her a key to her suite and a key to Sophie's suite that her bridesmaids are in.

"So are you nervous?", asks Lewis.

Taking a deep breath, she beams. "No. I'm good."

"That's great to hear. Well, I might go and start your preparations. If you did want to go check out the function room, you don't need any permission from the staff to do so okay."

"Thanks, Lewis."

"That's okay Harriet. And congratulations", he nods as she moves off.

"Thank you for everything. I'll see you later okay."

She smiles and makes the walk to the elevators. As she steps inside and pushes the button. She takes it to the 18th floor and finds

Room 252. Knocking on the door, she smiles as Sophie answers the door.

"Hey!!!", they say in unison, and as they hug, Harriet can feel Sophie's bump rub up against her. Harriet looks down and smiles at her bump. Sophie looks at her belly and covers it gently.

"I know can you believe it? We had a scan last week. Everything looks good."

"That's great, Sophie.", Harriet nods happily.

"Who knows, this could be you in a few months too?", Sophie smirks. Her comment prompts Harriet to stop and think. For the first time in the day, she is beginning to feel nervous about her nuptials. Pushing them away into her mind, she moves into the suite and sees Paige with Karen sitting on chairs.

Taking a seat next to them, she smiles. Her Aunt Wanda will arrive soon to do her hair and make-up.

"Hey ladies. Looking good."

They smile at her as Harriet looks at the stylists to thank them. "Thanks for doing this Monica and Stacey. I really do appreciate it."

Monica looks up from Paige's hair and smiles. "What are you kidding? I am happy to do this for you. After everything you did for me at my own wedding, I would do anything for you."

Stacey nods profusely, "And well, if I ever get married. I assume that you'll help me if I need it!!!"

Shaking her head merrily, they all giggle together as Sophie hands Harriet a flute of champagne.

"So Harriet, are you ready to start?"

Looking up from her phone, Harriet looks to the girls. "Wanda is on her way up. I showered before I left home. My dress is in the other room and my luggage is over there. So yeah. I'm pretty good hey."

Paige looks over to her older sister. "Wow Harriet, you're really organised!"

Harriet shakes her head at her. "Really Paige? Are you kidding me with this right now? This is what I do!"

❋ ❋ ❋

When Wanda finished Harriet's hair and makeup; her hair composed up into a simple 1930's side updo and make-up in modest but elegant tones, she put on her wedding dress. Stepping into the dress, she pulls it up over her. Designed by a friend, the dress is a beautiful white A-line, vintage-styled, organza dress with a tulle bateau neckline with hand-beaded lace. The bodice also adorned beaded lace and an asymmetrically cut skirt with scalloped frills spilling down the back's centre. For the first time in her life, Harriet feels like a true princess.

Looking at herself in the mirror, her face is glowing. She is still looking at herself in the mirror when Wanda gently taps on the door and lets herself in. Holding her hands up in a praying gesture, she places them against her lips. Her eyes glistening, she smiles at her god-daughter.

"Oh Harriet, you look so beautiful."

Moving towards her, Harriet's hands are trying to zip up the back of her dress, but Wanda gently places her hands on them and stands behind her. "Here honey, let me" as she gently pulls the zip closed. Taking a moment to look in the reflection of the same mirror that Harriet is watching her godmother in, they share a smile.

Wanda leans in over her shoulder and smiles. "I'm so very proud of you. You know that. And I'm so very honoured to be your godmother. You know that too!"

Nodding, she blushes with tears glistening in her eyes, her aunt continues. "I know that you and were Mother have a delicate relationship but no disrespect to my sister, but I always have thought of you as my own. I love you so very much Harriet! You are so amazing, kind and strong that I know you will be very happy!"

246

Taking her hand and placing it over her Aunt's, Harriet nods. "I love you, Aunt Wanda. Thank you. I couldn't have gotten anywhere without you and Sal."

"That's okay honey. We know. But we'd do anything for you; you're worth it. Don't ever forget that, okay dear!"

Wanda looks around and sees Harriet's shoes on the bed. "Right, enough girl talk. Let's get the shoes and veil on"

Crouching down, Wanda slowly lifts her dress as Harriet steps into her low-heel satin pumps. On the tip of the shoes, are round blue jewelled brooches which shape match her Swarovski crystal earrings and matching necklace. The veil is pinned into her hair by her Aunt and to finish, Harriet pulls on her garter over her thigh. Its white lace and blue ribbon matching the colour tones of her shoe brooches.

Stepping out of the room, she moves towards the small party that now has gathered in the suite. Greeted by her parents, her bridesmaids and some of her aunts, Harriet looks over her bridesmaids in their beautiful lilac 50's style dresses with lace bateau, full skirts and purple bows on the back. Their hair curled and waved, pulled up into a side ponytail.

Karen hands Harriet her bouquet. Fondling it in her fingers, she admires the florist's work and quality of flowers: each bouquet, including her own, a full of an assortment of white, pink-purple roses with little crystals entwined throughout with a purple ribbon tied around its handle.

Taking a deep breath, they are ready to go. As they all depart the suite, her father waits until its only just Harriet and him, left in the room. Taking his daughter in his arms, he gently hugs her and smiles. "You look beautiful honey."

"Thanks, Dad. You look pretty awesome. Love the suit!"

His belly jiggles. "Thanks, sweetheart. So you ready???"

She nods. "Yeah Dad –," she replies before taking a deep breath, confidently she confers. "I am."

"Okay. Well, I'll go on down. Your mother will be waiting. We'll see you at the church okay!"

Kissing her on the cheek, he steps away, and they exit the room. Joining the girls outside, they move to make their way downstairs to the hotel foyer to wait for their rides to the church.

❄ ❄ ❄

Damon is already at the church, and he looks nervous. Trying to put on a front, he deflects his thoughts by greeting and smiling as

guests pour into the church. Ignoring looks from his family as they all sit cautiously in the first row in front of the altar, he feels relief at the sight of Will's arrival and his presence beside him.

Watching Damon and sensing, he's nervous; Will tries to defuse the situation. Slapping his shoulder, he grins. "It'll be all over before you know it. Everyone gets nervous on the big day."

Smiling grimly at Will's comments, Damon begins fidgeting with his tie, and as he fits a finger in between his shirt and neck, he slowly begins to feel like he can't breathe. His hands are sweating profusely, he glances down at them as they shake haphazardly back up at him. Watching on, a concerned Will is nervous, and as he continues to stand beside the man whom his sister is about to tie her life with, a harrowing thought overwhelms him. That this may not be the happiest day of his little sister's life and that she may just be about to get her heart broken.

❄ ❄ ❄

Standing out front of the Plaza, Harriet is running over last minute details with the concierge and chef when her bridal car arrives.

248

Her bridal party had already at the church. Her father planned to ride with Harriet but her mother, feeling the need to create extra drama on the day, felt it unnecessary that Frank rides with Harriet when they should be at the church greeting the guests. Besides, Harriet was a fully grown woman; she didn't need her father to ride beside her.

Opening the door of the car, she slides into the dark blue Bentley rented just for her. Gathering up her dress, she organises the skirt around the back seat of the car before tapping on the partition for the driver to drive on.

Looking out the window, she takes a deep breath as the car pulls out onto the street. Trying to ease her building nerves, she looks out at the window. Straining her neck to look up past the city skyline, she searches through the clouds to make shapes. Only her attempts are thwarted, when she hears a familiar voice over the car's speaker.

"There's not many clouds in the sky today. The Harriet I know would take that as a sign."

Watching as the partition comes down, she turns to watch as Nate's face becomes visible in the rear vision mirror.

"I thought . . . I thought that you weren't going to -"

Nate looking at her, with deep concern as to why she's so interested considering she is about to marry another man, just continues to look at her. "Yeah well . . . Change of plans."

Closing her eyes, she wants to avoid seeing his face.

"Nate -"

Glazing back at her, he remains hopeful that she still might change her mind.

"Yes -"

Taking a deep, steady breath, she looks out the window at the scenery move by outside instead of meeting his eyes in the rearview mirror. "You're not going to interfere today, are you?"

Nate avoiding looking at her back looks out at the road and not at her in the rear-view. His jaw tightening, its muscle jumping.

"No . . . No, I'm not."

At his reply, Harriet feels a tear expel from her eye and fall slowly down her cheek. Wiping it away, she sees the church within the distance and begins to shift on the back seat to prepare her exit from the car. When the car stops, Harriet's father comes to the door and opens it. Leaving Nate firmly fixed in his seat behind the wheel. Taking her hand, Frank Lancer helps his daughter out, and Nate watches on from his seat as they begin their journey up the stairs for her impending walk down the aisle.

Watching her smile, as Paige drapes her veil over her head, Nate becomes lost at the view of Harriet in her beautiful dress. As her father loops her arm through his and they begin their walk down the church's aisle, Nate feels sick to the stomach. When the church doors close behind them, he realises that the butterflies from his stomach had finally all shrivelled up and died.

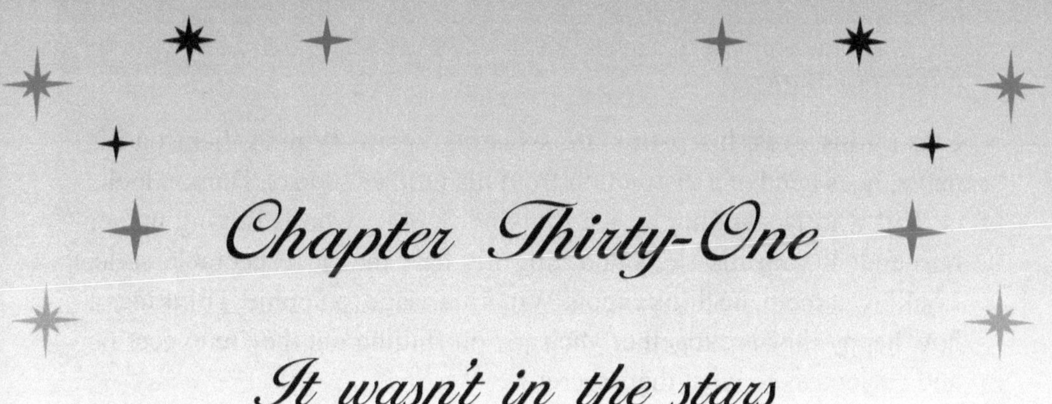

Chapter Thirty-One

It wasn't in the stars

Inside the church, lilac chiffon and silk drape each pew. Purple, pink and white roses decorate the altar and sit on the ends of each pew fusing together the elaborate affair she had planning so delicately for the last year. Beaming a radiant glow, she smiles as she looks around the church and waits patiently for Pachelbel's Canon in D to play so that her married life can begin.

Damon, fixed on the side of the altar, steals a look over at Harriet. She looks beautiful and ready. Any moment now, she will begin to walk down the aisle to him, and it's making him feel sick to the stomach. His nerves are getting the better of him, and hands are sweatier than ever, worse than that he can't get them to stop shaking. His mother, aware of his behaviour, is watching him with a judgemental eye. She's not happy one bit about him marrying a girl whom she has always believed is not of his family's standards. Harper, his sister, is watching their mother and can't help but glance back and forth between them like she's privy to an exceptionally intense tennis match. Harper, who is generally always happy and loves Harriet like a sister, is beginning to think that this isn't such a good idea as well.

Looking around at his guests, Damon eyes Lucy sitting beside his mother and as his eyes linger on her, Lucy manages to look up at him at the same time. Watching as she twitches uncomfortably in her seat, she looks back at him; she looks at him with concern written all over her face. This was his mother's doing. Lucy wouldn't be there otherwise.

Closing his eyes, his palms are sweating again. Wiping them on his pants, he is need of a distraction from his mother's looks, Damon looks at Will who is standing beside him and Sophie, who is tidying up her husband. Fixing his tie, smoothing his hair into a respectable style. Looking at them, he thinks about Will's marriage to Sophie. Thinking of how happy they are together, their joy on finding out they're expecting and curious as to what their secret is.

He is pulled from his thoughts when he overhears Will's phone buzz, and he answers, whispering into his phone.

"What do you mean; you're not coming to the wedding? Man, you're like another brother to her Nate. Someone else can watch the car."

Upon hearing Nate's name, Damon straights and looks at Sophie. "Nate's here?"

Smiling awkwardly, she nods her head as Will hangs up on Nate.

Damon turns to look at Will. "Nate is here? Why is Nate here?"

Will nods. "Yeah. He drove the bridal car."

Damon puzzled, looking out towards the entrance of the church. The church is ready for Harriet's descent down the aisle.

"I thought he couldn't make it," he growls.

Will is scratching his chin. "Nah. He couldn't get any of his guys to do it."

Truly confused now, Damon responds. "What about his getaway with Halley?"

Confused, Will shakes his head. "What getaway? When were they going away?"

It is this moment that Damon realises that Nate had been telling tall tales for the sake of avoiding coming to their wedding. Slowly, he begins to realise that Nate will always love Harriet and he will always be around, no matter what happens. He begins to feel sweat beading down his face. As Damon takes his place at the altar, he looks out at his bride and comes to the realisation that he is going to have to break Harriet's heart in front of her entire family. Looking at her relatives, he recognises Sal and the woman sitting next to him, his wife, Wanda. Looking around at his groomsmen, he sees Will take his place behind him.

Reaching the altar, Harriet smiles and hands her bouquet to Paige before taking Damon's his hand and walking up a step before the priest greets everyone. The priest keeps talking, and before they know it, the priest asks.

"If anyone objects, the time to do so is now or forever may they hold their peace."

Harriet is calm, and she smiles at Damon. Damon taking a breath, he nervously looks at her then turns to look at his mother and

Lucy, then Harper, Will and resting back to Harriet. Shaking his head, he nervously spills. "Wait -"

Harriet stops smiling and cuts a stunned look at him. "Damon???"

"Just -"

"Damon, what is going on -"

Hesitating on the spot, he has no other choice but to take her hand and lead her into the back room of the church.

"Can you all please just excuse us for a moment -"

Inside the side room, Damon closes the door as the wedding guests all turn in their seats, confused at the groom's behaviour. Will steps up next to the Priest.

"Ladies and Gentlemen, the bride and groom just need a moment. We ask that you be patient and the ceremony continues as soon as it can."

Inside the room, Harriet once-sweet glow has been replaced by fury. "Damon, seriously what are you doing? This isn't the -"

"Time, um yeah I know but -"

Looking at him, her chest burning, as it rises and falls. "But what?"

Wiping his sweaty hand over his face, he starts. "Harriet, I love you but -"

Losing the colour in her face, Harriet pales.

"I've been thinking that maybe . . . maybe this isn't what I want."

"This . . . isn't what you want?', she grounds out as she takes a long deep hurtful breath. "Damon. It's our wedding day. You realise that, don't you?"

"Yeah . . . but -"

"I should have known something you'd do something like this. You should've said something, like maybe I don't know . . . YESTERDAY!!!!"

Smirking back a laugh, he sniggers. "Just like you could've rung me with the heads up that Nate was driving your Bridal car!!!"

"Oh, of course. I planned that on purpose, didn't I Damon. Just to get a rise out of you!!! *I didn't know anything about it, Damon*!!!"

"Why is he here, Harriet -"

Watching him, she finally reaches disbelief. "I can see that on today of all days, nothing I say will matter."

Making a move towards her, he attempts to comfort her and stop her pain he's caused but is stopped when she takes a step back. Looking at her, he wants to say something. Anything.

"Harriet, I'm sorry, but I can't marry you."

Sucking back a heartbroken breath, she nods. Her eyes trail from down to her dress then up to her trembling hands to finally rest on her engagement ring. Edging out of the room, she looks for the exit, and upon departure, she glances over her shoulder and with a low, chilling and ravaged voice that he will never forget.

"*I don't understand.* One day soon, you'll have to explain this all to me. But right now, *I . . . I can't.* It breaks my heart just looking at you."

Picking up her dress, she disappears out of site down the side of the church towards the exit. Fixed in his spot, Damon has no choice but to let the best thing that ever happened to him disappear from his grasp. While outside, a perturbed Nate anxiously against the car for the service to finish when he sees Harriet run-up to the Bentley. Without acknowledging his presence, she

opens the door and gets in.

Shocked and concerned, he too jumps in and starts the car. Looking down at the steering wheel, Harriet eventually through her tear stained eyes looks at him in the rear-view mirror and sobs.

"Just drive."

Nate nods and as requested, drives off towards the unknown.

❄ ❄ ❄

In the church, the guests are growing concerned. Having just witnessed an extremely distraught Harriet run out of the church, their attention changes to Damon as he emerges from the side room. Watching as he approaches the middle of the altar and turns to face their guests, a nervous Damon looks down at them all. He notices immediately that his mother is smiling, her smile seemingly more wicked than ever but to her left, a disappointed Lucy can't bear to look at him. Joining Lucy in the disappointment department, is also his father and Harper whose purposely looking into her lap, shaking her head.

Moving his attention over to Harriet's side, he can see that they are getting ready to pounce at him. Harriet's father looks like he wants to kill, but he is being held back in his seat by Uncle Sal's hand on his shoulder. If Damon didn't believe that Uncle Sal was

involved in some way with the mafia now, his demeanour is now telling him that Uncle Sal could really make him disappear and it wouldn't be an accident.

Slowly he opens his mouth, staring down at all these people. With his voice shaking and his palms now a puddle of sweat, he manages to stammer out. "My apologies ladies and gentlemen but unfortunately Harriet and I, will not be getting married today. As a thank-you, we ask you to please continue onto The Plaza for drinks and dinner. The Bennett family will pick up the tab and once again, we apologise for any discourtesy."

And on his finish, he moves towards the side aisle and makes for the exit: Will, who has been standing who his family, is holding back his uncles and father from going after him, motions that he will go out and speak with Damon.

"So that's it?"

Damon stops, dead in his tracks outside the church.

"You've dragged all my family and Harriet's friends here today . . . only to not marry her?"

Damon turns and faces him. "Will, just leave it alone -"

"No, I won't leave it alone. Do you know much time and hard work Harriet put into this wedding? Harriet's spent most of her hard-earned savings, only for all 'you' hypocrites to go and embarrass her. You've made a complete fool out of her!!!"

Shaking his head, Damon denies the accusations. "That's not what I -"

"Oh come off it. Yes, you have, and now you've embarrassed the rest of us. So what it is, she's not good enough for you?

"Will, just let it go!"

Will shakes his head, angry he spits out. "No, I won't. We might not be as high and prestigious as you all think you, but it doesn't give you the right to treat us like you have. To treat Harriet like you have -"

"Why was Nate here, Will? He is always around Harriet? Don't you find that odd? He showed up at the wedding, Will. He keeps popping up everywhere. I can't keep competing with him anymore!!!"

Will stops and taking in Damon's smug, stuck up face, he flat out sucker punches him. "I don't care what your excuses are; if you knew you couldn't go through with it, you could've stopped the wedding months ago or yesterday!"

Sophie's who has been standing behind them approaches her husband after watching their entire altercation go down. Wiping his bloody nose, Damon looks up from his position on the ground at Will then to Sophie then to Harriet's family that have joined to watch the showdown between the two.

Exhibiting no remorse for his once friend and future-in-law, Will and his family exit the church. He remains lying on the ground at the entrance of the church, clutching his nose. Getting up off the church steps, he rights himself. Positive that his nose is indeed broken, he lets the blood run all over his suit until he's seen the last of her family leave. Taking a handkerchief out of his pocket, he stuffs his nostrils before disappearing out to the street to hail down a cab.

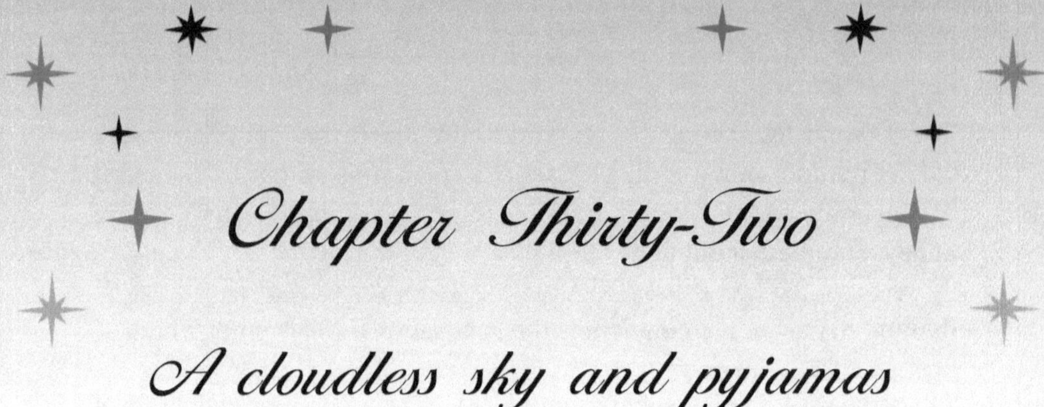

Chapter Thirty-Two

A cloudless sky and pyjamas

Nate pulls up in front of Harriet's apartment and on opening her door, he holds out his hand to help her out. Taking it as she gathers up her dress, Harriet steps out onto the sidewalk and fishes through her bag to find her keys noticing as people pass her by, wondering why she is standing on the sidewalk in Tribeca in her wedding dress when she should have been married by now.

She must look like a mess. She cried for most of the ride to home. Nate remained silent the entire the ride. Glancing back at her,

he remained both gutted and heartbroken for her as this was supposed to be the day she'd never forget. When she wasn't sobbing, she was looking up at the sky and realised that Nate was right. There was not one cloud in the sky today, and someone like her would take that as a sign.

Finding her keys, she walks up the steps to her brownstone apartment. Opening her door, she glances down at Nate before entering.

"Thank you."

His concerned eyes glance up at her. "For what?"

Pausing on her landing, she takes a deep breath and glances down at the wreck that is herself. "For not asking . . . for just driving."

Nate smiles, unable to hide it from her. "It's the least I can do."

She smiles back, and the first time since they left the church, she has some kind of colour in her cheeks. "Did you want to come in? For a coffee. I mean, it's the least I can do."

Shifting weight from one foot to the other, he looks away from her. Knowing that he shouldn't and that she probably needs some

time to herself, he turns her down. "Ah no. . . Um, thanks for the offer but I'm guessing you have a lot on your mind and you probably just want to be alone."

Rubbing her forehead, she pauses to think. "Actually. I'd love some company, any just . . . not my mother's."

Nate smiles and nods. His feet are betraying him as he finds himself following her inside. Walking into her lounge room, she puts her bag down on the hallway table. Looking around at the empty apartment which is now, amazingly back to being her own, Harriet looks down at her dress and wants to get out of it.

"I'm just going to change out of this thing. Won't be a moment. Just ah, make yourself comfortable."

Taking a seat on her couch, Nate realises that this is the first time he's ever been in her apartment. He looks around at her place, slowly taking note of all the photos. There are photos of family and friends. Photos of her and Damon in happier times but as he reaches her bookshelf, his eyes become transfixed on a frame placed behind a photo of Damon and Harriet at their engagement.

It was taken at her eighteenth birthday when he had slow danced with her. Her friends must've taken a photo of it because he never remembered posing for it. When you think about it, it was more of a snapshot to which Harriet must've discovered her on the camera days later.

Standing up, he picks up the frame and looks at it thoroughly. Standing arm in arm, they both are staring into each other's eyes with one hand of his on her back and the other one cupping her hand inside his against his chest. His mind races over the events of her birthday, and he nearly jumps out of his skin when he places the frame back in its sport by the sound of Harriet's voice from up the stairwell.

"Nate . . . um, could you come here for a moment please?"

Following the sound of her voice, Nate finds her standing in her bedroom attempting to unzip her dress but is unable to reach it.

"I know this is very awkward but could I get you -"

Nervously, he mumbles. "Erm . . . sure."

Walking up behind her, he is careful not to stand on her beautiful dress, her places one hand on her shoulder and one hand upon the zip. Feeling the warmth of his hands emanating throughout her, her body stills and her eyes travel the length of her arms to rest on his hand on her shoulder. Closing her eyes, his touch and close proximity reminds her yet again of their history.

With the zip proving to be a little more difficult than originally anticipated Nate moves so close to her that she can feel him breathing on her back. His sweet aftershave and gentle touch make Harriet shiver, and suddenly she is covered in goosebumps. And on hearing the zip come undone, she glances over her shoulder to smile sweetly at him.

"Thank you."

Awkwardly looking up at the ceiling, willing himself not to look down at her naked back, he nods. "Erm . . . That's ok."

Turning, she holds the dress up and covers herself her chest. Assuming that she'll be wanting to change, so he backs out of the room and on closing her door, he pauses. Fighting his inner urge to storm back into her room and cradle her in his arms, he instead makes the wise decision to sit on her couch.

When Harriet finally appears downstairs, Nate bites his tongue when he notices that she has changed into her pyjamas. Not just your usual singlet and pants, but her purple and pink spotty winter pyjamas. The ones she takes out of the closet on the days when she grew tired of people and their dramas and needed to just be by herself.

As she was putting them on, she was reminded of the first time she wore them in front of Damon. He, of course, teased her about them too but eventually grew to love them. In fact, she knew he loved them because, on the nights she wore them, he always made an effort to snuggle up to her more closely in bed.

Smiling at Nate as takes a seat upon on her window seat, she feels his eyes on her now; she glances up at him.

"I know, but it's the only thing I feel like wearing -"

Nate nods understandingly. "It's okay."

Feeling the need to drink, she stands and walks into her kitchen. Pulling out a bottle of white wine from her fridge, she yells from the kitchen at Nate. "Would you like a drink?"

Nate pouts, glances at his watch before yelling back. "Ah, sure. Why not."

Filling a glass to its hilt with wine, she puts the bottle back and grabs a beer for Nate then walks back into her lounge, hands him the beer and takes a seat down on the carpet leaning against her window seat. Looking down into her glass, she takes a breath before draining its content. Looking away from the glass, she looks to Nate who is looking back at her with concern.

"Nate, I just want to thank you again."

Astonished, he just nods. "No, it's fine . . . really."

"I also want to apologise for my shortness with you in the car before -"

After taking a sip of his beer, he mumbles. "No, it's okay. Truly"

"Soooo . . . how's Halley doing? I bet she'll get a real kick out of all this."

"Fine, I think, and I doubt she'd take comfort out of all this."

Puzzled, she looks up from her carpet. Confused, she looks at him with her eyebrows crinkled. "You think? Aren't you two still dating?"

Scratching his chin, avoiding her eyes. As much as he loves her and her eyes, they are looking at him in judgment, and he can't risk her seeing his vulnerability. At this point, he'd do anything for her if she'd only ask. But he couldn't have predicted what happened today and it was killing him seeing her in the state she was in.

Despite her facade, he knew she was trying to save face until she was alone. Alone to shed the tears that should have been tears of joy by now yet instead they're tears of heartbreak and the fact that what has happened is only going to make her question everything they shared and the state of their future? Well, that was driving him insane inside. Were they over? What actually happened?

When they last spoke, they fought. He told her not to marry him, and he also ended things with Halley. He came clean with Halley the very next day and as to where their relationship was heading, which was nowhere. Deep down, he knew that Halley had thought pretty much the same and that somehow she could never complete with Harriet. Her exit, however, wasn't so graceful and she definitely let him know.

Watching him, she can't help but pry. "Nate, you and Halley are still seeing each other, aren't you?"

"Oh um, no. Not anymore."

Feeling awful, she sighs. "Oh. Sorry. I . . . Er. . . I really should mind my own business."

"No, it's ok. Really."

Pushing inappropriate thoughts out of his mind, his eyes continue to deceive him by trailing from her to that goddam photo of them at her eighteenth, he can't keep an open mind. He has to leave. He needs to leave. Before he can excuse himself, he is interrupted by a knock on the door.

Putting her empty wine glass down on the coffee table, he watches as she stands and walks to the door. Opening it, she is surprised to Will standing on the landing.

"Will -"

"Hey -." Smirking, "You're in your pyjamas??? I mean, sorry. I just wanted to come by and check in. See how you're doing?"

Holding the door open for him, he enters and stands in her small entrance. "We all thought you might've gone back to the Plaza, but when you weren't there, Sophie said you might be here."

Avoiding his eyes, she looks down at her feet. "I couldn't. I just wanted to come home."

Touching her arm gently. "Everyone is so worried. Why don't I take you back to the -"

She interrupts "No, ah it's okay. I'm fine here. I think I just need to sleep in my own bed."

Respecting her decision, he nods. "Okay"

Harriet nods.

"Harriet?"

"Yeah?"

"I punched Damon -"

"You *did* **what**?!"

"I punched Damon. I thought it was rude of him to just stand you up like that in front of your family and friends . . . so I punched him. I um, might've broken his nose. Not sure didn't wait around to see."

Harriet smiles, choking back a laugh. "Thanks, Will. I wouldn't say this normally but the way I'm feeling, he deserved it!!!"

"It's weird though. Before I punched him, he asked me why Nate was at your wedding. Nate told him he wouldn't be available to drive the cars because he and Halley were going away. Yet he was driving your car?"

Feeling the tears beginning to well again, she wipes her cheek with a pyjama sleeve. "I don't know, Will. Honestly, I don't know what's going on."

"Well then. If you're okay, I'll head back to the Plaza and let everyone know that you want some time alone and then I guess when you're ready, you'll come out to Hartford. You know . . . cos we'd love to see you. All of us, even Mom."

Thinking that her mother would actually give her some kind of reprieve causing Harriet to chuckle quietly then smile up at her brother. "Thanks, Will."

Exiting, Will turns to walk down to his car but mid-journey, something stops him, and he turns. "Harriet -"

"Yeah???"

"I know . . . I know that we've never been close. Things happen, life gets in the way and well Mom, but you can talk to me. I um, hate to think that can't come to me if you need to talk."

Standing against her doorframe, Harriet nods. As a smile forms across her lips, she smiles gently at him and replies with, "Thanks, Will. I appreciate that."

Turning, he nods and makes his way down to his car. Waving she waits until he's driven off before she closes her door to return to her living room.

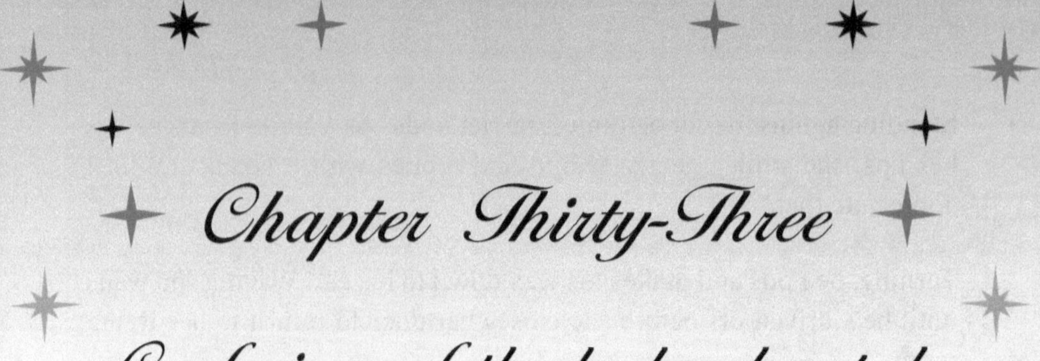

Chapter Thirty-Three

Confessions of the broken-hearted

"So, Will didn't want to come in?", Nate asks Harriet as she reappears in the lounge.

Taking a seat on her couch, she picks up her glass and fills it to its lip once more before snuggling back into a pillow.

"Ah, no. Everyone's at the plaza. He just wanted to check up on me. Make sure I'm ok."

Looking down into his beer bottle, he mumbles. "Is that all?"

"Yeah -"

Shrugging his shoulders, he senses it's time for him to leave too. She needs space and their proximity to each other right now is just messing with his mind.

"Soooooo . . . if you're okay and settled here, I might um take off."

Harriet nods. "Okay"

Nate gets up and walks to the door and placing her glass down on her coffee table; she follows him out. Opening the door, he is about to exit, but his curiosity gets the better of him, and he's probably the biggest asshole for even asking, but he can't help it.

Turning, he asks. "Harriet, why did Damon call off the wedding today?"

"Nate, please I don't want to talk about -"

"Just answer the question!!!"

"I *don't* **know**!!!."

"Then why would he care if I was there at your wedding? I'm sorry I couldn't help but overhear -"

"Apparently you weren't coming anyway, I mean, that's what you told Damon. And he knows about -"

Nate raises his eyebrows, shocked. "He knows??? You told him everything."

Flummoxed, amazed that Nate would even ask that, she replies. "Well of course I did. He was the man I was going to spend the rest of my life with; I told him everything."

Astounded, he angrily descends her steps. "If he knew, why did -"

"I don't know Nate. God, what do you want me to say? That he was wary of you. Well, he was!!! Then you show up as the driver of my wedding car. Maybe he thought -"

At the bottom of her stairs, he glances up at her. Stuck. His heart conflicted and choosing to be selfish; he continues to push the issue. "We well maybe he thought right. Maybe I couldn't stop thinking that I couldn't let that guy marry you unless you knew how I felt but then I saw you in your dress and how happy you were and I couldn't stop thinking -"

Her eyes mesmerised by his words, she watches on as he pieces his words together. Frazzled, he splutters. "How can I look into the eyes of the woman I love and tell her not to get married on her wedding day."

His attention now at his feet, he can't bring himself to look back up at her face. Just a glimpse is torturous enough.

"And then when we were in the car, you asked me if I was going to interfere and I said no -"

Harriet nods.

In almost a whisper, with half hope and half curiosity, he has to ask her. "Did he? Did he, did he call it off because you're in love with someone else?"

But unfortunately for Harriet, she can't help give him the answer she knows he longs to hear.

"No. I'm so sorry Nate . . . but I really wanted to marry Damon -"

Falling to her landing, she sits on the stoop and wipes her face from the tears that have been filling her eyes like a never-ending waterfall. She could end a drought with the number of tears she has cried so far today.

"I love him. I knew he was nervous and his mother was being overly painful, but once we were married, we assumed that -"

Nate takes that as a confirmation of his question, nods and walks to his car.

"Nate"

Pausing at his driver's door. "What?"

"There's something I need to tell you . . . something I should've told you ten years ago."

Nate waits.

"I'm sorry I didn't tell you earlier, and I hate it's come to this very opportunity to tell you the truth. But you need to know. I didn't get an abortion."

Nate's face becomes grim. "Then what -"

"I ran out on the appointment and drove all the way back to Dartmouth."

Confused, he moves away from the car door and directly up her steps to back inside the apartment. "I don't know about you, but I'd rather hear this inside than have whole of Tribeca hear about it!"

Stopping at the kitchen doorway, he leans against it with his arms crossed as he waits for her to enter and take a seat on her couch.

"So, what. . . What happened Harriet?"

She closes her eyes, blinks and nods an okay. Seated on her couch, she takes hold of a pillow and holds onto it for dear life.

"I freaked out. I couldn't stop stressing out about everything. What happened. How I treated you. What I did. What I said. How I felt. I was teetering on having it then giving it up but -"

"But???"

"But a couple of weeks later, I knew something wasn't right, and I started bleeding, so I drove to the hospital and -"

"And???" he asks, as he closes the distance between them and sits directly in front of her, on her coffee table. Reaching down, he takes one of her hand in between his and meeting his eyes, she finishes. "I miscarried."

Quiet, with a face as white as a ghost, Nate's stomach churning at the thought of her going through all of that, alone. "I lost a lot of blood. Too much. Doctors kept me in the hospital for a week."

Feeling sick, his horrified face emits everything he's feeling. "Why. Why. Why didn't you tell me?", he stammers out as a tear falls down his cheek.

"You weren't talking to me. I treated you so awfully. The things I said, I was so . . . I was so embarrassed."

"Your right, you did but . . . **you should still have told me!!!**"

Swallowing back hurtful tears, she wipes her face before glancing up at him. "It won't be another ten years before you talk to me like this, will it?"

Turning to look away from her, he drops her hand and stands. Wiping his mouth, he walks to her front bay window. Reflecting on everything that has happened from nineteen years ago to ten years ago to finally the events of a couple of months ago to today and suddenly he realises, that maybe there's a reason for his cowardly actions and it dawns on him. He's never going to be truly happy unless he walks away for good. It's time to cut ties for good.

"No, Harriet. It won't."

Wiping her tears away with her sleeve, she watches him as he turns back to face her. "I'm sorry that you've been to hell and back with this all especially on a day like this, but I can't do 'all this' anymore."

"I need to move on. I've been stalling for the longest time, thinking that you would come to your senses and run into my arms but I've finally realised that you've never wanted me. You've avoided me for the last ten years, and like a fool, I told myself to be patient, but I've been so reckless. I want to love someone who loves me back. I want someone who chases after me. More importantly, I don't want to be anyone's second choice."

Glancing away to a photo of her and Damon, he takes a deep breath. "I want to get married and have children someday too, you know but that's not going to happen if I continue to let myself be caught up in you. I have been in love with you for almost twenty years now and not once have I ever stopped loving you. I will probably never stop loving you. But you're no good for me."

Walking towards the hallway, he looks over his shoulder and ends with, "We've hurt each other so much already, and we were never really together. I'm not placing all the blame on you, but you're hung up on someone else and always were. It's Damon now, but Ryan then. And I'm done. I can't do this anymore. You need to find yourself and fix your relationship with Damon, and I need to move on. I'm sorry its taken me this long to figure it out, Harriet. I hope you find your happiness", before edging out of the room and exiting the apartment.

Silenced by his honesty, a quiet Harriet stands and watches him pull away. Taken back and hurt by his words, as harsh as they were, she deserved it. After all, she had kept the truth of her miscarriage from him all these years. Perched on her window seat, she sits there for some time. Her mind moving from Nate to rest on Damon and the events of the day. Placing her head against the cool glass window pane of her front bay window, she can't help but think of how the day started.

Having woke up refreshed, she was ready to be married and spend the rest of her life with Damon. Up until her arrival at the church, she hadn't once second-guessed the marriage. Nerves, well they're a common occurrence at most weddings but she never once thought the day would turn out as it had.

Standing, she makes the short walk up to her bedroom. Stepping inside, she gently closes the door before turning around to see her wedding dress, strewn across the bed only to pause and stare at the right side of the queen bed where Damon once slept.

Sitting on the bed's edge, she picks the dress and runs her hands over it. The beautiful handmade gown, its beaded bodice, and lace bateau, now reduced to nothing but a reminder of failure. With tear-stained cheeks, she feels a moment of rage wash over her, and she swipes the dress off the bed to the floor.

Crawling to the head of her bed, she yanks the cover back and slips into her side of the bed. Turning on her side, she lays her hand out over Damon's empty side of the bed. As she runs her hand over the space, she can't help but wonder where he is and if he's thinking of her. Does he miss her? Does he wish that he could just erase what happened today and start anew? Or was she just lying to herself?

Lying back into her pillows, she can feel the tears beginning to spill out once more as her mind attempts to piece together what went wrong between her and Damon? Were they perfect? Of course not! They had their differences, and yes, things were complicated, but no one ever said love was easy, right?

And oh god Nate. But she deserved that one, it was only a matter of time before the truth would come out. Their story was a tough one, and he's pretty much made her be the baddie in their story, but deep down, they both know it's not true. Things happen, and sometimes there's no going back. Sometimes, people become so invested in their work and their life that before they know it, the time has passed by and it's too late to do or say something.

But in all fairness, he had finally admitted to being in love with her all this time. Why he waited until tonight to actually declare it, was something she'll never truly understand. And not speaking to each other in ten years??? Where to start on that one! Firstly, its childish and but she had her reasons. Surely though; if you loved someone, I mean truly loved them with all your being, you'd cease any or all opportunity to sweep them off their feet. Though he had a point too. She was always walking *mostly running* away from him whether she meant to or not. If that doesn't scream doomed relationship than how else would you explain it.

Turning on her side, she looks out her window and up to her stars for solace. How what is that there was but not one cloud in the sky during the day but the night is painted in stars. Watching them shine, some brighter than others, her heart and mind fight to reason with each other. Deep down she will always hold a place for Nate in her heart. He's tied to her childhood, and he was her first love. He was a lot of firsts. *You never forget your first love.*

But as a woman, she loved Damon. She is in love with Damon, and while their relationship had now moved into unknown territory, she has to fix it. At least, find out what exactly had happened today. He had been acting strange yesterday. The night before yesterday, he mentioned something about going shopping with Harper, and when he got home, he was extremely quiet, and when he left last night to stay at The Plaza, he wasn't acting like himself.

Wishing that it was just nerves and he's realised he's made a horrible mistake, Harriet feels the need to hear his voice. Picking up her phone from the bedside table, she brings up his number and listens to the dial tone as it rings out, she gets his message bank.

"Hi, you've reached Damon Bennett's mobile. I'm available to take your call so please leave a message, and I'll get back to you."

"Damon, It's me, Harriet. I'm sorry for calling so late, but I just have to know if you're okay. There are things we desperately need to talk about, but for now, for tonight, I just want you to know that I love you and I still want to spend the rest of my life with you."

Choking back tears, her voice breaks. Trembling, she has to take a moment to put herself together before continuing.

"Anyway, that's all I want to say for now. I hope you're okay wherever it is you are. Please, call me back when you can. I love you. Night."

Hanging up, she places her phone on the side table. Curling into her side, she takes the pillow from what was once Damon's side, his smell still lingering on it, pulling it closely into her chest. Burying her face into the pillow, her eyes grow tired, and she falls asleep.

CLOSURE

Like time suspended,
A wound unmended –
You and I.

We had no ending,
No said goodbye;

For all my life,
I'll wonder why.

- Lang Leav

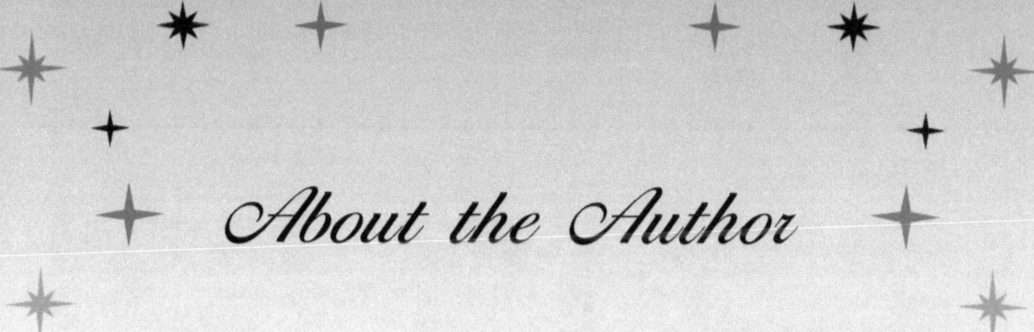

About the Author

Elizabeth J Marie's deep love for reading and writing began early in her life after her grandmother, an English teacher, helped to hone and pique her passion by introducing her to a range of genres and authors like Jane Austen and Charles Dickens, JRR Tolkien and Roald Dahl. Just to name a few. Marie is a school teacher who truly loves to help broaden and inspire young minds to read and write creatively.

Marie also loves being creative and one of her greatest passions when she isn't writing or teaching, is Graphic Design. A passion she wishes to become qualified in one day. She also enjoys watching movies and listening to music and becoming lost in the imaginative and magical storylines created to inspire our minds whilst piquing the interest of our eyes and ears.

She's Like the Wind is the first instalment of a three book series that Elizabeth is writing and she genuinely hopes that you enjoy it. She hopes that in some way that by looking to the stars, you too can draw inspiration or that they help to light the pathway to your next dream.